MW00880102

Beasts 3:

Unleashed

Natavia

SOUL Publications

Beasts 3: Unleashed   Natavia

Copyright © 2019 by Natavia. Published by SOUL

Publications. All rights

reserved www.nataviapresents.com This book is a
work of fiction. Names, characters, places, and incidents
either are the product of the author's imagination or are
used fictitiously and are not to be construed as real. Any
resemblance to actual persons, living or dead, business
establishments, events, or locales or, is entirely
coincidental. No portion of this book may be used or
reproduced in any manner whatsoever without writer
permission except in the case of brief quotations embodied
in critical articles and reviews.

SOUL Publications

Beasts, Mates, and Offspring

(Characters from previous Beasts book)

Ammon and Naobi- Goon's parents.

Dayo and Anik- parents of Chancy, Baneet (twins), Arya (adopted sister)

Izra and Adika- Monifa's parents

Fatima and Elle- Zaan's parents.

Goon (Akua) and Kanya- Akea and Kanye's parents (twins)

Osiris- Goon's nephew from Anubi. Parents were once Queen and King. Osiris's father, Baki, is Goon's half-brother by his father, Ammon.

Goon's pack brothers: Amadi, Izra, Dayo and Elle.

Ula- Amadi's mate

Geo- Baneet's mate.

Jetti- Geo's cousin

SOUL Publications

Keora: Adika's sister who was reincarnated into her daughter, Monifa.

Seth: A vampire demon who was with Keora in the past life. Their daughter is Rena. Seth is also Arya's interest.

Taj: a tiger shifter. Arya's other interest.

Fiti- a witch from Anubi who was ordered to kill Goon but couldn't. Instead, she sided with his pack against his enemy and fell in love with Zaan.

Kanye

I'm going on a killing spree.

I'm going with you, Akea replied.

We were standing in the foyer of the pack's mansion watching everything unfold right before our eyes. Anubi's warriors came to our home to capture my father. My father disobeyed Anubi's rules, leaving them without a king because he wanted to stay with his pack. But we had other problems. Someone stole a pharaoh's necklace from our store, A&K Jewelers. The unique piece wasn't for sale. We used it to attract customers.

"Wait a minute, Chancy. You cannot go with Osiris to Anubi! We will deal with Akea's bullshit later but now is not the time," Monifa said to

Chancy. Chancy offered herself to Osiris to free my father, but that was against pack rules because she was mated with Akea.

"You're a mated wolf," Chancy's mother said to her.

"Akea isn't a wolf! I'm not his mate. Matter of fact, Jetti is his mate. He screwed her while she was in heat! I smelled her stench when I went to their territory earlier. He betrayed me, so therefore I'm going to Anubi because I will not stay back and watch him father another wolf's pup," Chancy said.

Akea reached out to Chancy and Osiris pulled her away from him. I wanted to rip Osiris's throat to shreds. A deep growl escaped my throat and sharp fangs pierced through my gums. My mate grabbed my arm to calm me. My father's punishment would be worse if I attacked Anubi's new king.

"We saved you and welcomed you into this pack! How in the fuck can you desire your cousin's mate? We should've left you with the bloodsuckers because you're not a beast! You ain't shit but a bitch-ass nigga!" I shouted at Osiris. The ceiling shook and cracks sprouted up the walls. My beast was enraged and I had a taste for blood—my cousin's blood.

"Akea needs to be with his kind! He's not a wolf! He can't mark her and keep her for eternity. His soul will always desire another female. I can treat Chancy like the queen she is and give her everything! I can raise Destiny as my own. He doesn't deserve her. I will be back for Destiny. If you don't obey my rules, I will drain every drop of your father's blood until his soul leaves his body. We must go!" Osiris said.

Chancy had a change of heart. She pulled away from Osiris but it was too late. The warriors from Anubi disappeared with Osiris and Chancy. Akea punched the wall and part of the ceiling fell onto the floor.

"How can you let them take her?" Akea yelled at me.

"Our father will die if we disobey their orders!" I replied.

A jolt of electricity pierced through my chest and slammed me into a wall. My body was like a sponge to Akea's energy because we were connected. I sent it back to him but he placed a shield in front of him. Suddenly, my beast emerged and charged into him. Akea's energy formed as a shield to protect him from getting attacked.

"KANYE!" Monifa yelled.

Akea disappeared and I shifted back to my human form. I wanted to take his head off. Our father was captured and all he could do was think about Chancy and Osiris. The thought of them poisoned his mind. His thoughts led him to believe that Chancy would leave him for the wolf. His insecurities pushed her away. I couldn't make decisions for Akea's mistakes. He had to figure out how to get his family back while I dealt with our father in Anubi. The pack was yelling and shouting at each other about who was going to save my father. I headed to the bar in the basement to clear my mind. My anger was clouding my judgement. I wanted to kill every living being in Anubi to spare my father's punishment, but how could I go against the gods? Anubi flowed through my veins but so did my father's blood.

I poured myself a shot of Hennessey and threw it back so the warm cognac could sooth my throat. A sweet pine scent mixed with a potent musk filled my nostrils, causing my beast to growl.

My mate had that effect on me. Her scent was intoxicating and it tamed me. I worshipped my mate but she didn't take advantage of it. I turned around to face her and she smiled at me. Monifa's pregnancy glow made her more beautiful.

"Come here, beautiful," I called out to her. She walked into my awaiting arms and I hugged her. I buried my face into the crook of her neck and gently bit her. A slight moan mixed with a lust-filled growl escaped her lips. She pulled away from me and stared into my eyes.

"Don't use your witchcraft on me. Now is not the time," I warned her.

"You cannot kill everyone in Anubi. There must be another way. Your mission will kill you and not save your father," she said and I pulled away from her.

"So, you saw my fate?"

"You're the pack leader now. You have to lead with a strong mind and a pure heart. I cannot deliver our pups by myself. They need their father and going to Anubi will kill you. Please listen to me. I'm begging you to think of another way," she said.

"My beast has a taste for blood and nothing is going to stop him. I want them all dead! I want to crush Osiris's throat. That muthafucka laid in this house and hunted with us! He's the king and can turn this around but he won't because he wants Akea to suffer. This is personal and my father has to pay for it. Akea and Osiris need to fight it out like men and stop doing this female bullshit."

"Osiris's beast wants Chancy and nothing will get in his way. The only way they'll free Goon is if Chancy mates with Osiris. Even if Chancy hadn't offered herself, Osiris still would've taken her. So you see, Akea's vision was somewhat right. Osiris might be Chancy's soulmate. He's too adamant to have her. He craves her scent and will go against Anubi's rules to get her. He loves her, Kanye. I don't think Akea's love is strong enough to save her," Monifa said.

"So, you're telling me Akea never had a chance with her?"

"No, I'm telling you that Osiris will do anything to have her and his beast will be unleashed to protect what's his. We need to think of something else because we're doomed if Anubi turns their back on this pack," she said.

"I'm not giving up on my father to please the gods. My mother needs her mate. I'm not ready to be a pack leader. I feel so fucked up because I ignored him. What if I don't see my father again? I told myself I hated him after we had that fight but I didn't mean it. I thought the pack turned against me because I didn't want Arya around."

Monifa kissed my lips and wrapped her arms around me. As the new pack leader, I had to make two decisions: stay with my pack or save my father.

Father, I need you. What should I do? Monifa is carrying my pups and if I save you, my chance of survival might be slim.

A tear slid out of my eye when I made my decision. I had to save my father. Monifa pulled away from me sobbing. It wasn't supposed to happen this way but I was a warrior. I believed in sacrifice. If I died, I'd live through my pups' veins.

"I love you and our pups. But if I have to sacrifice myself to make this pack peaceful then I will. That is who I am," I said.

SOUL Publications

I got off the stool and kneeled in front of her so I could kiss her round stomach. Monifa pulled away from me and my heart broke into a million pieces as she sobbed.

"You don't love us," she said then disappeared.

What am I going to do? My mate will never forgive me.

Monifa

I sat on a log in the woods by a lake while staring at the full moon. The peace and silence calmed me. The mansion was in an uproar because of Goon and the jewelry store. I had to get out of that house before anger consumed me and triggered my beast. My mate disappointed me. How dare he make plans without thinking about me and our unborn pups? I had a bad feeling about Kanye going to Anubi, and that feeling settled in my stomach, causing goosebumps to appear on my arms. A tree in the woods fell over, knocking more trees down. My energy was destructive at times especially when I was hurt.

"Can I sit with you?" Baneet asked when she approached me.

I scooted down on the log so she could sit next to me. She was pregnant, too, but she was pregnant by a wolf from another pack. Baneet and I weren't as close as we once were because she picked Arya's side even when Arya was wrong. Arya always had evil ways.

"I don't think Geo stole from the store. The pack is holding me responsible and your mate wants me out of the mansion. Kanye is getting out of hand," she said.

"Don't disturb my peace with your non-sense. Of course, they're gonna hold you accountable. You're a traitor and you can dress it up however you like but you're the reason why Chancy was attacked and couldn't nurse her pup. I bet you were in on it, probably helped Jetti to destroy Chancy and Akea's relationship. You were always jealous of Chancy. I saw right through you but I pretended you weren't because I loved you. You're very wicked and you should do us all a favor and leave this pack."

Tears fell from Baneet's eyes as her sobs mixed with growls from her beast. Her beast wanted to challenge me but I wasn't worried about her. Baneet's beast was the least of my concerns.

"I'm wicked? You're the one who has the soul of an ancient evil witch! We all have demons. Arya is my favorite because she lives how she wants to. You all are stuck on this tiring tradition that doesn't have our best interest at heart. You know it's time to live by our own rules," she replied.

"Arya is your favorite because you both are jezebels. You bedded Zaan and Geo around the same time and Arya fucks anything, including demons. I believe in my gods, I just think they should let us live in peace. Get away from me while I think."

Baneet stood up and looked down at me with glowing brownish-yellow eyes. Her canines sharpened and her beast bellowed throughout the woods.

"One day you will see that you and Kanye don't belong together. If he was synced with you, he wouldn't be planning on going to Anubi while you're carrying his pups. Just think about it, Monifa. Open your magical eyes and pay attention. Arya is the first born and she's supposed to be his mate!" Baneet said.

My nails sharpened and the sickening sounds of my bones shifting echoed throughout the woods. Bats flew past the red moon. A deep and menacing howl caused Baneet to drop to her knees. The roots from the trees wrapped around her body as she cried for help. A gold spear appeared in my hand as I walked towards her.

"You look more delicious than a pregnant bear," I gritted.

The scent of her blood trickling down her arms from the tree roots squeezing her made my stomach growl. I sniffed the air and smelled a familiar scent, it was Kanye. The roots around Baneet disappeared and she collapsed on the ground, whimpering in pain.

What just happened? Why did I want to eat her? Her blood smelled better than any animal's I'd ever eaten before. What in the hell is happening to me?

Kanye appeared from behind a tree. He was only wearing a pair of gray sweatpants. Blood dripped from his mouth and chest. He used his nail to pluck out a ball of deer fur from his pretty sharp gold fangs. Baneet got up and ran, disappearing into the woods.

"What's up with her?" he asked.

"She tried to challenge me so I scared her. I want to be alone. This is the only spot where I can come to think and you're interrupting me."

Kanye sat on a log across from me and his ice-blue eyes glowed. I sat on a rock and pulled my legs up to my chin.

"I think we need to talk. I don't like how you left me in the basement," he said.

"Are you still going to Anubi?"

"Of course, I am. He's my father! Why are we even talking about this? As my mate, you should understand me. We're not supposed to argue with each other! This shit is getting whack. I understand your hormones are out of place but this isn't the time to argue. I don't want to leave with us like this," he pleaded.

"Go ahead and leave! I'm not stopping you! I should've stayed in Seth's world if I knew everything was going to happen like this. Now I understand why Keora's heart turned cold. It was to numb the pain because being good hurts! Being good gets you betrayed and feeling alone. Being good is also going to make our pups fatherless. I'm about sick and tired of being good! I don't want you to leave. If you leave and don't come back, it'll damage me for eternity. Please understand me. I love you so much and I can't deal with this."

"I won't leave my father to rot in a prison where they'll strip him from his strength as punishment," he replied.

Kanye was stubborn, so there wasn't any use in trying to talk him out of it. I wanted to use my sorcery and lock him away from everyone but me. I'd have to live without him for life if something happened to him. The thought angered me. I snatched off my wedding ring and threw it at him. His chest heaved and his stomach tightened while his beast growled at me—I pissed him off.

"Oh, that's how you feel? You mad at me because I won't bend down and kiss your ass?" he seethed.

"I want you to be here while I give birth to your pups! Call me selfish for wanting to share that moment with you. You win, Kanye. Do what you want to do. I just want you to know that I don't have to accept everything you do because we're mated for life."

"Can you put this ring back on? You saying I'm not coming back means you don't have faith in me. I'm the alpha of this pack and cannot make decisions based on how you feel. I will have to take this pack's feelings into consideration. My father isn't here, so I'm in charge. The decision I made is for everyone. Get out your feelings and wake up, beautiful. You can't call orders for an alpha and you know that. You're supposed to have more faith in me than anyone else. What if it was me? Would you want my father to stay here and let me rot in a cell or would you want him to be a strong pack leader? This is who we are and what we stand for! I will not back down, Monifa. Maybe this ring isn't for you if you don't understand that," he stated before he left.

Our argument was over. Kanye won and I had to let it go. No matter what, he was still my mate and I had to deal with whatever came with it. As an alpha, he can make any decision he wants if it's about protecting the pack. Also, a part of me knew Kanye was scared to be an alpha because he was afraid of making a mistake that would embarrass his father. Resculng Goon was also Kanye's peace; he wasn't ready to be the leader of the pack. A breeze past me and I caught the scent of a camp fire a few miles away. My stomach growled and suddenly I had a taste for flesh— human flesh.

I crept to the camp fire to stalk my prey. There were four Caucasian humans dancing around a camp fire while drinking beer. The music coming from the old pick-up truck was loud and the rattling sound of the engine pained my ears. I've never thought about eating humans but I was craving them. In the past, werewolves used to hunt the villages in Africa even though it was forbidden to eat humans. I waited until a couple went inside the truck to fool around. A woman sat on a log and lit a cigarette while her guy friend went into the woods. I leapt from the tree and quietly followed him. His back was turned towards me while he was urinating. After he was finished, he turned around and faced me.

"Jesus Christ, lady. You scared the holy shit out of me," he chuckled. He wobbled side-to-side, to keep his balance from falling; he was drunk. He backed into a tree when he saw my fangs. The loud music drowned out his screams when I went in for the kill. My sharp nails sliced through his neck, severing his head from his shoulders. After he dropped to the ground, I dragged his body deeper into the woods.

****

The pack stared at me when I came into the house because I was covered in blood. I heard sniffing, the pack knew the blood on me wasn't from an animal.

"Where have you been? It's three o'clock in the morning. You can't roam around while pregnant," my mother said.

"I'm fine. Everyone can stop worrying about me."

"Is that human blood?" my father, Izra, asked.

"Yes, I was trying to save this dying woman I came across in the woods. Someone left her there to die."

They wanted to ask more questions but I was already walking up the stairs. I went into my old bedroom and slammed the door. A picture of me and the pack from when I was a little girl fell onto the floor and shattered. My pups fluttered like butterflies and it brought a sense of relief over me. I just wanted to be happy with my gifts from the gods, but they were always taken away from me. When I went into the bathroom, I almost didn't recognize myself as I looked into the mirror. I clutched the sink as my head spun, almost causing me to pass out. When I pulled away from the sink I left bloody handprints. It suddenly dawned on me that I ate a human. I wasn't myself when I killed that man. My beast lured me to him.

The beast is overpowering my witch. What is going on with me?

I took off my clothes and a finger fell onto the floor from my bra. The horrific scene caused me to vomit.

Is that a testicle? Oh my god! Kanye will kill me if he knew I ate a man's dick.

"MOMMMMMMAAAAAAAA!" I screamed.

One hour later...

I was lying in bed eating grapes while my mother couldn't stop laughing at me.

"I cheated on Kanye. I feel so bad that I ate that man. It was an out-of-body experience, but he tasted so good."

"I promised Kanya I wouldn't tell anyone but she ate the limo driver when she was pregnant with Akea and Kanye. Carrying immortal children will make you so hungry that you'll find yourself eating something you're not supposed to. You have an appetite like a piranha. You'll even think about eating on us. You have to constantly feed yourself so you won't get that hungry again. Besides, humans hunt and kill animals all the time. Think of it as payback," she said.

"God, I wish I was just a witch," I mumbled.

"You'll kill your father's ego if he heard you say that," she replied.

The door opened and Kanye walked into my bedroom. My mother kissed my cheek before she left out of my room. Kanye closed the door and locked it. I knew he couldn't stay away long. He slid underneath the silk sheet and I scooted over to make room for him. Kanye grew two inches in height and probably gained twenty pounds. He was a full-grown beast and he had a new symbol on his chest to warn other males he was an alpha. He was his father's twin.

"Couldn't go to sleep, huh?" I asked and he sat up.

"I want you to put this ring back on," he said. I held out my hand for him and he smirked.

"You were bluffing. See what you do to me? I can't stay away for long," he growled against my neck. I closed my eyes and inhaled his scent. My heat phase was over, but my sex drive was still high. He sank his canines into my neck and my pussy throbbed. I moaned for him to stop biting me, but he ignored my request. He placed his hand between my legs and massaged my slit. He leaned in to kiss me but I pulled away from him.

"I have a confession."

"What did you do, Monifa? You did some crazy shit, didn't you? That's why you blocked us out your head when you went hunting?" he asked.

"Sorta. Please don't get mad. I had a human nut sack in my mouth, and before you fly off the handle, it happened when I bit into his upper leg. It's soooo disgusting. I'm about to get sick again." I jumped out the bed and ran to the bathroom. Kanye was standing in the doorway when I flushed the toilet.

"Sooooo, tell more about this beast you got inside you. Why you ain't never do that to my dick? I can handle it," he said with an attitude.

"Are you serious right now? You want me to bite your dick off?"

"My package is too big to bite off. It'll take you and your witchcraft to chew through this heavy meat. But fuck all of that, why are you eating humans? They're not healthy for you. They do drugs, drink alcohol and eat processed food. I want my babies to be healthy and not crying for McDonalds," he said.

I washed my face and got back in bed. Kanye wrapped his arms around me and kissed the back of my neck.

"You can go to Anubi if you take me with you," I whispered and he sat up.

"HELL NO!" he barked.

"You don't have a choice. Let me go with you or I'll work some magic around so you won't be able to do anything. I have a plan that will keep me, you and our pups safe."

I told Kanye the plans I had for Anubi without hurting anyone and he seemed skeptical about it. He paced back and forth scratching his chin in confusion, trying to decide if he was making the right decision.

"Fine. One fuck up and you will come back! I mean it, Monifa," he finally said.

I jumped in excitement and kissed his face. He didn't have much choice because I'd do anything to keep him safe. Even if it meant locking him up so he wouldn't be harmed. I know the pack would disagree with Kanye's choice but he needed me. He was strong and could handle a lot but him against Anubians would weaken his beast, making him vulnerable. I couldn't allow that to happen.

Chancy

Meanwhile in Anubi...

I stood before a crowd of hundreds of people inside a castle-style temple. The Egyptian statues of mummies, pharaohs and gods stood on each corner of the room where the king sat and watched over his people. The drawings on the wall weren't easy for me to understand but I could make out a few things. Many of the drawings meant peace, blood, afterlife and beasts. I saw those drawings when Akea made love to me. The crowd was chanting and a warrior told me to bow in front of a half wolf and half man statue. While bowing my head, a woman ripped my shirt and stuck something in my back. My skin sizzled and the smell of burning flesh filled my nostrils.

"It's okay, Chancy. You're branded as one of us," Osiris said as he helped me up.

"I only came here for one reason!" I whispered.

"And you will get your wish in due time," he replied.

The people left out of the king's room, leaving me and Osiris behind.

"I had to get rid of your scent. You smelled like a wolf and the only way to get rid of it is to brand you. Everything from your old life will disappear, but that's a good thing, right? You will love it here," Osiris said.

"What have you done to me? What about my daughter?" I yelled.

"A warrior will go to your pack in a few to retrieve her. Trust me, Chancy. I really have your best interest at heart," he said. Osiris pulled me into him and kissed me. I hated myself for enjoying the kiss. My mission was to save Goon but it was also to show Akea how bad he hurt me.

I couldn't get over him. The way he made love to me reminded me of a wolf. He was aggressive, passionate and took charge of my body like an alpha. It had been a while since we made love and I missed the way his eyes turned colors when he was deep inside me. Akea didn't notice it, but his eyes turned blue and gold when he climaxed. I always joked with him about him having a beast hidden somewhere inside him. Osiris pulled away from me with disappointment in his eyes.

"Why are you still thinking about him?" he asked.

"It's only been a day! I still love him!"

"Then why would you give me your body if you still belong to him?" he seethed.

"You know why I'm here, Osiris. Let's skip this fake-ass honeymoon phase and get down to the real deal. Take me to Goon's cell so I can check on him."

"I'm afraid I can't do that right now. The warriors have him in a special dungeon. How about I talk to someone and see if you can visit? Queens aren't allowed in the dungeon, it's a rule. The werewolves haven't mated in a while and let's just say they'll try to break free when they see your beautiful face. I'll arrange something. I'm new to this king thing, too, Chancy," he stressed.

"Okay, fine."

Osiris was right, he had just become king and I was barking a lot of orders at him. I decided to give him a break for a day, but I also had plans on how to sneak into the dungeon.

"Follow me," Osiris said. He grabbed me by the hand and pulled me down the hall. At the end of the hall sat two stone doors. The doors were so huge, four men had to pull it open by thick rope.

"This place reminds me of a movie. It's beautiful."

"You can see the Nile River if you look through the window," Osiris replied.

"Where is this place?"

"It is hidden by the Nile River. It's invisible from those who don't belong here. It's sorta like heaven except we're not dead. It's a whole different world and I want to show you everything," he said while gazing into my eyes. When we walked through the big double doors I was in awe. The room was set up like an ancient loft. Fruit grew on the tall plants and a big platter of raw meat sat on the table. The bed was made out of cotton and silk and surrounded by curtains draping from the ceilings. The furniture was made of real gold and big gems were embedded into the walls.

"This reminds me of Aladdin."

"I don't know who that is but is that a good thing?" he asked, placing a necklace around my neck. It was a heavy medallion with a wolf's head.

"That belonged to my grandfather, Ammon. It's a very special piece to Anubi and I want you to have it," he said.

"I've heard bad things about Ammon."

"Me, too, but he was a king and we can't erase that. Besides, the necklace was a gift from his mate, Naobi," he said. Osiris took off my clothes and I covered my breasts. They were leaking with milk for my pup. I was relieved from remembering the bottles I had in the fridge for her.

"I need my baby."

"You will have her. I promise," he said. He kneeled in front of me and gripped my hips. His sharp nails scratched my buttocks, leaving three bloody marks on each cheek. His teeth pierced through my clit and I howled in pain. I collapsed on the floor.

"What the hell!" I screamed. Osiris ran to me with a sheet and pressed it against my pussy. Suddenly, the blood that had formed disappeared and the pain was gone.

"What was that?"

"An ancient tradition. My father told me, 'she's not able to give you strong pups if you don't bite her fruit,'" he replied.

"You all are weird," I chuckled.

"Of course, it's weird. Nothing thousands of years ago made sense but we still carry on the ancient tradition. The gods are always watching," he said. Osiris led me to a bathing area. I sat in the warm square-shaped tub which was made out of clay. The tub was deep enough to be underneath the water without leaning back. Osiris sat on the edge and stared at me.

"I fell in love with you the first time I saw you. I won't give up fighting for you. Enjoy your bath and I'll bring you a glass of goat milk," he said. Osiris kissed my forehead before he left out of the room. I closed my eyes and thought of Destiny and Akea. My eyes watered but I refused to let the tears fall.

What have I gotten myself into?

Akea

"**W**hat are you doing in my room? Get out before Geo knows you're here," Jetti said. She had just come in from a shower. I snuck into her bedroom to avoid Geo's pack. The stolen jewelry was the least of my worries because I lost the love of my life to Osiris. I snatched the towel off Jetti's body and my heart shattered into pieces.

Who have I become? I feel nothing for this wolf or the pup she's carrying if it belongs to me. The pup was conceived out of lust, not by love. She betrayed me.

"You betrayed me!"

Chancy was supposed to be the only woman to carry my children. She would never forgive me for sharing what I gave her with Jetti.

"Geo was going to kick me out of the pack because he didn't have enough money to take care of me and my pup. I was tired of working low-paying jobs like a slave. I never had to work when my mate was alive. This is the only way I can survive on my own," she cried.

"You did all of this for financial gain? I gave you money for helping me with Destiny! I would have given you anything for that but you trapped me. Chancy will never forgive me for this and definitely not my pack. We are at war with each other now!"

"You made it so easy. I thought you were this powerful sorcerer who could see through everything but you were blinded by lust. You wanted me as much as I wanted you. If you didn't, you would have seen my plan. I ended up falling in love with you so I no longer feel guilty about what I did. This baby is innocent and this was meant to happen," she said.

Jetti walked over to me and grabbed my hand. She placed it over her stomach and I felt the connection. Jetti wasn't carrying a pup, she was pregnant with my son—a warlock.

"I know this baby isn't a wolf. He gives me a different energy," she beamed and I pulled away from her. She placed her hand on my shoulders when I sat on her twin-size bed. Geo's pack was very poor and they were living in the eighteenth century.

"I want my son after you give birth," I whispered.

"WHAT!" she shouted and I stood up.

"You think my son will be raised in a swamp? I'm not taking care of you, so this is the last resort."

"Who will nurse him?" she asked.

"He's not a pup. I will figure it out."

"GET OUT!" she screamed.

There was a loud bang on the door followed by a growl. Seconds later, Geo burst into Jetti's bedroom with glowing eyes. His face formed into a snout; he was in mid-shift.

"What are you doing in my house?" he growled.

"I came here to talk to Jetti. I'll leave when we're done."

Geo charged into me and we fell through the bedroom window; we landed in the backyard. Jetti screamed for us to stop but it was too late. Geo's teeth sank into my throat and a gold dagger appeared in my hand. I stabbed him in the stomach and he howled in pain. My dagger burned him; the smell of his flesh sizzling reminded me of burnt wood and animal carcass. Geo's pack came out the house like a stampede as the skin on my neck pulled together to heal from his bite. They all came to a halt when the ground in front of them split. The trees collapsed on top of their house, smashing it to the ground. A dark cloud covered the sun and although it was morning time, it looked to be midnight. A lightning bolt struck the ground causing a fire. I chuckled when I saw the fear the werewolves had on their faces. Geo paced back and forth, locking his eyes on me through the fire. I could no longer see them when the fire blazed, just their silhouettes.

This isn't over! You destroyed our home so now we will have to destroy what you have, he thought.

"You stole our jewelry and I want it back or else you all can meet your fate," I shouted.

We don't have it! I don't fear any of you. Your pack is not the only werewolves with a strong bloodline. This is far from over, punk! Geo thought.

"I'll be ready once you put the fire out!" I shouted before I disappeared. When I got home, Chancy's mother was on the couch, tears falling from her eyes. I rushed to her and she snatched away from me.

"Chancy came back for Destiny while everyone was asleep. She left this letter behind. She's the queen of Anubi. This is all your fault!" she cried.

"She came? I didn't have a vision of her. You're lying to me," I said.

Chancy's mother backed away from me, but it was too late. She was hypnotized when I looked into her eyes and demanded she tell me the truth.

I was ashamed to use spells on pack members but her mother was holding the truth from me.

"I took Destiny to a warrior from Anubi. He was waiting for her in the woods. Chancy stayed in Anubi so you wouldn't be able to see her whereabouts," she admitted.

"STUPID BITCH!" I shouted. I wrapped my hands around her throat. The energy in my body exploded. The objects in the house floated around to the ceiling. A plant flew past me and crashed into the window. Chancy's mother's nails sharpened and she slashed my face. My blood evaporated into the ceiling. Suddenly, blood was pouring from the ceiling like rain.

"Why did you take my daughter? This pack was supposed to protect her! I told everyone not to give Destiny to anybody unless it was her mother! What did you do?" I shouted.

Someone tackled me from behind. The items floating near the ceiling fell. The house stopped shaking and the blood from the rain decorated the living room floor. Chancy's mother fell onto the couch, gasping for air. Kanye stood over me with a displeased look on his face. Monifa stood behind him in confusion.

"He tried to kill me!" Chancy's mother screamed.

I heard the pack coming out their rooms, all heading downstairs. Chancy's father ran to her mother and she told him I tried to kill her. He shifted then charged into me but Kanye interfered.

"Wait, Uncle Dayo. I heard what happened. Your wife took Destiny to a warrior from Anubi. How are we supposed to know if they took her to Chancy? Your wife betrayed pack rules," Kanye told Dayo.

"Yeah, and putting your hands on my mate is a rule, too! Fuck this bullshit. We're moving out. This pack hasn't been the same since y'all grew up and started fucking each other. You should've stayed away from my damn daughter! You tricked her with your witchcraft bullshit and made her get pregnant. Now she's in Anubi with your punk-ass cousin and getting ready to marry him. You want to put your hands on my wife? How about man the fuck up and take responsibility for your own shit. Your father isn't here to save you, muthafucka. You're a man now," Dayo said to me. Uncle Izra stepped in between us and Dayo growled at him.

"What do you want? I'm not up for any of your shit right now," Dayo warned Izra.

"Your dumb-ass mate needs to mind her business. Destiny is Akea's daughter! Y'all just the damn grandparents. She gave Destiny to a damn stranger and you can't see why he choked her? I would've took her head off if it was my daughter. It's about that time where you tell your mate she needs to make decisions with the pack, not on her own. She's been doing it for a while now," Izra said.

"Destiny needs her mother's milk. I believe Osiris really cares for her and Destiny. He wouldn't send someone to hurt the baby and we all know it. Akea has another child to think about, so let Chancy do what's best for HER daughter. He lets Jetti play mother with Destiny and now he wants to have a fit because she'll have another father? We have bigger things to worry about like getting Goon back to this pack," Chancy's mother said. I wanted to curse her, make her age so she could rot in hell. Regardless of my mistakes, I loved my daughter.

"But I was a damn good father! And nobody can't take that away from me. If Chancy wants to be with Osiris, fine! But I still need my daughter in my life!" I yelled. Monifa rubbed my back and told me everything was going to be okay.

"Why are you siding with Akea?" Baneet asked Monifa.

"The same reason why you sided with Geo while they were stealing from us, bitch!" Monifa yelled.

Monifa's mother told everyone to calm down but I was frustrated with the whole pack. My mother didn't come to my defense and that's what crushed my spirit. She didn't see anything wrong with what Anik did. I went to my room and slammed the door. In the corner of my room was Destiny's crib. Her baby scent was still in the room. A tear slipped out of my eye when I grabbed her pink blanket. Kanye came into my room. I wiped my eyes and cracked a smile so he wouldn't think I was soft.

"Father said real men cry, bro. You can be soft for your daughter," he said.

"Jetti is pregnant. She's carrying my son and he's going to be just like me. I lost my daughter and my fiancée, but I don't think Geo is responsible for our jewelry store. This pack just ain't the same anymore. Father has only been gone for a day but it feels like years. I miss him. What if we can't get him back?"

"Can't isn't in our vocabulary. Our last name is Uffe. Uffe means wolf man. You are a wolf at heart and I need you to get in touch with the man deep inside you. We are not pups anymore. We can't cry to our parents about everything. Our father has been showing us what to do in times like this for years but we weren't paying attention. I spent all my life mad at everyone for thinking I was a bad seed. You spent all your time hating that you're a warlock. Those times are gone, brother. If Chancy wants to stay, let her. You can't force love, and if it's meant to be she'll come with you. Far as Jetti, she's still our enemy and will never be welcomed in this pack, so you don't have to worry about her again, just your son," he said.

"I'm starting to hate this mature Kanye," I chuckled. He playfully punched me in the arm and I fell off the bed and slid into the wall.

"Damn it!"

"You'll be aight," he said and left the room.

I laid back on the bed and closed my eyes so I could imagine my life as a beast. It was a feeling that could never go away and for years it haunted me. Nobody understands how lost I was with trying to figure out who I am. I was insecure with Chancy because she deserved someone of her kind. Warlocks are more human than beasts. I developed an urge to sleep with another woman and because of those urges, I'll never make Chancy happy. I had to let her go because being with her made me question my capabilities of pleasing her. She deserves a mate for life and me not being sure if I could dedicate my life to her hurt more than anything. I pulled out a small bottle from my pocket before I closed my eyes and drifted off to a peaceful sleep...

"What the hell!"

I looked around the dimly-lit temple and saw hieroglyphics. On one drawing, a man with the head of a wolf was wearing the pharaoh's neckless that was stolen from me and Kanye's jewelry store. I heard a deep howl coming from the shadows in the corner of the room. A white paw and long snout emerged from the dark corner. A gigantic pure-white wolf stood in front of me with a gold medallion around his neck that matched Kanye's when he shifted. One of the beast's eyes was ice blue and the other was gold. Moments later, the wolf shrunk into a man; the man looked like me and Kanye.

"What the fuck?"

"Have a seat, brother," he said. I closed my eyes and told myself to wake up.

"Brother? It's only me and Kanye."

"I live inside you. It's time for me to come out. Unleash me, Akea, so I can fight this war for you," he said.

"You're lying! This is fucking impossible. After all this time? Why am I able to see you now?"

"You might have never seen me but you always felt me. Why do you think your life feels incomplete? The feeling of not knowing who you are is because another life is inside you. You're fighting my existence. Look around you and read the drawings on the wall. This is the temple of the afterlife," he said.

"You're dead. You can't live inside me," I replied.

"I'm not dead. I'm trapped between the afterlife and your life! We share the same body, but you won't let me out!" he yelled.

"I'm going through a lot of shit and now I'm hallucinating which is normal for me," I chuckled to myself.

"I have lived in this dark temple for twenty-one years and you keep rejecting me! Let me free. Great danger will come to you if you don't let me fight your battle," he said.

"How can I do that?"

"Stop fighting it and release me."

"Okay, I will. Now, get me out of here!" I told him what he wanted to hear so I could wake up, but I didn't. I was still stuck inside the temple.

"This isn't a dream, Akea. You'll wake up when I'm finished!" he yelled before he disappeared. I banged on the walls of the temple but nothing happened. Even though my strength was gone I felt at peace. There was something about the temple that gave me hope by making me see things I'd overlooked...

Kanye

I ran into Akea's bedroom when I heard him yelling "get me out of here!" My brother was going through it. I could see it in his eyes that he wasn't the same and him choking Chancy's mother proved it. He was on the floor when I approached him.

"Akea! Wake up!" I slapped his face but he didn't budge.

"This ain't funny, bro!" I yelled out again. He was still breathing, but his heart rate was faster than normal and his body was hot. His shirt was ripped across the chest area and I saw a marking that matched the one on my chest.

"What kind of bullshit is this? You keep messing around with that weird witchcraft and look at you." I opened his mouth and a sharp fang cut my finger.

This can't be real. I'm gonna fuck him up when he wakes up.

"Get up, bro!"

I punched Akea in the chest and he and opened his eyes. Akea had two different colored eyes. I remembered seeing those eyes when we were younger. We had got into a big fight when we were thirteen years old. I thought it was some kind of magic he used to scare me off. I watched as Akea stood up and went to a mirror. He was my height and had the same exact body as me. His hair grew on his head into a big curly fro that fell into his face. He also had a goatee like mine. I was looking at a replica of me minus the hair. The pack could tell me and Akea apart because I was taller and weighed more, but now it would be impossible for them to know with Akea's new body.

"What have you done? You look just like me!"

"Calm down, brother," he said when he turned to face me.

My voice used to be deeper than Akea's but not anymore.

"Nigga, you better tell me something. Now is not the time for this bullshit, Akea! You couldn't wait to practice your sorcery later?"

"My name is not Akea. It's Djet," he replied.

"An Egyptian dog's name? Really, brother?"

"It was written for me on the wall in the Temple of Afterlife and it's wolf, not a dog. But we can talk later. I need to get to Anubi before Osiris mates with Chancy," he said.

"You must be smoking some ancient crack! You did all of this to scare Osiris? You got me, Akea. I will kill him for you if I have to but Father wants us to be happy with who we are and you are not a beast!"

"This isn't Akea, brother. Mother was pregnant with triplets but I didn't make it. Somehow, my soul latched on to Akea's body in the later years. I can't really explain it but it has something to do with our father," he said.

"What in the Beloved type of shit is this? So, you're telling me you're dead but you're inside my brother's body? I'm ready to beat him out of you," I growled. Akea crossed his arms and leaned against the dresser. I wanted to rip his heart out of his chest.

"Change back or I'm going to fuck you up in this room. Mother is already emotional because of father's imprisonment and you want to lie about her having three sons but she only gave birth to two? I swear you don't want to get on my bad side, brother."

"We don't have to tell anyone. You can tell them it's sorcery but I want you to know the truth because we are a team. I need to see our father so he can fix this. Do you know how hard it is not having a body? I have to live through a warlock who is in denial about everything. Who are you to strip me from finding out the truth? You can have your magical brother once I complete my mission," he said.

"Okay, prove to me you're not Akea. We can settle this once and for all. I want you to hunt. Akea doesn't like the taste of blood and even when he got inside my beast, he still couldn't stomach it. Let's go," I barked. I opened the window inside the room and jumped through it, landing on my feet. Akea was right behind me.

"Not bad, but I'm still not convinced."

"I'm not done yet," he replied.

We took off running towards the woods while our bodies transitioned to our beasts. Akea's wolf was pure white and had gold symbols embedded into his fur. My beast was the same except for my black coat with gold markings. White wolves meant spirit, guardianship and loyalty. Legend has it that you're guarded and safe when you see a white wolf in your dreams. My beast was opposite—black werewolves were a sign of danger and death. Many feared black wolves because we were vicious hunters and warriors. Djet had a half moon symbol on his neck and I had the other half. Both halves made a full moon.

Our father knew about this? I asked through our minds.

I was inside of mother's womb but somehow I ended up in the Temple of Afterlife. But I'm growing, becoming a man. The dead doesn't grow. I believe I'm cursed.

We will go to Anubi the next full moon but I need to know about Akea. Is he alive?

He's alive in the temple. He'll be safe but he might be disappointed when he finds out the truth. The afterlife temple forces us to see our truth.

Djet spotted four deer a few feet away. They were drinking water from a small pond. Without thinking, he charged into them but they ran and got away. My beast galloped through the woods while my heavy paws thumped against the ground. Two deer were in front of me. I leapt across a log and my body slammed into them, knocking them down. Djet jumped over my head and grabbed a deer by its throat. I dragged the other one to him so he could eat. Djet was weak, probably from Akea not eating the kinds of food his beast needed. I shifted into my human form and watched Djet maul the deer into shreds.

"Father would bite the shit out of you for hunting like a pup."

Djet lifted his head away from the deer and his once snow-white fur was coated in blood.

I never hunted before.

"I gotcha," I replied.

Monifa appeared in the woods. I forgot to bring her a glass of warm milk and honey.

"What's up, beautiful?" I asked her.

"Awww, Akea. You look magnificent! What a great way to win Chancy back. She used to dream about a white wolf when she was younger and has been fascinated by them ever since. Kanye should be this romantic," Monifa called out to Djet.

"Baby, that's not Akea."

"Are you out here smoking again? I thought you were going to quit?" she giggled.

"Beautiful, it's too much to explain," I replied. Djet shifted into his human form and Monifa gasped.

"Whoooaaaaa, you showed your dick to my mate!" I covered Monifa's eyes and her laugher echoed throughout the woods.

SOUL Publications

Djet snatched a small bush from the ground and covered himself. He walked over to Monifa and kneeled in front of her. He knew she was a witch and could see all he had been through. I uncovered her eyes and she placed her hand on Djet's forehead. Minutes later, she pulled away from him and he stood. Monifa hugged Djet and told him he'd find what he was looking for. I wanted to know what she saw but I decided to ask her later. I didn't need any more distractions until our father was safe.

"Let's head back to the mansion," I said.

"Good idea," Monifa replied.

Djet went into Akea's room to shower and I went into my bedroom to talk to Monifa.

"We need to go to our house before we leave," Monifa said.

"I kinda think we should move back into the mansion. We need to stick together, and besides, my father would want this. Let's talk about that later, what did Djet show you?"

"I saw his life in a temple where he roamed the halls. The afterlife temple is for the dead but Djet was the only one alive. He was very alone. It saddened me because I saw a vision of him crying for his parents when he was a pup. His only way out of the darkness was living through Akea. Djet is cursed but I couldn't see who cursed him. What if your father did this to him? He had to know about the other pup," Monifa said.

"My father would never do that," I replied.

"Your father is powerful enough to band his son for twenty-one years without anyone knowing. What if your father isn't as pure as we think he is?" she asked.

"You don't know what you're talking about," I replied.

"Well, we will find out when we get to Anubi," she said.

Father, I hope you didn't do this to Djet. I hope Monifa is wrong.

Goon

"**S**o, you're the great beast Anubi speaks so highly of? Look at you? You're weak!" a warrior said to me. I was chained against the wall in a dungeon that was underneath a temple. My body was covered in blood and there was a big wooden bowl underneath me to drain my blood. The guards whipped me every hour. I was weak and thirsty. My wounds stopped healing a few hours ago. I didn't regret not being the king of Anubi. I'd rather spend my last days with my sons and mate before I ruled a kingdom that my father once ruled. I could smell the stench of blood in the dungeon and a few rotten corpses. The chains around my wrists were cutting into my flesh. I coughed up blood and the warriors laughed. The door to the dungeon opened and the guards bowed their heads. It was the king of Anubi. A warrior pulled the door to the cell open and Osiris stepped in. He nodded his head in approval when he saw the deep scars on my skin.

"Leave us alone!" he called to the guards.

"That's not a good idea," someone said.

"GO!" Osiris yelled and they ran out the dungeon.

"I'm going to make sure you pay for what you've done to my home. You left my mother and father here to die. The great beast everyone talked about and worshipped failed his people! Now I have no one left because of you. You've killed my grandfather and my uncle Dash. Meda was right about you! She hated you so much for everything you did. My father needed you! What kind of beast are you and why did the gods give you the spirit of the ancient beast?" Osiris seethed. I spit blood into his face and he punched me in the rib cage.

"That's the best you got? You think I'm afraid of death? I've lived many lives and I always come back! I don't fear nothing!" I spat.
"That bowl of blood is going to bring great fear to you once I'm done with it. My father wanted me to be like you, fearless. But Seth showed me

something when he possessed me. Even the evil fear something, so don't fix your fucking mouth to talk about fearless. What about your granddaughter, Destiny? I wonder what she'll become if I drowned her in your blood," he said.

"What did you do?"

"Oh, now you're interested in what I have to say?" he asked.

"You wouldn't hurt Chancy if you loved her."

"She can have more pups—my pups," he replied.

"It's not too late to turn your heart around. You will die if you don't! You don't know shit about me and what I've done. My father was killing off his own kind and I saved them! Dash put my mate in danger while she was carrying my pups. You blame me for your parents' deaths? You are to protect your family and you've failed! I will die to protect mine but something tells me you're not the warrior your father trained you to be. Real warriors do not blame their mistakes on others! Kanye's beast will show you how a real man fights for his pack! I'd never chain a man up to feel above him. I'd rather fight him until one of us takes our last breath. Your legacy will not be honored, not even in death."

"This is just the beginning. You'll be begging for your life by the time I'm done with you," Osiris said. He slammed the door to my cell when he left the dungeon. The candles blew out and it was pitch-black.

I'll never die!

Monifa

The next day...

Me and Kanye snuck downstairs while the pack was asleep. They didn't know about our plans because they would have tried to talk us out of it. Goon's pack brothers had a plan but we had an even better one with Zaan, Djet and Fiti. Fiti was a witch from Anubi and didn't talk to anyone much but Zaan because she was shy. As for Djet, only me and Kanye knew he wasn't Akea. Kanye didn't want to upset his mother anymore.

"Listen, the secret portal is three hours away from here. We will drive because the pack can track us down on foot. Fiti, I sure hope you're right about this secret passage," Kanye said.

"It should be the right one," Fiti said.

"What is the plan again?" Zaan asked.

"Ignore him," I told Kanye. Zaan smoked exotic weed all day and could barely spell his name. He and Kanye had been close since they were pups despite being exact opposites.

"I'll drive," Kanye said.

We got into his truck which was parked on the side of the house. I sat in the front with Kanye. Zaan, Djet and Fiti sat in the back. Fiti was chanting something but I couldn't make it out. Fiti was old fashioned. She was sent from Anubi to destroy Goon but it wasn't in her heart. She stayed with us because of Zaan. Kanye placed his hand over my stomach and smiled at me. His smile was intoxicating. Djet was quiet while looking out the window.

"This is going to change the pack for good. We're about to break a lot of rules," I said.

"Rules are meant to broken," Kanye replied.

It was ten at night when I looked at the clock. We were going to New Jersey. Kanye was blasting rap music and Zaan had the car filled with smoke. A person appeared in the middle of the road and Kanye slammed on the brakes. The background was pitch-black and foggy with only the outline of the person's body showing. They were wearing a cloak and my heart almost skipped a beat when red eyes glowed at us. All I could think about was the bloodsucker, Seth who captured me because I harbored his ex-lover's spirit inside my body. Kanye and Zaan growled. The shadow came closer and tapped on the window.

"Monifa? Is that you?" the voice yelled out. "It's me, Rena. I need your help!" she said.

I got out of the truck and the rest of the pack followed. Rena took the hood off her head and I was relieved it wasn't her father, Seth.

"What happened?" I asked.

"My father's bat is missing," Rena replied.

"I don't get it," I said.

"His bat is very precious. Bad things can happen if it gets into the wrong person's hands.

His bat was used for many rituals, including bringing evil spirits back to life. I'm so happy I don't have to walk so far now. I was on my way to you because the thief who stole the bat left this behind at his club. I need your help because I know you can possibly tell me who this belongs to," she said. Rena pulled out a gold bracelet and Kanye took it from her. He sniffed the bracelet.

"How did they get in?" I asked.

"This is Arya's scent," Kanye said and gave the bracelet back to Rena.

"You remember that bitch's scent?" I asked.

"I know everybody's scent and I know that bracelet. I gave it to her when I was fourteen years old," he said. Me and Kanye didn't get along back when he had a crush on Arya, but the thought still made my stomach turn.

"Why would Arya steal Seth's bat?" Fiti asked.

"I don't know but I need her out of my father's life before she causes him to go back to the dark side. She thinks he loves her but he only wants to be intimate with her. I need that bat back before it brings out something very evil and undefeatable," Rena said.

"So, vampires aren't psychic?" Zaan asked.

"Only with humans, bro," Kanye answered.

"I'm sorry, Rena, but we can't help you right now. We have a lot going on," I said.

"What about your Egyptian calendar? Six days from now will be Festival of the Dead. Family members will gather around and summon their loved ones back to life to feel their presence, but the spirit will be reborn if a sacrifice is made. Unlike the afterlife cycle, these spirits are wicked. I find it odd that our bat is missing days before y'all's tradition," she said.

"We don't follow some of those ancient traditions," Zaan said.

"Anubi would never call an evil spirit," I replied.

"Anubi isn't the same anymore, Monifa. It's not a safe place. Some of us practiced witchcraft by making sacrifices. I was forced to be one of them," Fiti said.

"We will worry about this later, Rena. Right now, we have bigger fish to fry," I said.

"Just be on a look out," she said.

"Want us to give you a ride?" Kanye asked.

"Sure, you can drop me off at the nightclub," Rena replied.

Rena's father nightclub was only twenty minutes away. We headed for New Jersey after we dropped her off. All I could do was think about Arya and what she was up to; why had she tried so hard to go against her pack? I wondered if she was still trying to get to me because I mated with Kanye. Arya thought she was supposed to have him but he was my soulmate and nothing could come between us.

****

We arrived at an old and abandoned factory in New Jersey. I smelled fresh blood mixed with dead animals. We stepped out of the truck and Kanye's teeth sharpened. Black wolf hairs covered his face and arms.

"Wolves are in this area," Kanye said.

"They stink," Zaan replied.

A loud howl came from inside the building and Fiti hid behind Zaan. Djet and Kanye shifted at the same time with Zaan following behind. Me and Fiti stood off to the side, prepared to join the battle if we had to. Twenty wolves emerged from the old factory building. The alpha male was gray, indicating he was an older werewolf. He shifted to his human form, he was a dark-skinned man with long gray locs. He had a youthful face but his hair told another story. He also had scars covering his body.

"We don't allow outsiders on our territory!" the man warned.

"What are we going to do? We are outnumbered," Fiti whispered.

"It's not about quantity. It's about quality. These wolves are starved and damaged. They can't defeat anyone," I replied.

SOUL Publications

It's important that we cross this threshold. We've come in peace!

"We don't want you here! Now leave before it gets ugly," the man replied to Kanye. Kanye's beast stepped forward and Djet stood beside him. The old man's pack backed away from him. They were too weak to take on Djet and Kanye. The old man shifted into a beast the charged into Djet but Kanye caught the gray beast by his neck and slammed him onto the concrete. The others growled at Kanye and he let out a warning howl. His husky howl shifted the building. Debris from the building formed a dust cloud. I covered my nose so I wouldn't inhale the chemicals. Kanye's beast kneeled so I could get on his back. He ran past the wolves and Zaan and Djet followed. A werewolf tried to sneak up behind Fiti as she rode on Zaan's back but she turned him to dust.

Now do you see why you're supposed to be home? This is too much action for you. I know you can handle all of them but you're pregnant with my pups!

We ran past what was left of the old factory until we came to a waste area. Flies were everywhere and vultures were eating on dead wolves and even humans.

"Is this the portal?" I asked Fiti.

"Yes, according to the map in my spell book," she said.

"Spell book maps are created from our visions. What if your vision was wrong?" I replied.

"It can be wrong or it can be right. But I think those wolves back there were guarding the portal. It's not just a coincidence those wolves were guarding the area," she replied. Kanye's beast huffed, he was annoyed from the flies flying around us.

I think she's right, Monifa. They were guarding something, Kanye thought.

Something in the waste area caught my eye. There was a pile of branches next to a sewer. The werewolves from the other pack surrounded us and the old man walked towards Kanye. Djet blocked him and was ready to attack but Kanye called him off. They didn't seem as aggressive as they were minutes ago; they were calm and willing to call a truce. The old man kneeled in front of Kanye.

"Are you two the sons of Akua, the wolf god?" the man asked.

He's our father, Kanye replied.

"I was once a doctor in Anubi and I helped Naobi deliver your father. This was many ages ago. Your father lived many lives because he's a god. We were banned from Anubi because we were loyal to our beliefs but your grandfather betrayed us all. We've been here in this very spot for twenty-two years. Please forgive me," the man said. He pulled his locs away from his face to reveal the Anubi symbol on his neck.

"My name is Pateo. My mate is underneath that pile of sticks. She died two weeks ago from wandering off. A truck ran her over. I begged Anubi to open the gates so someone could help her but they don't answer those who are kicked out. Are you here to go inside?" he asked.

"Yes, they have Akua held prisoner," I replied.

"Oh noooo, nothing good will come out of punishing a wolf god. You have to hurry and save him," Pateo said.

"We need a way in," Fiti replied.

Pateo pulled out a gold rod with Egyptian writing from his knapsack and gave it to Fiti.

"Hold it up to the North star and read the words on the rod. It will take you to Anubi. You can keep it, I have no use for it anymore. None of us can go back," he said. Pateo's neck still bled from Kanye's bite. I climbed off Kanye's back and covered Pateo's neck with my hand so it could heal and he thanked me.

"I'm very sorry for what the old king did to his people," I said and he smiled.

"Anubi is cursed and has been for many years now. Ammon's blood still flows in the walls of his temple. All the good you do won't work unless you give pure blood to the temple so it can heal and spread tradition again. We need healing," he said with a shaky voice.

You will be back home soon, Father. I promise, Kanye thought.

Beasts 3: Unleashed   Natavia

SOUL Publications

Arya

My knees were aching from scraping across the wood floor inside of Seth's kitchen. My scalp was on fire from Seth pulling my hair but I couldn't get enough of his taste. His intimate face made me wetter than I'd ever been. His bottom lip was tucked in his mouth while showing off his fangs. I swallowed him and a growl mixed with a slight whimper slipped from my lips. Being intimate with Seth was a dark fantasy I had. He made me love to me as if he hated me but his eyes showed a softer emotion. His cum dripped from my lips after he exploded down my throat. He pulled me up by my ponytail and sank his teeth into my neck. Seth loved the taste of my blood and it made him more aroused. It was two o'clock in the morning when Seth called and demanded I come to his mansion. I left out of bed with Taj to have sex with my secret lover. Taj treated me with respect and he made me feel special but we weren't intimate. Taj wanted to wait until we were serious before we crossed that path.

"We gotta hurry up before Taj awakes," I reminded Seth. His eyes turned red and his eyebrows frowned. He punished me when I mentioned Taj's name. Seth turned me around and held me down on the countertop.

"I thought we weren't going to mention his name when it's my turn!" he gritted.

His sharp nails dug into the flesh of my buttocks, causing me to flinch in pain. He pulled away from me and the kitchen was quiet. I was afraid to turn around because Seth didn't tell me I could. It seemed like ten minutes passed when I felt his hands parting my pussy lips. My nipples hardened and nectar from my fruit drizzled along my inner thigh. My nails scratched his marble countertop when he teased my slit with his girth. He covered my mouth from behind before he violently shoved his dick inside me, plunging into my wetness. He pushed my leg up to the counter so he could go deeper. He bit my shoulder to taste my blood again. His bite was intoxicating. Seth turned me around and picked me up. I wrapped my legs around him and he carried me to the wall.

He entered me again and my teeth expanded along with my nails. He moaned into my ear when I clawed at his back. My hair grew wild and beast hairs appeared on my skin. My moans turned into growls. The feeling was beautiful. I loved him and wanted him to be with me but he was a bloodsucker. Seth's kind were sex machines and very rarely fell in love. Still, I wanted to prove to him I would love him either way.

He choked me up against the wall and went deeper. Our bodily fluids splashed onto the floor. I closed my eyes and enjoyed the massive orgasm Seth gave me. He cupped my breast and bit my nipple, a spec a blood dripping from his mouth. Every bite made me wetter and made me crazy.

"Please fuck me harder. I need you," I moaned.

"You don't need me, Arya. You only need to cum," he whispered in my ear.

"WHAT IS GOING ON?" a voice said. Seth turned around and I opened my eyes. Rena was standing in the kitchen with her mouth gaped open.

"What are you doing here, Rena? You're supposed to be at the club," Seth said and pulled out of me.

"I came here to warn you about that wicked bitch! I ran into Monifa and her clan and showed them this bracelet and Kanye said it belonged to Arya. She stole your bat! Maybe she wants to awaken the wicked because she enjoyed you being a demon. She's nothing but a whore, Father," Rena said.

"Excuse me? I haven't worn that bracelet in years! I left it at the pack's mansion in my old room after I moved out. I hated that darn bat and your father knows it!" I yelled at her.

"You'll do anything to live in our world but things have changed. My father is embracing the god that he is and you're trying to ruin it. You hate to see anyone making progress if it doesn't concern you. I'll kill you if wicked souls roam this Earth. Demons do not disappear, Arya," Rena replied.

"I didn't take that creepy old bat. Is this a game? Are you trying to frame me so I won't be with your father? This is pathetic!"

"You are what's pathetic. You have Taj but you'd rather be one of my father's many whores. Do you think you're the only one my father sleeps with? He has sex parties here every week! You are disgusting," Rena spat. My beast emerged and was ready to attack. Seth grabbed me by my wolf's tail and slung me into a wall.

"ENOUGH!" Seth yelled.

"I'm out of here. I'll never forgive you if you bring back that demon who tarnished your life and took everything from you, including my mother!" Rena said to her father. She left the house with the door slamming behind her.

"Go home, Arya," Seth said. He flew to the second floor of his house and slammed a door behind him. I grabbed my clothes and ran out of the house. Rena needed to die! She was the reason why her father didn't want to be loved.

****

Taj was sitting on the steps in front of my cabin when I pulled up in the driveway. I looked at the dashboard and it was four o'clock in the morning. He was a heavy sleeper and usually I could leave for two hours without him noticing. I desperately wanted to talk to him about Seth. Taj needed to share me if he wanted to be with me. I wanted both Taj and Seth and nothing was going to stand in my way.

"Where were you?" he asked.

"I was out hunting."

"Do I look like a fucking fool to you, Arya? I can't name one damn wolf who uses a car to go hunting!" he yelled. Taj's eyes were emerald and they glowed in the night. Black tiger stripes covered his face and his body swelled; he was ready to shift. I backed away from him. My beast wasn't a match for his gigantic tiger.

"I went to the twenty-four-hour grocery store for a steak. Why are you questioning me?" I asked.

"You were out fucking," he said. I threw my hands up in frustration.

"Okay, fine! I was out with someone else. You don't touch me and all we do is kiss like we're some fucking humans. I'm an animal and so are you! It's in our nature to be sexual. What are you afraid of?"

"You look beyond what matters just to concentrate on getting fucked. I know about your past and I know the pain you have been through growing up in a sex slave ring so I wanted to show you a different picture," he replied.

"I don't want a different picture! I don't want to change, Taj! I enjoy having sex and you have to deal with it until you're ready to man up. I should've known you were a pussy when I saw you shift into a cat. We need to stop acting like we're interested in doing things like we're human."

"Do you love him?" Taj asked.

"Love who?"

"The man you're sleeping with."

"Yes, I do," I replied and he chuckled.

"But you're not into doing human shit. Sneaking around and lying about what you're up to is what humans do, dumb-ass. I'm out of here," he said. Taj snatched off his car door instead of opening it—I'd pissed him off.

"Wait, Taj. Don't leave!" I ran to him.

His roar paralyzed me. I should've taken heed to his warning and stay away from him. I stood still and watched him leave out of my driveway.

What did I do wrong? Why can't I live freely and do what I want? I'm tired of doing what everyone else thinks is right.

Eight hours later...

"Do you hear me talking to you?" Baneet asked me. She was sitting on the ground while my beast laid next to her eating lunch.

I'm busy, Baneet. Leave me alone until I'm finished!

"But Geo wants to see me and I don't know what to do," she said.

Do what you want to do. Goon's pack cannot control you.

"Can I move here? The pack isn't talking to me that much because they think Geo stole from Kanye and Akea's store," Baneet replied. I pulled away from the deer carcass when I caught a whiff of another wolf's scent. Geo came out of the woods by the small lake behind my house. Geo was very attractive but he didn't have much. Baneet hated Akea for what he did to Geo's home. Geo and his pack slept in mud because their home burned down. Baneet ran to him and jumped in his arms. He kissed her and hugged her tightly. I wasn't concerned about Baneet and Geo's relationship like the pack. I left them and went into my house so I could shower. Taj was heavily on my mind but I loved Seth. Seth's real name is Utayo, but he was given another name when a warlock turned him into a demon bloodsucker. My beast didn't crave Taj's beast, only his human form. We could never mate because our seed would die in my womb. But, Seth could give me children and love me for eternity if he allowed himself.

What do I have to do to make him love me?

I heard screams mixed with howls while I was showering and I panicked.

Baneet!

My beast emerged and its nails scratched the tile on the bathroom floor, causing me to slip into the sink, knocking it onto the ground. The pipe burst and I cursed myself because I might be overreacting. I burst through the backdoor and came to a halt when I saw the commotion in my backyard. Baneet cradled Geo's naked body in her arms. The werewolves that surrounded Baneet were different than any werewolves I'd ever seen. Their paws were covered in gold plates and they all had a pyramid-like symbol embedded into their shiny and well-groomed fur. I howled to warn them off but the leader walked towards me; his stride spoke "alpha" and his growls were intimidating. His brown and gold eyes were familiar. My beast lowered to the ground in surrender. My beast wasn't a match for the alpha. He and his pack would've torn me to shreds. The beast disappeared and Osiris stood in front of me. I was confused.

What does he want with me?

I shifted into my human form and he smirked at me. It was something different about him. Osiris had eyes of a lost and afraid wolf when I met him but now his eyes showed confidence. I wondered if he mated with Chancy. Baneet told me about everything that was happening at the pack's mansion, including our mother giving Chancy's baby to warriors in Anubi.

"What are you doing on my territory? I don't have Anubi's blood flowing through my veins so your business doesn't concern me!" I gritted to Osiris.

"Because you can help me. Remember our time together? You've forgotten Seth possessed my body and me being inside you? You're just like me, Arya. Unloved and alone. Do me a favor and I'll grant you whatever you want," he said. Osiris cupped my chin and forced him to stare into his eyes. I gasped when his eyes turned red. I didn't understand what was happening. The demons were dormant according to Seth but Osiris must have awakened them.

"I felt empty. Ibuna made me feel something I have never felt before and that's revenge. When Monifa healed me, I thought I was going to be happy but she made me feel again. I don't want to feel sadness and rejection anymore. So, I have a plan for you—for us. You kill Goon's pack and I'll give you back the bloodsucker you fell in love with," he said.

"And if I don't?"

"I'll kill him and make you watch," he said.

"I cannot kill a whole pack! You have lost your mind. Get away from my house or else I'm going to alert G—"

"Alert Goon? He's locked away and bleeding like a slaughtered pig. Goon cannot do anything for you. Do you think I fear Akea and Kanye? They don't have nothing on what I've got planned! You don't have a choice, Arya. You can either die along with them or be with the demon bloodsucker your pussy craves," he said.

"You're a traitor!"

"And so are you, beautiful. I don't want to go against you. I want you to be on my team. You know that pack is disappointed in you for all of your sins. You'll never fit in with them so there is no need to spare them from death," he said.

"Are you the one who stole my bracelet? Framed me so it could look like I stole Seth's bat?"

"A man never shows his hand. Just know Rena wants to kill you and she will. I'll handle her and anything else you want me to do if you plant these beads in the pack's mansion. The beads are poisonous and will put the pack into a deep sleep they can't wake up from. I found it in my aunt's temple, along with this," he said. Osiris handed me a spell book and I was confused.

"What is this for? I'm not a witch!"

"Meda taught sorcery to those who weren't born a witch. Sacrifices have to be made if you want the power from the spell book to stick with you for eternity," he said.

"What kind of sacrifices?"

"Blood from a pup. Baneet is pregnant I see," Osiris hinted.

"She's my sister."

"She's useless. Her loyalty is to another pack and by mate's law, you cannot betray your mate.

She'll leave you hanging before she goes against him. You have to be selfish if you want to overcome all of this. Only the strong survive. I'll be watching you so make the right choice. Do not fail me," he spat. Osiris disappeared along with his warriors from Anubi. Baneet screamed and cried while Geo laid in her arms.

"Help me carry him into the house. He's losing a lot of blood. Osiris's pack attacked him from behind," Baneet cried.

"Let him die, sister. His other mate can mourn his death. He never cared about you, just your money. His pack has been freeloading off of you for far too long."

"Osiris wants to bring back the demons and you're gonna help him? Monifa was right about you! You don't care about anyone. Seth was healed and you're about to put him in a dark place so he can love you? Demons don't love, Arya! The pack loves you and that should be good enough," she said.

"What do you know about love? You stole from Akea and Kanye! You pretend you don't know about their missing jewelry but I know you did it. You stole their jewelry so Geo's pack can have as much wealth as Akea because you're jealous of him and Chancy. Where is the pharaoh's necklace?"

"I don't have it!" Baneet screamed. Geo choked on blood as Baneet sobbed. He was dying.

"I'm going to alert the pack of your plan," she said. I picked up a rock and struck Baneet across the head twice. Her body fell on top of Geo's. I grabbed her by the ankles and dragged her to the basement of my cabin. After I was finished, I stripped her from her bloody clothes then tied her to the stairwell. I couldn't imagine killing Baneet because she's all I had but I couldn't let her stand in my way.

"I'm going to be Queen of Ibuna and I'm going to take you with me," I whispered to Baneet. I covered her body with a sheet while she rested. I had a mission and that was to poison the pack, including Anik and Dayo who raised me. The only decision left to make was whether to sacrifice who I thought was family for living my fantasy with Seth.

I'm so sorry but I have to do this...

Rena

I woke up to the sounds of glass breaking and more noise coming from downstairs in my father's mansion. I quietly slipped out of bed and grabbed my black cloak. The growls and howls had almost deafened me when I flew downstairs. In the middle of the hallway lay five werewolves with ripped out throats. Blood was everywhere and I ran into the kitchen where the louder growls were coming from. I burst inside and four beasts were attacking my father.

"Run, Rena!" he yelled before he took a chunk out of a beast's throat. Another beast charged into me and I slammed it into the wall. My sharp nails cut through its throat but he was still alive. I screamed in pain when the beast bit my shoulder. My father was fighting the beasts but they pulled him outside through the back door of the kitchen.

"FATHER!" I yelled. The beast slammed me through the wall and jumped on top of me. His big paws pounded my head into the floor. His nails opened the flesh on my face. I grabbed him by the snout and snapped his bone in half. He fell against the wall and I flew upstairs. The beast leapt in front of me, his snout twisted with a bone poking through his cheek. He couldn't bite me anymore but his large brown paws could kill me. I noticed the Anubi symbol on his chest.

Why are Anubi werewolves attacking us?

"Stand back!" I yelled.

The large beast ran towards me and I closed my eyes and asked for forgiveness. I didn't understand what I'd done to deserve this punishment but I had too much pride to beg for my life. But nothing happened. When I opened my eyes, the beast was lying on the floor shredded to pieces. My heart was beating out of my chest. I made a promise to my god that I wouldn't use any magic but my father told me it was a gift from my mother. I believed her gift was wicked so I kept it inside me. Osiris appeared next to the mangled beast. He prayed for him before he turned the beast into ashes.

"Why are you doing this?"

"I owe your father. Pay back is a bitch, Rena," he said.

"He was forgiven from his god! He was possessed himself when he possessed you! We want peace not war." Osiris grabbed me by the throat and held me against the wall. He was strong and emotionless just like my father was when he was a demon.

"You stole my father's bat?"

"I can't steal what's mine," he replied.

Osiris's hand slid underneath my cloak—I was naked. He rubbed my pussy then sniffed his fingers like the animal inside him.

"You're a virgin? Wow, a bloodsucking virgin at that. I thought you all were jezebels," he said then dropped me on the floor.

"I'll do anything you want me to do. Please let my father go," I begged.

"Your father brought me into his world and now I'm finishing what he started. This isn't about you or your blood-sucking piece of shit father. This is about my grandfather. I'm going to turn Anubi to Ibuna and no one can do a damn thing about it!" he yelled. Osiris disappeared and tears fell from my eyes. Osiris didn't know what he was doing and it was sure going to backfire. Only true vampire gods can rule Ibuna.

Oh no! He's going to sacrifice his soul and get inside my father's body. He's going to reincarnate himself.

I thought of the person who could help me. Blood seeped through my wounds and I was too weak to travel on foot. I went downstairs and grabbed my father's keys to his car. I was getting weak and needed blood.

Please be home.

****

An hour later, I pulled up to a luxury high-rise downtown. It was almost ten o'clock at night. My father's club opened at midnight and I had to figure out if his assistant could run his club while I found my father. I saw a tall man walking down the sidewalk wearing a track suit and tennis shoes. His emerald eyes glowed when he saw me getting out of the car. I was weak, the drive took all the strength I had left. Taj ran to me when I collapsed on the sidewalk.

"What happened?" he asked.

"I'm hurt, Taj. I was attacked by werewolves from Anubi. Osiris is still wicked. I don't think he was ever healed. He tricked us all. Osiris's destiny is to be wicked anyway so there is no cure for him. We need to kill him." Taj picked me up and carried me inside his building. I spit up a glob of blood on the elevator floor. I was dying but I held on long enough so Taj could alert Monifa's pack of Osiris and the plans he had for their ancestors' kingdom.

Kanye

"**W**e've been traveling for a whole day and nothing! I think that old wolf lied to us. What if this is a trap?" Monifa asked.

We were in the middle of a small forest along the Nile River. Anubi was a replica of Egypt minus the humans. We found a resting area and Monifa laid in the grass. Me, Zaan and Djet went to the river for water. I could see the tall temples of Anubi but they were still far away.

"I regret bringing Monifa with me. Look at her," I told Zaan.

"Yeah, she's holding us up. We would've been to Anubi by now. Maybe we leave her here with Fiti until we get back," Zaan replied.

"Fuck no. You've lost your mind if you think I'm going to leave my pregnant mate out here. We don't know Anubians like that and what if someone is watching us? Do you think they'll leave the portal unguarded?"

"Bro, nobody is following us. We would've smelled another beast. Monifa is going to get us caught," Zaan whispered.

"I have a plan."

Djet stepped into the water to cool off. It looked refreshing but we didn't have time to swim around.

"We should rest until the sun is up. It's late and I'm tired," Fiti said when she walked over to us. I looked back at Monifa and she was asleep with her hand resting on her stomach.

"I agree. We can rest for a bit but we have to wake up when the sun begins to rise."

I used an old wooden bowl by the river to take Monifa her water. Her snores were mixed with a slight growl. I moved a loc of her hair out of her face so I could take in her natural beauty. She opened her eyes when I kissed her lips.

"Why are you kissing me like you'll never see me again?" she asked when she sat up. Her stomach grew and her face was a little fuller than before. She placed my hand over her stomach and weakly smiled. Monifa didn't look well and I hated myself for allowing her to come with me, but I wanted her to have peace instead of worrying about me.

"I'm tired and weak. We've been walking in circles and my feet are sore. I don't think I can make it," she said.

"I want you to go back home."

She smacked the bowl of water out of my hand and growled at me.

"I don't want you to agree with me. I was expecting you to tell me I can do it. You need me here to protect you and I won't leave you. I have to make sure you make it back to me, the pack and our pups. I apologize for complaining and I won't do it again," she said. Monifa pulled my face to hers and stared me in the eyes. She was trying to figure me out but I couldn't let her see my plans. I had a way of blocking her from looking into my future. She pulled away from me when she couldn't find anything. Zaan and Fiti were playing around in the river. I remembered a time when me and Monifa kidded around but mating changed us. Djet was drawing a symbol in the sand with a stick. I wondered what Akea was doing along with my father.

"I feel old," Monifa said.

"Yeah, me, too, but we'll feel our age again after all this bullshit is over. I'm gonna rip Anubi to shreds and they can kiss their temples goodbye."

I heard a noise coming from the bushes behind us—it smelled of an animal. Our stomachs growled and I realized we hadn't eaten in almost two days. I shifted into my beast and crept between the bushes. There were four camels resting by the trees.

Zaan and Djet! I need you two. Follow my scent and do it quietly so you won't scare our food. I'll take two down and the rest is up to you two.

Bro, what are you going to do with four kills? Zaan asked.

My mate has an appetite of three male beasts!

Zaan and Djet's beasts appeared alongside of me moments later as we stalked our prey. I jumped out the bushes and pounced on a camel, snapping its neck in a matter of seconds. The other three ran but I caught my second kill by the throat and crushed its windpipe. Zaan and Djet made their kills, too. Monifa sat next to me while I used my teeth to chop through the camel's stomach. She pulled chunks of meat out of my mouth to eat. Fiti sat aside and watched us. Zaan dropped a camel's heart into her lap.

"I don't eat raw meat," Fiti laughed.

"This tastes better than deer. It has more fat," Monifa said with a mouthful.

An hour or so later, the camels were devoured except for the bones. We split up but not too far so we could rest. Djet decided to sleep in a tree so he could be on the lookout. There weren't any signs of werewolves in the forest, not even other animal carcasses. Monifa found us a sleeping spot between two big fallen trees.

"This place feels so familiar. Almost like we've been here before," Monifa said.

"That's cause we're a part of this. I thought it was going to be magical with diamonds floating around in the water but it looks normal. I see why my father picked our home before this."

Monifa laid across my lap and I looked down at her. Her breasts swelled and her nipples poked through the thin material of her shirt. She wasn't wearing anything else. Monifa wanted to sleep naked but I didn't want her to since we didn't have much privacy but I was regretting it. She placed my hand between her wet center. Monifa spread her legs wider for me so I could slip my finger inside of her. The eyes of her beast glowed and her center flowed like the Nile on my fingers. I craved her—I needed her.

Straddle me.

She read my mind. Monifa took off her shirt and tossed it behind us. Her cantaloupe-sized breasts bounced as she positioned herself on my lap. She roughly grabbed my face and kissed me. The nails from her beast gently scratched my cheek. Her round ass was planted firmly into the palms of my hands. She moaned as she deepened

99

Beasts 3: Unleashed   Natavia

our kiss and my dick pressed against her wet pussy.

"I need to be inside you. My dick is about to explode."

She moved her hips, teasing me while smearing her essence on my shaft. The scent of her female was taunting. She pushed me onto the forest's soil so she could take advantage of me. I rubbed her stomach and she blushed. Monifa bearing my pups was the best gift that could be given to me. A deep growl, loud enough to reach the temples in Anubi escaped my lips when she eased my dick inside of her. The hairs of her beast poked through her skin and her teeth expanded from her gums. She moaned and growled while riding me. Monifa's tight pussy squeezed my girth, almost popping the thick veins in my dick.

"FUCCCKKK!" I growled. My nails scratched at her thighs and her nails scratched at my chest, drawing blood. She gasped when I sank my teeth into her neck. The more pressure I used, the wetter she got and exploded on my dick. Tears fell from her eyes and she jerked when I pummeled into her pussy. Sweat beads dripped down her cleavage and her skin was hot.

"You feel so good, Kanye."

She was on the verge of exploding again but I wanted to taste her. I laid her down and kissed her lips while rubbing her swollen clit.

"You still can't handle the pleasure?"

"It's too intense," she panted.

She pushed my head away when I sniffed at her entrance. Monifa covered her mouth to muffle her cries. My tongue slid into her and she bucked her hips. A man was no longer pleasing her. My beast ate between her slit without manners and remorse. I feasted on her essence and the folds of her mound until she squirted in my mouth. Her body went still and she breathed heavily when I made her cum again. Her pussy tightened around my tongue and pre-cum oozed from the tip of my dick. Her scent grew stronger and filled my lungs and my beast took over. Careful to protect her stomach, I laid on top of her and entered her again. She bit my shoulder and her nails scratched my back as I stroked her.

Don't fuck me back. I want you to feel all of me while I enjoy my pussy.

She laid still sobbing; she wasn't crying because I was hurting her. She cried because I felt too good inside of her. Our love poured through our souls during intimacy. She screamed to the gods how much she loved me as I deeply stroked her.

Forgive me for what I'm about to do but I have to. This is the only way you'll stay safe.

Before she could react and see a vision of my plans, I bit her again but it wasn't an intimate bite. It was to put her to sleep so I could send her back home without her putting up a fuss. Anubi wasn't good for Monifa's pregnancy and I worried she'd deliver the pups early due to the stress she was putting her body through. After she closed her eyes and stopped moving, I pulled out of her and dressed her. I called for Fiti to help me before Monifa awakened. The last thing I wanted to do was go to war with my mate.

Monifa

I woke up with a headache and a throbbing pussy. My vision was blurry and my body was sore. Kanye was more than a lover during intimacy. He wasn't afraid to let the animal out of him during sex. It was one of many gifts of being an immortal. When I sat up, I was fully clothed inside of our bedroom. Me and Kanye had our own home together outside of his father's mansion. We lived in a six-bedroom house. It was plenty of room for me, him and our pups.

"I better be fucking dreaming! Kanye is going to deal with me if he fucked me over!" I said aloud. I closed my eyes, thinking my sorcery put me into a deep sleep. Sometimes I overwork myself by using a lot of magic and it forced me to have dreams that seemed real while being in a deep sleep. I heard someone come into my room and I opened my eyes. Fiti was standing next to me with a plate of raw meat and a glass of milk.

"Where in the fuck is Kanye?" I asked.

"We traveled back to our starting point so we could come back home. It delayed his time to get to Anubi. Who knows how long it'll take for them to get there. I'm so sorry, Monifa, but Kanye was worried about you. After he put you to sleep, I blew sleeping dust onto your body so you could sleep through our journey back. And before you kill me, just know I had to obey Kanye. He's the leader and I was raised to always listen to the leader," she said.

"Kanye needed me to disguise their identity. How is he supposed to make it into the temple without getting killed?"

"I disguised them. I'm not as strong as you so I worry my spell won't stick. I expressed my concern but Kanye told me he would rather die than to bring you along with us while carrying his pups. He's not worried about himself at this point, just you, the pups and the pack. You can't force an alpha to do what's not in his heart. I believe in him but you have to, too. Giving him your support will make him stronger and fight harder to come back home," Fiti said.

"I was selfish but what is love if you can't be selfish about your mate?"

"Yes, of course, but sometimes being selfish can bring harm to love. I worry about Zaan but instead of arguing with him to come with me, I prayed our gods look over him and keep him safe. I feel much peace doing so and now I only have good visions," she said.

"You're right but I'm still gonna kick his ass."

We burst into laughter. Fiti opened my eyes to what was important. Kanye was on a path to becoming what he was born to be.

"I have a change of clothes in the spare bedroom along with a bathroom. Take a bath or shower if you want to. We're going to the pack's mansion after we're done. Something needs to be done about Arya. Rena thinks she's responsible for stealing from Seth. This is all connected somehow and I'll figure it out."

"Kanye wants you to rest," she said.

"Kanye is being selfish. Remember what you just said about it bringing harm to love. Well, I'm not incapable of finding out the truth. Let's get ready."

Fiti left the bedroom and I went into the bathroom. Kanye left passion marks on my neck and chest. I could still feel his touches and smell his masculine scent. His soul was with me. I don't know what he did to me but he provided a feeling of serenity.

I hear you, Kanye. Do whatever you have to do and make it back home to just not me, but to the rest of us who love you.

I will. Love you, beautiful, I could imagine him replying back. With Kanye being in Anubi, I couldn't hear his thoughts but he could hear mine. We were disconnected.

Two hours later...

"Does the mansion look different to you?" I asked Fiti when we approached Goon's estate.

"Yes, I smell snake poison. Wait, don't go near the door!" she yelled.

"What is the matter with you? I don't smell anything."

"We use it in Anubi to terminate prisoners. Snakes are strong enough to put a wicked witch to rest. They plant the balls in the ground of the dungeon and it can kill you. The smell might be faint to you because you're not familiar with it. It smells fresh, maybe been planted an hour ago," Fiti said. I ripped off the sleeve on my sweater and covered my nose and mouth. Fiti did the same. I opened the door to the mansion and the house was quiet. I ran upstairs to my parents' bedroom and they were sprawled out on the floor. My father was choking as foam seeped through his nose and mouth. I grabbed a sheet and ripped it in half. I covered his nose and mouth then my mother's. She had a heartbeat but it was slowing down. I wrapped them inside another sheet and dragged them down the spiral staircase and out of the house. Fiti appeared next to me with Chancy's parents. We went back inside to get Zaan's parents. It was early morning and they were sleeping when someone poisoned them. Fiti went back inside the house for others while I tried to heal our parents. We weren't too late. Fiti managed to get everyone outside but someone was missing.

"Where is Kanye's mother?"

"She's not in the house, Monifa. She left this behind," Fiti said and handed me a letter.

"His mother went to Anubi by herself. I wonder how she got through. We have to find her before someone does something to her," I panicked.

"Something bad is in the air and I'm not talking about the poison," Fiti said.

"We have to get everyone into the company van and take them to my house. This home isn't safe for anyone until we get rid of the poison."

"It'll take days for it to go away.The poison is aged and I mean hundreds of years old. Goon's father got it from a wicked witch. They call it a silent killer. Someone from Anubi planted that inside the house to kill us all. We are at war with our own kind but our souls will burn for disobeying the gods," Fiti said.

"Kanye was right. Our gods have failed us. It's time we pick our own beliefs because Anubi is hell now."

I left Fiti in the front yard of the mansion so I could get the van. Seeing Kanye's sports car parked inside the garage brought back memories. The human girls at school used to wait in front of campus for Kanye to pull up while blasting his rap music. After school, we'd come home to our parents greeting us. Akea's car was parked next to Kanye's and I giggled because Kanye thought Akea's car was nerdy. Akea had stickers from all the groups he joined in school. The wind blew and a breeze swept past my nose. I sniffed the air to inhale the scent again and it was fresh. The scent belonged to Arya. I left out of the garage to follow the trail. It took me to the back of the house and down the steps to the heating and air conditioning room. The door had a security code and that bitch knew it because she used to live with us. Fiti appeared next to me.

"Arya did this. She made the poison travel through the vents. Why would she try to kill us? Even her own parents."

"Get through to her," Fiti said.

"I can't see visions of her. She's not our kind. She belongs to an Indian tribe. Our gods are different and so is our traditions. That's why she's so dangerous. She can sneak past us and we don't hear her. To see through her, you have to be in her presence."

"We will go to her after we take the pack to a safe place," Fiti said.

"I'm going to put on my Timbs and whoop her ass human style," I spat.

"Whatever Timbs are, do you have another pair? You must teach me to whoop ass human style," Fiti said.

"Yes, Chancy has a pair at my home. Let's hurry up and get out of here," I replied.

The pack should've killed Arya the first time she betrayed us and now she's trying to kill us. Her life shouldn't be spared anymore!

****

"Are you sure Arya was behind this?" Anik asked.

Me and Fiti worked for hours to wake the pack up. Everyone was sluggish but they were all alert. We were sitting next to the fireplace trying to come up with a plan. Kanye's mother going missing was very unexpected but I would have done the same thing for Kanye.

"That little whore almost killed our child!" Ula said about Arya.

"That child doesn't belong to you! You found her abandoned in the woods. The woman you speak of belongs to me. I'm mad at Arya, too, but do we have to kill her?" Anik asked.

"How can you fix your lips to tell me this pup isn't my child when you get to claim a whore you didn't give birth to neither? One more insult and I'll turn you into a fur rug! For months, we have been dealing with Arya's betrayal, and excusing her behavior isn't going to solve anything. She tried to kill you, too. Do you understand that nothing is going to stop her but death?" Ula asked Anik. Anik went into the guest room and slammed the door.

"Don't slam nothing in my daughter's house again!" my mother called out.

"My mate is brainwashed. She still thinks of Arya as that little girl but she's far from it. I think she needs to be put to rest so this pack can be peaceful again," Dayo said. The rest of the pack was lost for words. They were tired of hearing about Arya. They were also used to her betrayal.

"A lot of my oils went missing. I should've known Kanya was up to something. She was too silent. I think she took my oils to hide her scent. We've failed our brother. We failed each other. Pity to think we were going to live peacefully but we can't rest until blood is shed. I need to sleep," Ula's mate Amadi said. He grabbed their pup from her and went to the bedroom at the end of the hall.

"I'm going to Anubi. We should've killed those muthafuckas when they came on our territory to imprison our brother. We've gotten soft over the years. We made ourselves believe we could live like humans but aren't humans! We are fucking beasts! We're animals! We kill, fight and protect our pack! For years we tried to hide the real meaning of what we are so our kids could feel normal. Look at what it has done to Akea. We need to do what we have to. We cannot sit here and let Kanye die alone. Goon is our pack brother and we should've been in Anubi," my father said.

"It's more to life than being an animal!" my father's pack brother, Elle, yelled.

"Oh, shut the fuck up, Elle. The only time we hurt is when we live like humans! Tell me I'm wrong so I can snatch your tongue out of your mouth!" my father spat.

"Izra, hush! This is why we're crumbling. We are always fighting and I'm sick of it. Elle is your pack brother and has been since you were a young wolf! He raised you, so watch your mouth and show respect," my mother scolded my father.

"It has to be another way to Anubi," Dayo said.

"Yeah, it is but you have to fly to Egypt and find a secret passage to Anubi. Egypt isn't like it was decades ago. Humans took over and built over our passages. I wouldn't know where to look," my mother said.

"Doesn't matter. I'm ready to book our flights," Elle said.

"I know exactly who can help us," I replied.

I told the pack about the banned wolf we ran into in New Jersey who could help them. Anubi had to be reborn again to right all of their wrongs.

****

"You didn't have to leave your mate to come with us," I told Ula.

"And pass up seeing Arya get her ass whipped? Chile, I've prayed every night that hotbox gets the punishment she deserves," Ula said.

"So, just to be certain. I ring the doorbell and snatch her out the house by her hair, drag her down the stairs then stomp on her? Now, do I stomp to squash the turd or do I stomp as in I'm jumping for joy?" Fiti asked.

"Chile, what in hell do y'all smoke in Anubi? I will not believe you all are this old fashioned. What is stomp on the turd?" Ula asked Fiti.

"We have beetles in our temple the size of turds. So, we call them turds. Do I stomp her like I'm killing a bug?" Fiti asked. I covered my face to stop myself from laughing.

"No, sweetie. You stomp like you caught her sucking Zaan's dick. Now I know for a fact you know what a dick is cause ain't nothing but jezebels in Anubi," Ula said.

"Can I just turn her into ashes? It will take me days to study this spell," Fiti replied.

"You and Zaan are a match made in heaven. I understand it now and, sweetie, it's okay. How about you stay back and I drag her out the house," Ula said. We stepped from behind the tree where Arya lived. Her front door was wide open and drops of blood was on her front steps. The inside of her cabin was dark. Ula told me to wait outside while she checked the home out. I didn't put up a fuss because she didn't want me in harm's way in case something was lurking around Arya's home. Five minutes later, Ula came out of the house carrying Baneet's necklace.

"Arya isn't here. I checked her closets and it seemed like she took some stuff with her. Baneet is with her but that's all I could sense. Something wicked has been on this territory and I'm not talking about Arya," Ula said.

"MONIFA!" Fiti called out from behind the cabin. We ran to her and she was kneeling next to Geo. Geo was barely breathing; his wounds were fatal and his eyes were lifeless.

"Help me," he whispered.

I walked over to him and kneeled beside him. A knife appeared in my hand and I held it to his throat.

"Why should we help you when you stole from us?"

"Arya is trying to kill your pack," he wheezed.

"We need to help him, he's lost a lot of blood. I think he's been out here for a while," Fiti said.

"I have to see if he's deceiving us. Geo's pack is greedy and full of manipulative thieves."

"Grab my hand, so you can see through my eyes," Geo begged. Ula nodded for me to see Geo's memories. I picked up Geo's bloody and cold hand to see what happened to him. He showed me Osiris and the werewolves from Anubi. Osiris promised Arya the life she wanted if she sacrificed her family. I also saw a vision of Arya striking Baneet across the head then dragging her into the house. Osiris was indeed wicked and used Arya as a pawn because he wasn't brave enough to come back to our territory. Arya betrayed us.

"She betrayed us for love when we loved her!" I cried.

"Some will do anything for love. It's a disease to those who don't know what to do about it and use it as a weapon," Fiti said. I healed Geo's wounds but he was still weak from losing a lot of blood. Fiti gave him a bottle of natural herbs and made him drink it. We pulled him up and leaned him against a rock.

"I've done a lot of things but I didn't steal from your pack. Baneet gave me the money because she wanted to impress my other mate. I'd rather sleep on concrete before I beg for someone's help. Akea destroyed our home and all I asked is that he fix it because I didn't steal from him. He gave me a job," Geo said.

"I know you didn't steal from us. I saw it through your vision. We have bigger things to worry about right now like dealing with Osiris."

"We need to find Seth. Maybe Arya is with him," Ula said.

We were ready to leave but Geo called out to us. He was standing up when I turned around. He was still a little pale but was improving fast.

"Take me with you. I have to retaliate for what those werewolves did to me. I won't let it rest. I also need to find my mate because she's carrying my pup," Geo said.

"I don't know if Kanye would approve of this since he's not here," I replied.

"We came together once to defeat that fucked up experiment Arya helped create. It's not about us being friends but alphas do not turn their backs on each other when there is a bigger threat against us. Osiris has a lot of help and all you have is Goon's pack," he said.

"Give me your hand," I replied.

Geo gave me his hand and I cut a dash across his palm with my nail to draw his blood. His blood dripped into the muddy soil underneath his feet.

"The earth will swallow you whole if you betray us."

"You cursed me?" he asked.

"It doesn't matter if you're a man of your word, does it?" I replied.

"Cool," he said and shrugged his shoulders.

We disappeared deep into the woods. Ula had a sanctuary hidden where she practiced spells. We went to her place to figure out our next plan because Geo couldn't go around the pack, especially Baneet's father. They would have torn him to shreds.

I hope you're safe, Kanye.

****

Ula's sanctuary was by mountains and an old farm. The place was creepy but I could tell it used to be nice because of the mountain view. My pups were moving around, so I had to rest myself.

Kanye would raise hell if he knew I wasn't resting.

"Are you feeling okay?" Fiti asked.

"Yes, I'm fine. I'll take a nap shortly."

"You need to eat something," she replied.

"I will soon."

"Why are we here?" Geo asked. He was still a little weak. He laid across the floor and covered his eyes with his arm.

"We're here to figure out our next move unless you want to go to Monifa's house so the pack can kill you," Ula said. Geo turned over with his back towards her.

"What is our plan?" Fiti asked.

"We don't have one yet but we will soon," Ula replied while snatching books off her bookshelf.

My cell phone rang and I forgot I had once since me and Kanye didn't need it to communicate.

"Hello," I answered after fumbling with the phone.

"Yo, this is Taj. I've been trying to contact you since last night. Rena is hurt. She was attacked by werewolves from Anubi. What in the fuck is going on?" he asked.

"I'll be over soon and tell you everything," I replied.

"I need blood. A lot of blood so she won't wake up hungry and turn me into a meal. There is a blood bank near the hospital. I can't leave her alone. Those sons of bitches might come back to finish her off."

"Okay, see you shortly," I said and hung up.

"We have to go see Rena. She's hurt very badly."

"You three go ahead. I'm going to stay back and see what I can find from these books. There has got to be a way to stop the lost souls from resurfacing again," Ula said while throwing things across the room. I kissed Ula's cheek before we left her small house.

"I don't understand how this shit is supposed to help me find Baneet," Geo said.

"Would you shut the fuck up? We have to solve the bigger problem before the small one," I replied.

"Her carrying my pup isn't a big problem to y'all? She was right about the pack. Y'all hate her," Geo said. He was ready to say something else but his lips glued shut.

"I'll turn your mouth back to normal after we get blood for Rena," I said. Geo scratched at his mouth while we walked through the woods. I was concerned for Rena. We were connected even after all the circumstances with Keora. Keora wasn't a good being when she was alive but she gave me life when my mother couldn't conceive. I loved her for what she did for me so I'd do anything for her, including making sure Rena was safe.

Akea

"**G**ET ME OUT OF HERE!" I banged on the wall of the temple.

"Why are you doing this to me? I don't deserve to be here!" I yelled. My voice echoed throughout the temple. I've walked in circles, looking for a way out. I was alone and afraid of dying without anyone knowing what was happening to me. I closed my eyes and rested against a statue of a pharaoh. The temple eased my mind for a few hours but after sorting everything out I wanted to go home. A hand touched my arm and I opened my eyes.

"Why is this happening to me?" I asked.

The stranger carried a staff with small balls at the end. He was bald with black eyes and had a lot of stitching into his skin with drawings covering his body. He reminded me of death.

"You need to see the truth, Akea. You will not get out of here if you live a lie. You've missed the message the gods have tried to show you," he said.

"I'm a warlock and the son of a warrior from Anubi. What else am I supposed to see? Get me the fuck out of here before I strangle you! I need to get to my daughter!" I yelled. The old man sat next to me and rested his head against the wall.

"You're trying to fight a battle that isn't yours to fight. I want to show you what you have missed but it's up to you to put the pieces of the puzzle together," he said.

"I'm gonna put my foot together with your old ass if you don't get me out of here! I need to see my daughter!" I yelled.

"Destiny isn't your daughter, Akea. Her real father put you in here so he can rescue her. You took what belonged to him out of greed. You didn't have desires for Chancy until you felt the soul of his beast haunting you. Chancy loved you for a long time but you didn't pay her any attention; your brother did, though," he said. I burst into a fit laughter.

"Your theory sounds true but I feel for Chancy," I replied.

"Your brother made you desire her because she was in love with you. He was the one who paid attention to her. You broke his curse when you broke her heart," he said.

"Why does he live inside of me?"

"He can't live inside of Kanye. They are both beasts. You are the link between them," he said.

"Why was Djet cursed?"

"I can't tell you. The gods want you to be a man and learn on your own. Kanye is finding his path by going to Anubi and you should find yours while you're here. I want to show you something," he said. I got up and followed the old man down a long hallway. We stopped at a tomb inside the wall. He placed his staff on the tomb and it opened.

"A mummy? Let me guess, this is supposed to be me. This is sorcery and I'm being hypnotized into believing that I'm in this place when really I'm still asleep in my bed."

"Unwrap him," he said.

"I've seen movies like this. This person is going to be me and I don't care enough to find out. I feel dead just by being here."

"Do it now!" he yelled and banged his stick against the floor. Tired of the old man, I unwrapped the body and there was nothing.

"I'm tired of your games." The old man chuckled and shook his head.

"My games are learning lessons. A tomb without a body is a life without meaning. Why do you want to go back when you don't know the meaning of yourself? I can use your company since Djet is gone," he said.

"Djet has no meaning because he's dead! I'm alive and I need to get the hell out of this spell."

"Djet is more alive than you'll ever be. Maybe the wrong brother was cursed because you don't deserve your life! I know your secrets, Akea. I also know you don't value your life. Now, I want you to tell me why you think you're in this temple?" he asked.

Tears fell from my eyes and I remembered the first time I met Djet. I thought it was a dream or maybe even me wanting to become a beast...

Eight years ago...

It was me and Kanye's thirteenth birthday. The pack was celebrating in the woods because of Kanye's big kill. Kanye proved to our father he could hunt alone after he took down a black bear. He wrestled the bear in human form and used his teeth and nails to kill the animal. The pack praised Kanye. I was humiliated because I couldn't impress our father. My sorcery meant nothing because I didn't have the blood of a beast. I left the camp fire and roamed the woods until I came to a lake.

"I want to be a beast!" I yelled out to the moon.

I hated Kanye and wished I was born by myself. He was going to be an alpha and I wasn't

SOUL Publications

going to be anything but a spell book-carrying witch. The pack didn't love me so I figured my life didn't matter.

"Akea, what is the matter? The pack is looking for you," Chancy said when she came from behind the bushes.

"Why do you keep following me?" I asked.

"Because I think you're cool. Being different than us is a good thing," she said.

"Easy for you to say."

"We're playing hide and seek. Want to play with us? You can use your powers to find all of us. At least you have an advantage," she giggled.

"GET AWAY FROM ME!" I yelled at her.

"What did I say wrong?" she asked.

"Everything! Of course, I'll have an advantage because I'm a witch! I always have to find everyone. Why can't nobody find me?"

"I'll always find you," she said.

"Leave me alone. I hate you! I hate all of you!"

She tried to hug me but I pushed her away and she scraped her knee. Chancy got up and ran back to the camp fire. I knew my father would punish me for what I did to her so I went swimming. When I got to the deepest end, I purposely drowned. The feeling of being depressed and not knowing why I craved to be a beast so much forced me to hate myself. I wanted to die. I tried to make myself drown but a force inside me pulled me back up to the surface. It was like someone else was inside of me. I laid in the grass by the lake, exhausted from swimming around. I'd fallen asleep. I saw the boy inside the temple who looked like me but before I could speak to him, my father woke me up...

I looked inside my hand and there was the bottle I drank from before I took a nap. The remedy was something I made a few years ago just in case I had one of those urges again. I committed a sin. Suicide in our tradition was only done for sacrifices.

"You don't deserve to be in your father's presence," the old man said.

"It still has nothing to do with Djet! This is my body!"

"It has everything to do with him. Why should he remain cursed and put away so you can live? The gods took him from his mother's womb and placed him here so you could live. It was either him or you and they chose you. You disappointed them when you showed them they made the wrong choice," he said.

"I don't understand why they couldn't let all three of us be born," I replied.

"Your father broke the gods' hearts so they punished him by taking away his son. Your father betrayed us all. He was never supposed to live amongst humans. He belongs to Anubi. With each life he lived, he never fulfilled his destiny," the man said.

"So, you're telling me that all of this is because of my father's choice to live his own life? He doesn't know of Djet so how can he make the right decision to make this right?"

"The gods want his decision to come from his heart so he doesn't need to know of Djet. Djet paid for his father's sins and now it's your turn.

You don't like it here? Get used to it! Djet is finally free and he will appreciate his freedom," the old man said.

"We both know this shit isn't right! I'm not supposed to be here!"

"The gods think otherwise. I've told you before, you don't deserve to be free when you don't cherish what you have! Djet cherishes life. Get used to your home," he said then disappeared.

Father, what have you done?

Goon

"**H**old him down!" a warrior yelled out. The warriors of Anubi were attacking a man.

"I'll never be a prisoner in this world! Kill me now!" the man yelled. A warrior stabbed him in the stomach then pushed him into a cell. I could smell the scent of his blood. His blood wasn't of a werewolf nor human. He walked to the bars of his cage and stared at me.

"I know I'm not going to make it out alive if they're killing their wolf god. Tell me something, Goon, did you try to fuck someone else's mate again?" he asked.

"Seth?" I chuckled.

"Fuck you, muthafucka!" he yelled through the bars.

"I bedded Keora many lives ago and you're still uptight about that? I can't even remember her scent."

"Why are you in here?" he asked.

"Why would I talk to a demon who possessed my son? I'm gonna use the last breath I have in my body to snap that frail neck of yours."

"We can fight once we're free. That demon is not inside of me anymore. Monifa healed me. My real name is Utayo. I hate to be reminded of what I used to be. That bitch-ass nephew of yours came into my home while I was asleep. This world will crumble if my daughter is hurt. I'll kill all of you!" he shouted. My limbs were numb from the chains and my lips bled from dehydration. I'd rather die before I beg the Anubians for water.

"We're going to die down here, demon. You ain't doing shit," I chuckled.

"Crazy son-of-a-bitch! I'm gonna wear that pretty black fur of yours after I skin your stanking beast! It'll look very good with the all black suit I have in my closet," he said.

"Your threats bore me."

"I have a front row seat to your death, poodle. Look at you, losing a lot of blood and don't have enough strength to break free. I dare you to break out of those chains, wolf man. Your beast is weak!" he chuckled.

"My beast is gonna die a warrior while you sit and rot in your cell like a banana. Look at you, that small stab wound made your skin pale. You're dying already."

Seth walked away from his cell and sat in the corner of the cage. He took off his shirt and wrapped it around his wound. Unlike beasts, bloodsuckers couldn't heal fast without drinking blood.

"We have to get out of here for our kids. We can kill each other later but we have to help each other," he said.

"My sons aren't weak. I trust them to fight but I don't trust a demon. I'd rather die like a man. I'll never help the enemy. You tortured my son! You almost took him away from me. I want to kill you," my beast growled.

"I wasn't the demon who possessed your son. I wasn't myself when I did those things and my god forgave me for all my sins. I'm a free man now and I'm sorry for what I did to Kanye. Everyone has a little evil in them so we all have a demon inside us. Look at your world, how is it any different from what Ibuna used to be? Your kind kills each other every day. You must've sinned because they are punishing you for something. We gonna get out of here. I have no beef with you anymore although I dislike you very much. You're an arrogant muthafucka," Seth laughed. The door to the cell opened and I closed my eyes to pretend I was asleep. Seth laid on the floor and did the same thing. The scent of the beast who came into the dungeon caused me to get an erection. I felt betrayed, angry, aroused and worthless. The figure's eyes glowed in front of me.

Maybe I died and that's why I'm talking to that bloodsucker. No way Kanya is brave enough to come to Anubi by herself.

"What did they do to you?" she cried.

"What are you doing here? Get the fuck out and go home!"

Kanya was hardheaded and had been for many years. Her beast always found a way to challenge mine. Many times, I almost shifted and bit the hell out of her because of her stubborn ways.

"Your mother helped me get here. She told me how to sneak into the dungeon but she didn't tell me how to get you out of here," she said.

"Where is my mother?"

"She didn't come because she doesn't want to interfere with fate. Naobi said the answer to freedom is right in front of you. I don't know what to do," she cried.

"Go home, Kanya. I'll never forgive you if something happens to you."

"I can't go home. Our sons are either here or on their way here. I cannot sit home and worry about who is coming back and who I'll have to bury. I'm not leaving this place. Someone is coming," she said then ran off.

I gotta get out of here but I'm too weak. I have to do something and fast. Akea and Kanye cannot take on the Anubi by themselves and their mother isn't strong enough to defeat male warriors.

"Let me know what you decide because I can't stay here. I don't know what those punks did to my daughter," Seth said.

"Under one circumstance."

"What?" he asked.

"Fight me after all of this is over."

"Bet," he replied.

I'm gonna rip his throat out!

Chancy

"**K**ing Osiris wants you to wear this gown," the servant said.

"Not until he let me see my daughter's grandfather!" I yelled. Three servants jumped on me to force me to wear the gown. I'd been in Anubi for almost three days and it felt like prison. Osiris didn't want me to leave his hall or even go outside of the temple. He was in control of what I ate, how I bathed and what I wore. I was done playing his games. He wasn't himself anymore. His eyes seemed soulless and his voice dripped with anger. Maybe it was because I was still in love with Akea. Osiris didn't give me time to move on. He wanted to mate with me but my pussy didn't throb for him the way it did for Akea. I loved Akea since I was thirteen years old so getting over him would take years. How could I not love someone who helped me create a beautiful being. I wondered what him and Destiny were doing and if they missed me, too.

"OUCH!" a servant screamed when I bit her arm. Osiris threatened to have them punished if they couldn't get me to comply to his rules.

"Get off of me, bitch!" I yelled and punched the other woman in the neck. She slid across the floor then fell into the bathing pool. The third servant shifted into a beast. I grabbed a knife off the meat tray and prepared to fight the beast in human form. The beast charged into me and I wrestled her on the floor. Her heavy paws struck my face and blood splattered on the wall. She howled when my knife slashed her snout. They dragged me across the floor by my ankle. I haven't been able to shift since I came to Anubi.

What did they do to me? Why am I not shifting?

I kicked at the beast's wound but she didn't budge. She growled and grunted while slinging me around. I fell over my dinner tray and the beast jumped on me. She wasn't trying to kill me. She wanted me to surrender to their rules.

"Let me go!" I screamed.

I remembered a time when Kanye and Goon were wrestling in the woods. Goon was in human form while fighting Kanye's beast. Goon wrapped his legs around Kanye's beast's throat and applied pressure to weaken him. It took Kanye a while to slow down but it worked. The beast howled when I mimicked what Goon did to Kanye. She fell on top of me gasping for air. She tried to bite my shoulder but I dodged her. I grabbed the knife beside me and stabbed her.

"Don't fuck with me! None of you!"

I'd lost my mind. For the past few days, I had dreamed of a white werewolf. I couldn't understand why I was dreaming about it again. I used to dream about seeing him in the woods but now it was of him lying on top of me. The darkness of the woods hid his face but revealed his glowing eyes in my dreams. I wondered what all of it meant.

"Let her go!" one of the servants cried out but it was too late. The woman's beast disappeared. She laid between my legs naked with blood covering her body. She was dying so I snapped her neck to put her out of her misery. The two servants ran out of there screaming. Before anyone could come, I made a run for it. I ran down the hall and people screamed because of my bloody gown and the knife in my hand.

"Stay back before I kill again!" I warned a warrior who approached me.

"Put the knife down or you'll be punished!" the warrior said. He lunged into me, wrapping his large strong hands around my neck. The warrior slammed me onto the ground and held my hands behind my back. Osiris walked down the hall with his clan following him. He ordered for the warrior to let me go.

"She killed Lita!" he yelled at Osiris.

"And you're the king, huh? You call the orders now? Let my mate go!" Osiris growled. The warrior stepped away from me in confusion.

"Your father would've thrown her into a cell for what she did to Lita," the warrior said. Osiris threw red dust into the warrior's eyes and he screamed. His skin sizzled and blood dripped onto the floor.

"No man will lay a finger on my mate!" Osiris warned the warriors. I took off running down the hall to find an escape door out of the temple. Osiris caught me and pulled me into a small room filled with paintings and statues. A few Anubians were sitting on the floor chanting at the big half man and half wolf statue. It was their prayer room. Osiris told them to leave so we could be alone.

"What happened to you? Anubi fears you."

"Because I'm the king and make my own rules. Why do you want to leave me? I'm trying to give you everything. You miss your human world and fancy cars? Anubi is a better place for immortals like us! I'm going to make you love me," he said. Osiris grabbed at my naked breast and I smacked his hand away. He gripped my face, squeezing until tears filled my eyes. He bit my neck, drinking some of my blood. Maybe it was a spell because his bite aroused me. My pussy throbbed uncontrollably. My body was surrendering to his while I saw images of another world—a world filled with darkness, black shadows and red eyes.

"We can be the king and queen of Ibuna and Anubi. Both worlds are joining and we can be unstoppable. I'll give you anything you want, Chancy. Just let me inside you," he whispered in my ear. My body yearned for his. I needed him more than anything. I couldn't explain why or how I began feeling this way but it happened. Osiris saved me from self-destructing from Akea's disloyalty.

"He never loved you. I can feel your pain and see the sadness in your eyes. He only wanted pleasure, not your mind, body and soul. Let him keep Destiny and we can start one of our own. I want you to bare my children and I promise I won't hurt you," he said. Osiris's words were like music. Destiny was better off with Akea and Jetti. I kissed Osiris and he kissed me back with my blood on his lips. He pulled the string on his silk pants to release his thick girth. I begged him to enter me. I needed him inside me. Black bats covered the statue the Anubians were praying to and their eyes were the color of blood. The black shadows I envisioned were surrounding us. They were welcoming me into their world.

"They approve of us," Osiris said with a mouth full of my breast. The shadows were comforting.

"This world is yours, my queen. You belong to us," Osiris said. He placed me against the wall and pried my legs open. When he entered me, I saw visions of the white wolf again. A tear the shape of a diamond fell from the wolf's eyes then he disappeared.

You should've saved me a long time ago. Now you can stop invading my dreams. I'm finally free.

Osiris and I made love for what seemed like hours. I no longer belonged to Goon's pack. Anubi was my home for eternity.

Kanye

"**W**e're late," Djet said.

"She should've never left. This is Chancy's fault. I'm here to save our father," I replied. We were inside a vent system for air circulation. Fiti drew us a map of how to sneak inside. We were a little behind because we traveled back to the portal to send Monifa and Fiti back home. We followed what appeared to be Chancy's voice while traveling through the vent. Djet's beast's growls echoed throughout the tunnel as he watched Osiris fuck Chancy.

"I gotta kill him," Djet stated. He tried to break through the wall but I tackled him.

"Calm the hell down! She's possessed now. Those shadows are demons and this is a ritual for soul sacrificing. He made her give up her soul.

She's not Chancy anymore. Our father can figure out what to do after we free him but for right now, fuck her. Her revenge bit her in the ass or should I say neck? Chancy is our enemy now. She's gonna side with Osiris until she's pure again."

"I heard her thoughts. She told me I should've saved her a long time ago and that she's finally free. I came to her and proved to the gods I was worthy of living outside the Temple of Afterlife and this is how she repays me? I'm gonna kill the both of them," Djet said.

"Why is he talking like he's not Akea? I think this beast spell is making him crazy," Zaan said.

"It's a long story, and if I told you wouldn't believe me," I replied.

"I can't go out there like this," Zaan said.

Fiti turned Zaan into a teenage girl with braids and beads. Djet was an older man with a bald head and long beard. Fiti didn't change much about me. I had the same body but I was darker with a lot of facial hair. I also had a scar on my face.

"You looking a little thick back there. What that pussy do?" I joked. Zaan punched me in the chest and I roared in laughter.

"You really gotta joke during a time like this?" Zaan asked.

"We might die here, bro. This could be our final moment," I replied.

Zaan lifted up his silk skirt and a weird scent whizzed past my nose.

"You definitely got what humans refer to as wolf pussy. Is that a braid on your bikini line?" I asked. Zaan touched his center before he sniffed his hand. I cringed and Djet gagged.

"Bro, your pussy is sour," I said.

"The stinkier the better. Do you think I want a bunch of male beasts sniffing up my ass?" he said then walked off.

"Just don't go into heat!" I called out.

Once we got to the end of the tunnel, it was time for us to part ways. Fiti turned Zaan into a female so he could get closer to Chancy. Men weren't allowed in the queen's chamber unless it was her mate. Zaan's disguise was also to be Chancy's servant. I was the king's warrior and Djet was just a religious Anubian who practiced witchcraft. Fiti knew the ins and outs and promised us our disguises were beneficial.

"Around this time tomorrow we will meet right back here and hopefully I'll have my father. Please do not fuck this up. Kill if you have to but that should be your last resort. I don't want to go to war with Anubi before I get to my father. Anything goes after I find him," I said.

"Got it," Zaan said. Djet was silent but I needed to know if he was on board. I was concerned about him ruining our mission.

"Father first. Chancy second," I replied.

"What about my daughter?" he asked.

"I'm sure she's safe. But if she isn't, do what you have to do," I said.

"Be safe," Zaan said. He reached in for a brotherly hug, pressing his breasts against my chest. I pushed him off and he chuckled.

"I don't roll like that, bro. We cannot waste time. Fiti said these disguises might not hold up for two days. No fucking around," I warned them. We went our separate ways. The tunnel split in five directions. I took the path furthest to my right and it led me to a bathing room. Naked females were everywhere. Anubi had a lot of beautiful women. After I jumped out the vent, I tried to sneak past them but they saw me.

"What are you doing here?" a woman asked.

"I had a lot of wine and found the wrong room. Please forgive me," I said.

"Ladies, seize him!" she called out. They ran after me. Some were naked and some were half dressed. I headed for the double doors at the end of the room. One of the girls jumped on my back and I slung her off. A few daggers flew past my head, grazing my cheek.

You better not shift! You better not shift! They'll know who I am if they see my beast.

My beast wasn't listening to me. Black and gold hairs began covering my body and my hands grew bigger with sharp nails. I climbed up the wall and across the ceiling. They were still following but I was losing them. I saw a statue hanging from the ceiling and hid behind it until the coast was clear. Anubi's women were warriors, too. They were fast and aggressive, the same as male beasts. I jumped from the ceiling when the females disappeared down the hall. Two warriors came out of a room behind a curtain. They growled when they saw me standing in the hallway.

"Why are you in this wing?" he asked.

"Is there a problem?" I replied.

The warrior was ready to respond but he was cut off when two doors opened and it was another warrior.

"The king wants us to transfer the wolf god to the ritual temple tonight," he said.

"The king is asking for us to commit suicide. The wolf god is still strong and can kill all of us," one said.

"He barely has blood in his body. Osiris will be our wolf god once he drinks Goon's blood. After we're done, we can throw his carcass to the wild boars," he replied.

"Osiris will never be a wolf god and everyone will be punished," I said.

"The king will cut out your tongue if he hears you! We have to obey him, even if it's wrong. Our family lives here and he will slaughter them if he finds out you're not siding with him," he replied. Osiris was being a dictator instead of a king. He threatened the warriors' families if they didn't obey him. Anubi had a little hope after all.

"You saw what he did to my cousin moments ago? Rad will never be able to see again. Black shadows with red eyes are in this temple. He brought demons to our world and wants us to kill our only hope. Goon can save us and the prophecy is written in the hidden temple that Osiris doesn't want anyone to go near," the warrior said. I wanted to ask more questions but my father once told me that you learn more when you stay quiet.

"Osiris has loyal warriors on his side. We will die trying to save the wolf god."

"Warriors are supposed to die when fighting for something they believe in. We aren't supposed to fear death. Anubi has made us cowards but we're in a war. Anubi is going to be hell by the time he's done with it and your soul will belong to him. You want to be a slave or a warrior to save our world?" I asked.

"Who are you?" one asked.

"A warrior," I replied.

"He's right, Warden. We gave an oath to Anubi and to King Baka before he died. I want my parents to see me as a man of god and not a traitor," one said. Warden was the warrior who Osiris sent to alarm the others about my father and I didn't trust him. The other two were on my side but Warden was lost between being a king's warrior and a warrior for his family.

"Sorry, I cannot disobey the king and I will have to report this," he said. He turned his back to walk away and I grabbed him a chokehold. Warden pushed me against the wall but I had a firm hold on him. My teeth sharpened then pierced through his neck. Blood gushed from his mouth and his body weakened after I pulled a chunk of flesh out of his throat. He dropped to his knees with tear-filled eyes, holding his throat to stop the blood from pouring out. His eyes were begging me to help him. He dropped to the floor with his lifeless eyes open. The two warriors backed away from me.

"Are you going to make this hard for me? If so, y'all can join him."

"Warden is the king's head warrior. How did you kill him so easily?" one of them asked.

"I didn't come here to socialize. Are you with me or against me?" I growled.

"With you," one said.

"Prove it," I replied.

"How?" he asked.

"Cut him up and burn his body. If I go down for murder, so will the both of you," I said. They grabbed Warden's body and pulled him behind the curtain. It was a slaughter house where they butchered their meat. They laid Warden on a table and began cutting his body parts.

"I didn't like him anyway," one said.

"What are y'all names?"

"I'm Tiko and this is my brother, Jasiah," he said.

They resembled a lot but Tiko was taller and maybe a few years older. Jasiah looked to be around eighteen years old. I could trust them and I didn't trust many. Tiko and Jasiah wanted Anubi to be peaceful. After they chopped Warden's body, Jasiah threw it into a pit and burned him.

"What now?" Tiko asked.

"We find Goon and heal him."

"How can we heal him?" he replied.

"You'll see."

"We cannot go in the dungeon. Osiris has a specific team for them," he said.

"Them?"

"Yes, they captured Seth, the vampire god," Tiko replied.

It was clear what Osiris wanted to do. He wanted my father's blood and Seth's body to control both worlds, Anubi and Ibuna.

"Are we saving Seth, too?" Jasiah asked.

"Only because Osiris will use him to destroy this place," I replied.

"I think I know someone who can help us into the dungeon. Follow me," Tiko said. Everything was looking up for me and it was easier than I imagined. I just hoped Zaan and Djet were on the same page.

Rena

I woke up to arguing coming from the living room. IV's were hooked up to me and my body still had bruising from the fight. The last thing I remembered was Taj carrying me to his penthouse suite. I was light headed and needed to drink blood. The IV's were to help me heal but I needed more because I was starving. I snatched the blood pouches off the IV pole. My fangs pierced through the pouch and the warm blood flowed down my throat. Taj ran into the bedroom when he heard me choking.

"I have fresh blood for you in the fridge," he said. He grabbed a towel out of the bathroom and wiped me off. I was completely naked and Taj tried to cover me.

"There is no need for that. I want you to see me," I said, and he chuckled.

"Is that you talking or the vampire?"

"A little bit of both. As you know we're very flirtatious and something tells me you like it," I replied.

"Monifa and a few others are here. Apparently, Arya has gotten herself into some deep shit with that Osiris guy," Taj said.

"Arya needs to die!" I spat.

Taj handed me an oversized T-shirt with a pair of boxer-briefs. He told me to come out to the living room. Monifa, Fiti and a young man were sitting on Taj's couch.

"How are you feeling?" Monifa asked.

"A bit out of place. I'm relieved to know my father is still alive," I replied.

"You can communicate with him?" Monifa asked.

"I had a vision of him in my dreams. He's in a dungeon with Goon, but Goon is not doing well. He's dying from losing a lot of blood."

"The visions you dream of are true?" Monifa asked.

"Only when it comes to my father and the others who are a part of Ibuna."

"Are you a witch, too?" Monifa asked.

"I haven't accepted that part of me yet. I wanted to share it with my mother but she's gone forever."

"Accepting it can help you save Ibuna. We need each other's help so we can get our loved ones back. Kanye's mother is in Anubi and the rest of the pack is going there, too. You have to bring your people together so they can fight with us. If Osiris wins, both worlds will be consumed by emotionless, lust-filled demons. Your mother would be proud of you," she said.

"What are we supposed to do?" I asked.

"Get to Arya and save Baneet. I think she's planning on using Baneet's baby to summon a demon," the man sitting next to Fiti said.

"And who are you?" I asked.

"Geo, Baneet's mate."

Taj excused himself and went into his bedroom. I noticed something was bothering him. We practically dragged Taj into the middle of our war. He had no ties to Anubi and Ibuna. I knocked on his bedroom door and he was taking his shirt off. Taj was so beautiful and his tall athletic body made me sick with butterflies.

"We will leave your home as soon as I get ready. I'm sorry for coming here," I said.

Taj turned around to face me, his emerald eyes glowing, chest swelled with brown and black hairs. He made a purring noise but it wasn't the typical cat purr. It was deep, raspy and short. My nipples ached and my legs turned to noodles.

"I'm happy you came so I can keep you safe," he said.

"You're always protecting someone. Maybe it's time for someone to protect you. I appreciate you." Taj smiled and let out a raspy chuckle.

"I need someone to protect my nine-hundred-pound tiger?" he asked.

"Your heart, Taj. I'm sure you can handle yourself."

Taj walked over to me and hugged me. He pulled away from me and kissed my forehead but I wanted more. I wanted Taj the moment I laid eyes on him but my father gave vampires a bad reputation. We were more than creatures who enjoyed sex.

"Do you still want to be with Arya?" I asked.

"It's hard to explain. Don't worry about me, though. I'll be fine," he said.

He still wants her.

"Okay, I'll see you when you come out," I replied.

I left out of Taj's bedroom in embarrassment. Monifa was discussing something with her friends when I walked past them and into the guest bedroom. Monifa appeared in front of me, scaring the shit out of me.

"Damn it, you don't use doors?"

"Why should I when I can just come in?" she replied. She sat on the bed and unbuttoned her hooded cape. Her stomach was bigger from when I saw her days ago.

"I think you and Taj are cute together," she said.

"Taj doesn't want me because I'm a bloodsucker. He'd rather date a misguided whore. What do I have to do?"

"Nothing. He'll come around after he gets over Arya. Her beauty captures men of all species," she said.

"How does it feel to be in love? Or are you and your mate just together because it was predicted?" I asked.

"I used to think the same thing. Me and Kanye told ourselves that we weren't in love and just wanted each other because it was destined to happen. It proved us wrong. Love isn't perfect. We argue a lot, and sometimes I want to rip his dick off, but that's just it. Only someone you care about can get to you that way. But then there is that part where he gives me butterflies and makes my heart race. Love makes the body explode from many orgasms without penetration. Sometimes I can feel him when he's not around. His scent lingers with me and a few times I cried because of how much I love him. This also comes with love," she said while rubbing her mid-section.

"My father loved my mother but he didn't know how to show it. I think Arya reminds him of her. If she really loved my father, why would she help Osiris hurt him? Those are the type of things that make love seem fake," I replied.

"No, those are the things that happen when we're lost. Arya can't love anyone because she doesn't love herself," she said.

"Thank you, Mother," I replied and she giggled.

"I actually don't mind you calling me that even though we're around the same age."

"Sometimes when I talk to you I can feel her," I replied.

"Me, too," she said.

A sweat suit and a pair of cute Nike sneakers appeared on the bed beside her.

"So, I can do that if I practice witchcraft?" I asked.

"Yes. Don't be afraid to carry her trait."

"I don't want to do anything that will remind my father of Keora. He's been happy and I don't want to ruin it," I replied.

"One day you're going to need it," she said then disappeared.

I went into the bathroom to shower. My father's nightclub was opening in a few hours. I wondered if the manager had everything under control. Being in the club would bring me closer to my father. I wasn't sure how I was going to save him. What could I do and how could I get into Anubi? After the shower, I got dressed in the clothes Monifa gave me. Taj was waiting for me by the front door. Monifa, Geo and Fiti were gone.

"They left?"

"They had to get back to Ula," he replied.

"You don't have to go to the club with me. I know how much you hate that place."

"I'm going wherever you go," he said while punching in a code to lock his door.

"The bathroom, too?" I joked.

"If I have to. Why not?"

He pressed the button to the elevator. When the door opened, he grabbed my hand and pulled me into him. I deeply inhaled his cologne and he smelled better than he looked.

"Do you have a little boyfriend or something that works for your father at the club? I would hate for him to see the way you look at me," he teased and I elbowed him. Taj's grunts mixed with a purr was so adorable. I began having thoughts of having a family with him; perhaps a son identical to him with the same laugh.

Do I want offspring? Naw, I'm not ready yet? Or maybe it's just Taj that make me feel this way.

We stepped out the elevator on the basement level of the building. Taj pressed a key to his truck then opened the passenger's side door. He helped me climb in and the scent of his leather seats was a wonderful smell although it would've smelled better with blood covering them. My stomach growled. I needed more blood.

"How long have I been asleep for?"

"A day and a half," he said when he climbed into the driver's seat.

My father's club was thirty minutes away. The ride there was a silent one. I wondered what he was thinking about because I couldn't hear his thoughts. I closed my eyes and fell into a small nap on our way to the other side of the city...

Rena! Are you okay? my father asked.

Yes, I'm fine. I'm on my way to the nightclub. Taj is looking after me. What are they doing to you?

I'm sitting in a cell. I need to feed. If I don't, I'm afraid I won't be able to cooperate with Goon's plan to escape, he said...

"RENA!" Taj shook me. I opened my eyes and we were in the parking lot of the club. Something about it seemed odd. Plenty of cars were outside but I couldn't hear any music. I got out of the truck and he followed me. The club goers were facing the center stage when we walked in. The clicking of heels across the marble disturbed the quiet inside the building. Arya stepped into view with a smirk on her face. She was wearing a black suit, almost identical to my father's, but the suit was tailored for her frame.

"Bitch, you're dead!" I yelled at her. I charged into her but she disappeared.

"Do you think Osiris's power is going to stop me from whipping your ass? Show yourself, whore!"

"Why do you want to fight your stepmother? I thought we could be a happy family," she shouted. I looked around the club but she was nowhere to be found.

"I guess the pussycat isn't afraid of pussy anymore," she said through the club's speaker.

"This is childish," Taj said.

"Osiris gave me a gift and I'm going to give it to your father so he can be the man he used to be," she said.

"My father doesn't love you!"

"He will love me after I show him I'm capable of pleasing him," she said.

"Where is the book Osiris gave you? He's playing games with your mind, Arya. That book is going to poison you with a bunch of unnecessary evil shit. Soon, you won't know who you are! Let's just talk about this like adults!" Taj called out.

"I'm tired of talking! This is my mate's club and you two aren't wanted!" Arya yelled.

"Is this bitch serious? She really thinks because my father fucks her in the ass that she's entitled to our business?" I asked Taj and he shrugged his shoulders.

"I don't want to mess up my pretty face from fighting a gutter rat, but you don't know too much about being beautiful and wanted, do you? You want Taj but his dick doesn't get hard for you and I wonder why. A man like Taj needs a woman who knows how to please her mate. What do you know, Virgin Queen? How can you make a big and strong man like Taj cum until he has nothing left? I how badly you want him inside of you. Well, that's too bad because he still looks at me the same way he did when we slept together. I'm leaving but I will be back!" she said. In frustration, I flipped a few tables and smashed some bottles. Taj reached out to me but I pulled away from him. Arya had a hold on him, too.

"We have to bring these humans back. Somehow, Arya has hypnotized them," Taj said.

He doesn't care what Arya said to me? Those humans aren't my concern. They can wait until we talk about this. Am I not pretty enough? He would've taken up for me if Arya was wrong, right? Who am I kidding? Taj is stuck on Arya. I wouldn't be surprised if she poisoned his mind, too.

"Arya isn't a witch. How was she able to do all of this?"

"Osiris gave her a spell book. I've heard from Monifa's friend that Anubians have been practicing witchcraft but they have to sacrifice their soul. I could be wrong, though," he said.

My father's club manager was lying on the floor with his eyes staring straight ahead. He was breathing but he couldn't move.

"This is so bad. What are we going to do with them?"

"Lock them inside until we figure out what to do," he replied.

I locked all the doors to make sure no one could get inside and harm anyone.

"Where to?" he asked.

"Take me to my father's house."

"Are you sure you want to go back there after what happened to you?" he asked.

"I'll be fine. I just need to be alone."

Taj shrugged his shoulders and started up his truck. I was silent on the way there because of my feelings for him. It was complicated between us. While looking out the window, Taj grabbed my hand. I wanted to reject him but I was like a bee to honey with him.

"You're beautiful, too, Rena. Don't think I haven't noticed those pretty brown eyes, succulent lips and cute round chin. You also have a small mole on the corner of your eye. I just don't want to be cursed," he said and I pulled away from him.

"Cursed?" I spat.

"Hypnotized by lust. You really can't blame Arya for her ways because your father got inside her head. Vampires are like ecstasy pills. You can't think straight after being with one. That's not love, Rena. Using sex to control someone is what I consider a curse," he said.

"Arya let my father feed on her body because she knew the affects he would have on her. She begs him to drink her blood knowing what it will do to her. Get your head out of her ass so you can see my father is not to blame! I think you cannot grasp the fact that you've been a good man to her and she still fucked and sucked on someone else. Get over it, Taj!" I yelled at him.

"Have a nice night," he said.

That's when I realized we were in front of my father's house. I'd been so angry with Taj that I wasn't paying attention to my surroundings. I slammed the door when I got out of his truck. My father's home was dark and the grass and trees around his home were either withered or dead. The front door squeaked a little when I went inside. The dead Anubian werewolves' bodies were now a pile of ashes. I went upstairs to my bedroom and opened the window for a cool breeze. I heard a loud thump coming from the roof. The branches from the trees rattled against the house.

Maybe a heavy tree branch fell.

I took off my clothes and laid across the bed. While staring at the ceiling, I heard a loud thump again. The thumps were getting louder and pieces of the roof slid off the house. I laid still. The Anubians were back to kill me. I sat up in bed when a huge shadow stood in front of my window. Green rays of light shined through my room from emerald glowing eyes. A heavy paw landed on the floor just underneath my window, causing my dresser to fall over. A long tail knocked the mirror off my wall. The gigantic tiger walked over to my bed. My bedroom wasn't small, but the animal's body made it seem like a shoebox. Taj shifted into human form. He stood in front of me completely naked. His masterpiece hung between his legs. Taj's body reminded me of a wooden sculpture. He laid across my bed as I stared at him. I didn't think he'd come back to me since our argument and the way he criticized my kind. His long locs were sprawled out on my bed.

"I apologize for saying those things. I'm kinda embarrassed to admit my feelings for Arya. I was falling in love with her but as you can see she didn't feel the same way about me. She wants to live in darkness to hide from her true colors and I have to accept it," he said. I was relieved Taj was able to admit to having deeper feelings for Arya.

"Does it hurt?"

He looked at me and smirked but it was forced. I could hear the disappointment in his voice.

"Yeah, it does, especially hearing her talking about fucking him. Shit like that does something to a man's ego," he said. I laid next to Taj and pulled the cover over our bodies. He wrapped his arm around me and snuggled his face into the crook of my neck. Taj wrapped me tighter into his embrace and made me feel safe.

"I was going to sit outside your house and make sure nobody came in but I couldn't let you go to sleep angry with me. I also couldn't stop replaying what you said to me back at my loft. You told me someone should protect my heart. I've been around a lot of women in my lifetime but nobody has ever said that to me," he said. Taj pulled away from me and gripped my face. I was clueless on what to do or say. He placed his lips against mine and kissed me. I wrapped my arms halfway across his back and slipped my tongue between his lips; his tiger purred while caressing my buttocks. Taj pulled away from me and turned me over onto my stomach. His locs tickled my skin while he kissed me from my neck to my backside. He spread my cheeks and massaged my slit with his nose. My teeth ripped a hole in the pillow when Taj's tongue plunged into my wetness. Taj wasn't the first man to orally please me. I'd fooled around with a few men in my past but none of them entered my body. Taj's tongue was different—animalistic. He snatched me away from the headboard then turned me over. He purred against my clit while stroking my pink bud with his thick tongue. The pleasure was unbearable. His razor-sharp canines grazed my skin, making me more aroused. I grabbed a handful of his hair and rode his face. His purrs and suckling woke something inside me. I wanted his blood. Taj groaned for me to explode on his tongue. My body convulsed and throbbed while I experienced a pleasure that I've never had before.

"STOP!" I yelled when he pinned my legs down. My appetite for blood was getting worse. My vision blurred and my gums ached from my fangs protruding. Taj's heartbeat must've had surround sound because my ears were sensitive. I could hear the blood flowing through his veins.

No, Rena, don't bite him! You'll prove he was right. But the sound of his pulse is driving me insane. Damn him for awakening this side of me. I need him.

I lunged for Taj's neck and he placed me in a chokehold. We rolled onto the floor but somehow, he landed on top of me. He held my arms above my head while his erection pressed at my center.

"LET ME GO!" I panicked.

Taj rubbed his hardness against my slit—he was taunting me. He knew being aroused made my hunger for blood worse.

"Please, let me have a taste. I'm too ar—"

"Aroused? Soaking wet?"

He fingered me while his thumb plucked at my clit in a fast pace. The rhythm of his beating heart made me scream. Taj covered my mouth and I bit him, a drop of his blood causing my stomach to cramp. I needed more. He pulled away from me and I jumped on him. Taj slammed me into the wall and I wrapped my legs around him.

"STOP!" he laughed.

Taj didn't fear me. I actually think he enjoyed me wanting his blood.

"If you weren't a virgin, I'd fuck the shit out of you. I'm so hard for you," he moaned against my neck. I went for his neck again but he aggressively wrapped his hand around my throat.

"I gotta leave or you'll be carrying my cub. I don't want to have it this way," he said. Taj dropped me onto the floor. He shifted into his tiger then leapt through the window. I laid on the floor panting and out of breath. The thirst for his blood finally subdued but I wanted him even more than before. I grabbed the sheet that had fallen off my bed and wrapped it around me while I laid across the floor.

I can't let him get away like this. I'm going to apologize to him after this urge goes away.

Chancy

A young girl came into my room while I soaked in vanilla and rose-scented water.

"Leave the towel on the chair."

The girl didn't budge. She stared at me with my towel still in her hand. I wanted to smell and look good for Osiris because he had a surprise for me.

"Chile, are you disturbed? Put the towel on the chair then get the hell out of my room!" I yelled at the servant. She dropped the towel on the chair but she didn't turn away from me.

"What did he do to you?" she asked.

SOUL Publications

"Who are you talking about?"

"Osiris. How did he get you like this?" the girl asked.

"It's spelled, d-i-c-k. It changed my life. I've never been so carefree until Osiris showed me a better world. A world with no emotions, stress or tears. I'm healed again."

"Do you miss your daughter?" the girl asked. She sat at the edge of the pool and put her smelly toes into my bath water.

"What daughter?"

"Destiny," she said.

"Oh, you mean the baby who betrayed me. She nursed from another wolf, and you know what that whore did? She fucked Destiny's father. If it wasn't for Destiny, me and Akea would still be together. She's better off without me. She's with her no-good father."

"You can fight it, Chancy. Osiris poisoned your mind. He's making you forget who you are. Soon, you'll be emotionless," the girl said.

"Do you know who I am?" I asked.

"Yes, I saw you when you first came here. You were strong-minded and nobody could break you. I thought you were going to be my hero but you're just like Osiris now. Do you know what happens when you put a rotten fruit next to another fruit? Well, the rotten fruit will turn the others bad, just by being too close. You've got to get rid of the rotten fruit," she said.

"And you have to get rid of that nasty smelling body of yours. Matter of fact, get in the tub with me. Tell me all about the rotten fruits," I laughed. The girl's eyes filled with tears.

"Let Osiris change you so you won't ever have to cry again. Let the dark shadows take away the pain. You'll be free," I said.

The servant girl stormed out of my bathing room. I leaned my head back against the stone wall and closed my eyes...

Destiny was running through the woods. I couldn't see her face, but judging by her height, she was around three years old.

"Get back here before you hurt yourself!" I yelled.

"Daddy is here!" her small voice yelled back.

She disappeared behind a row of bushes. I climbed through the bushes of red and white roses. They were the healthiest flowers I'd ever seen although the thorns were sharper than daggers. After I made it out of the bushes, my white gown was saturated in blood. I was weak but Destiny was in danger. A giant black shadow stood in front of her. I screamed and cried for her to get away but the shadow took her and she disappeared. In frustration, I screamed and pounded my fists into the soil.

"Bring me back my baby!" I yelled.

I closed my eyes and wished death would take over me. The soil turned to mud because it was saturated with my blood. Someone called my name.

"Chancy, wake up!" the voice said.

I opened my eyes and saw Akea. He was so handsome. He was dressed in gold silk garments.

He grabbed my hand and pulled me off the ground. The blood on my dress disappeared. Akea pushed a braid out of my eye while he caressed my face, but something strange happened. One of his ice blue eyes turned gold and a white wolf stepped from behind him.

"Why do you keep doing this to me? What does this wolf mean, Akea? Why am I seeing him again?"

"Because you need him to protect you. He's going to save you," he said.

"Why can't you save me? What is wrong with you! Why do you keep hurting me?" I cried. Akea wrapped his arms around me and the white wolf disappeared. He pulled away from me and wiped the tears from my eyes.

"I love you, Chancy," he said.

"I love you, too, Akea."

"I hope one day you seek the truth. And promise me you won't fight it. Destiny is our destiny. She's the link to us and the key to our happiness. But I need you to fight, Chancy. You have to be pure again because the next time the

thorns are going to kill you," he said, looking towards the rose bush. When I turned around, the bushes were gone but Osiris stood where the bushes used to be. Blood dripped from his lips, the blood belonged to me.

"Take a closer look, Chancy. What looks good to us isn't good on the inside. There was never a rose bush there," Akea said before he disappeared...

"CHANCY!" someone yelled and pressed down on my chest. I fell asleep in the tub and went underneath. Osiris picked me up and carried me to the bed. His red eyes stared at my breasts, making me uncomfortable. He sat me on the bed and I scooted away from him.

"What happened? I saw you underneath the water. You didn't have a pulse when I pulled you out," he said.

"I had a dream," I replied.

"Bullshit! We don't dream with our new gifts," he said.
"Maybe I had too much wine," I said.

"I brought you something," he replied.

Osiris picked up a gold cup with red rubies decorating the stem of the glass. The smell of fresh blood was enticing. Osiris slid on the floor between my legs. He kissed my thigh as the coldness of his fangs grazed my skin.

"Drink the blood, baby," he coached while rubbing between my slit. I put the blood to my lips and took a sip. My chest was on fire and Osiris smiled at me when I fell to the floor. He grabbed me by the hair and dragged me out my room and down the hall. Osiris's warriors watched my naked body with lustful stares. Their thoughts scared me and all I could do was think about Akea and the white wolf. I'd rather them kill me than be a man's sex slave.

"You called out Akea's name when I pulled you away from your bath. I should've let you die. I thought you turned but you're not fully there yet. Don't worry, I have something in store for you," Osiris seethed.

"Kill me now because I'll never be your slave. Your poison won't stick to me because you are not original. You are a fake bloodsucker and demon so all of your plans will fail. You're a coward. Akea will always have my heart!"

"He has your heart but I have your body, and soon, I'll have your mind. What do I need your heart for again? Your heart doesn't make my dick swell but that juicy mound between your legs brings me fantastic pleasure. My warriors are going to break you in. I tried to make this easy for you but you won't have any dignity or morals. You'll be chained for three days! You will be a heartless bitch by the time they make you loose and worthless," he said. I kicked and screamed while he dragged me down the hall. The skin on my back and legs were peeling. He was stronger than before and there was nothing I could do for him to release me. He took me to a small room that reeked of blood, urine and feces. He pushed me onto the floor.

"You're against me, too. Just when I thought I was going to spare that little weakling baby of yours. Oh yeah, I didn't tell you? Your daughter is waiting for me to sacrifice her little soul. I will be the new king of Ibuna, too. Both worlds combined will be named, Nomed. You're a smart little jezebel so I know you can make out the word backwards. I'll have excess to so much power that I can rule over the humans, too. You could've had it all right by my side!" he shouted. Osiris kicked me in the stomach, knocking the wind out of me. I coughed up a glob of blood.

"You're dying, Chancy. I gave you snake poison but don't worry. It's not as strong as the poison Arya used to kill the pack. Everyone is dead! Who do you have now?" he asked.

"I have the gods," I replied.

"The gods are dying with Anubi. Anubi is what keeps those assholes alive. You didn't know that, did you? You believe in things you have no knowledge about but I'm not surprised since your mother is a different breed of wolf," he said.

"Let me die in peace. You are a bigger fool than I thought if you think I'm going to beg you for my life. I will see my daughter in the afterlife."

"You won't be accepted. You're stained with a demon's blood," he said. Osiris left out of the room, locking the door behind him. I couldn't move my legs. The poison was paralyzing me.

How did I get here? Why is this happening to me? The pack is dead and that's why nobody has come to save us yet. I'm going to die with them but I'll see them soon. We're going to be together again.

The cramps in my side worsened and those black shadows swarmed around me. I thought Osiris was sending his warriors to take advantage of me, but he was talking about the shadows, the souls of his demons. They wanted me to surrender again. Voices filled my head, telling me to give in so I could live with them. The room had writings on the wall. One writing said, *Death is freedom.* I was sitting in a room Osiris sent his people, forcing them to convert. I balled myself up in a corner and closed my eyes. Their cold hands were touching me, grabbing my breasts and touching my center. I hated Osiris so much. I wanted to break down and cry but I couldn't. A part of me was still emotionless. The door opened and the shadows disappeared. An older man walked into the room with a bowl of water and towels. He kneeled in front of me and I backed away from him. My hate for men was growing and I wanted to kill them all. I spat in his face and his eyes glowed. His eyes were two different colors. He had eyes like the white wolf in my dream. The stranger had a bald head and long beard. He caressed my face and I moved away from him.

"I don't want any water."

He cut his wrist and let his blood drip into the water. I wondered if he was a part of Osiris's evil cult.

"More poison? I'm dying already! I don't need anymore!" I screamed at the stranger. He looked at me with a raised eyebrow. If looks could kill, I would be visiting the afterlife.

"Drink this. My blood will heal you," he said.

"You want me to trust you after everything I've endured?"

"Why did you let him enter your body? You showed him your weakness when he was inside you and now he's punishing you. This will heal the poison. You're turning blue and your eyes have blood in them. Drink this," he said.

"I don't want to heal. My family and daughter are dead."

"Your family isn't dead. I know I'm going to upset Kanye by telling you the truth but I have to.

It's the only way I can get you to trust and believe me," he said.

"Your eyes are familiar."

"You see me in your dreams, beautiful. I'm your protector," he whispered.

"Akea?"

The stranger backed away from me with disappointment etched across his face.

"It's me. Fiti disguised us so we can blend in and save you and my father," he said and I sobbed.

"I'm so sorry, Akea. I wasn't myself when I had sex with Osiris. It's like he had some type of control over me. You know I'll never love another man. We need to get to Destiny. I also have to tell Kanye about Arya poisoning the pack."

Akea caressed my face while I broke down. I weakly wrapped my arms around his neck and he squeezed me. Akea's presence was different and it wasn't because of his disguise. He was passionate but maybe because of the circumstances. I wondered if he was going to remain the same way when we got back home because I needed him very much.

"How do I know you're really Akea?" I panicked again. Maybe it was a demon that was tricking me into sacrificing myself.

"Remember that romantic picnic you planned for us? You wore that sexy yellow dress that hugged your curves? I whispered in your ear while you were eating and told you my heart beat the same as yours? Our heartbeats are identical. You got teary-eyed because you didn't think we were going to come true. I ignored you for years and I want to spend the rest of my life making up for it," he said.

"What made you give me a chance? I used to do everything to get you to notice me, but you always had your head in a book or something. Then one day out of the blue, you went to the movies with me. I've asked you so many times before but you made up excuses. Was it something I wore? My fragrance? Make-up? Tell me what it was so I can do it again. I want you to love me again."

"That wasn't me who hurt you. I'll explain later but you have to drink this," he said. I took the bowl from him and took a few sips. Goon and his sons' blood was magical which made them unique. I was beginning to feel my legs and the cramping eased a little. Akea took off his dashiki robe and wrapped it around my body. He told me to stay back while he looked out the door.

"The coast is clear. Let's go," he said.

He picked me up and ran down the long hallway with me in his arms.

"You used your magic to break into the room?" I asked while he jogged.

"No, I know how to escape temple rooms. We'll talk about it later," he said. Twenty warriors were coming down the hall. They yelled for Osiris when they saw Akea holding me.

"Hold tight, Chancy," he said.

"We'll break our bones if you leap out the window. Teleport or something. We don't have much time!"

The warriors were getting closer. Akea leapt out the window and we landed in a tree. He hurriedly grabbed me and jumped to the next tree. The warriors crawled out of the temple in beast form. There was so many of them.

"Damn it I can't shift!" I screamed when a wolf lunged for Akea's neck. Akea tossed me into a tree and told me to hold on while he fought them off.

"Use your powers! Make them all disappear!" I screamed when five werewolves jumped on him. We were in a small wooded area surrounding the temples of Anubi.

What has gotten into you, Akea? You're going to get us killed!

Suddenly, the five werewolves went sailing through the small forest. A white wolf, the size of Kanye's emerged. I was dreaming. I should've known better than to think someone would find me. Osiris said the pack was dead and I believed him because Goon was still locked away. The white wolf with two different colored eyes was tearing the army of werewolves to shreds. The werewolves were coming out of the temples to defeat him. They were biting and clawing at him, his once pure white coat covered in blood. I closed my eyes and covered my ears and prayed for myself to wake up. I couldn't have been dead; the dead don't dream. The sounds of bone crushing and snapping made me cringe and the smell of blood and flesh filled the forest. Out of nowhere, a beast snatched me out of the tree with his teeth and ran through the forest. The beast tossed me over his shoulders before he sped up his pace. I turned around and saw seven werewolves chasing us. The white wolf took on a lot of beasts by himself and I could feel his energy slowing down. His heavy paws shook the forest and knocked down smaller trees as he ran towards safety. I heard loud growls and whimpers coming from behind us. When I looked, I saw a familiar beast. He shredded Osiris's warriors like paper. I screamed in excitement when me and Zaan's beast locked eyes. He shifted back to his human form after he killed the warriors. Zaan was disguised as the girl servant who came to me while I was taking a bath.

"Get out of here! I have to sneak back into the temple. I hope nobody saw me. Kanye is gonna shit a brick, Akea! Chancy was supposed to be saved last. He told you to be careful and now look. There are plenty of dead warriors in the forest because of you. I was cleaning behind a dead body when I heard someone scream about a white wolf fighting warriors in the forest. Hopefully Osiris doesn't pin the white wolf on our pack," Zaan said.

I got off Akea's back and ran to Zaan, squeezing him tightly. It was good to know some of them were still alive. It gave me hope, maybe the others were alive, too, and Osiris was lying to me.

"Kanye is mad at me?" I asked Zaan.

"Not really but you caused Akea a lot of pain when you offered yourself to Osiris and now look at you. Osiris doesn't care about us. He used Monifa to bring him back from Ibuna so he can get inside of Anubi," Zaan said.

"You haven't smoked in a while, have you?" I replied. Zaan was difficult to understand when he smoked weed, but he was really a smart guy.

"I'm going into a weed coma after all of this bullshit is done with," he said. Zaan kissed my forehead before he ran off to the temple. Akea's body was already fully healed. He was no longer disguised as the bald man.

"No sense in being someone else when they already saw me," he said.

"You're just now using your magic? You almost died back there."

"Our disguise goes away if our bodies are critically injured. The healing is what makes it disappear. That's why Kanye didn't want us to do anything stupid but I had to save you first," he said.

"What happened to your powers, Akea, and how are you able to shift into a wolf? I've been having these weird dreams lately and all of sudden you show up as a white wolf with those same eyes. Your hair has grown and so have you. You look just like Kanye, and at first, I could tell you two apart. I loved you the way you were. You didn't have to do this for me."

"Would you just shut the hell up for a fucking minute!" Akea yelled. I was hurting for Akea because of what he did to himself. He had personal issues with being a warlock but I didn't think he would make himself lose his magic to become a beast.

"I don't want to talk about Akea right now and I damn sure don't feel like explaining who I am. Do you prefer a warlock? If you do then maybe I can take my ass back home and let you deal with his bullshit. I only came here for my daughter anyway and I needed you to help me get her which is the only reason I saved you first. You showed me who you really are after you fucked that bloodsucker. I heard your thoughts and you enjoyed it."

"Why are you talking like you're not Akea? You're scaring me!"

"My name is Djet. We are triplets. I've been cursed for twenty-one years and the only reason I was able to resurface was because the gods don't think Akea is worthy of being free. I don't know how to explain it but my soul latched on to his the night he drowned. It's hard to explain but we need to get Destiny," he said.

"So, this is what you're gonna do? After everything I went through. This is what you do to me? Invade my dreams and mess with my head? I guess you're going to say your triplet fucked Jetti, too, huh?" I asked. Akea walked away from me. He was naked from head to toe. His back muscles moved with every stride and he had muscular legs. I ran behind him, cursing and screaming at him for lying to me again.

"You're just like Osiris! You are trying to manipulate me because you have the magic to do so. Are you trying to tell me Destiny doesn't belong to you? Have you lost your mind?"

Akea turned to face me and that's when I noticed his gold sharp canines. I was beginning to think Akea was obsessed with wanting to be like Kanye.

"You never questioned how a warlock impregnated a werewolf with a pup? Destiny is a pup, Chancy! Explain that to me? Unlike our father, Akea is not a hybrid. So, I ask you again, how can a warlock and a werewolf mate and she gives birth to a pup? Let me guess, I'm Akea and I worked some type of magic to change Destiny's DNA?" he asked.

"It's not impossible. Have you ever heard of genetics?"

"Warlocks are and will always produce either a witch offspring or a hybrid. Destiny is neither! She's my daughter and that's the end of it!" his deep voice barked.

I followed Akea in silence. We walked for what seemed like hours until we found a small hidden temple in the forest. He went inside first to make sure the coast was clear. He seemed familiar with the place and that's when I noticed a backpack in the corner of the room.

"We found this place before we snuck into Anubi. We can stay here until it's time for me to sneak back inside to meet Kanye and Zaan. I'll be out of your hair soon," he said, getting dressed. He pulled up a floorboard and there was a set of stairs. They must've mapped out their hideouts before coming to the temple. Akea grabbed my hand and there was an old rug lying across the floor surrounded by old books. On the other side of the room was a resting and bathing area.

"Kanye said this place belonged to a witch," Akea said.

"Probably an evil witch. The skeletons hanging from the wall are gross. The witch must've used this place for some kind of sacrifices."

Akea made a small bed for me. I couldn't keep my eyes off him. He was very handsome but now had a more masculine look to him. His hands were big and looked strong enough to crush a throat in mere seconds. The scent of him was alluring. His coily fro suited his face and strong jaw line.

"I love you, Akea. If you're happy with the new you then I'm happy, too," I said and he chuckled.

"Get some rest, Chancy. I'm gonna sleep upstairs," he said.

"It's hard for me to believe your story. It doesn't make sense to me and I'm really trying to take it all in but I can't. You used magic while we made love. I know it was you."

"You can't conceive with magic. The night we made love and your womb expanded wasn't magic. You were ready for me. Akea not understanding what it's like to be a beast must've thought it was his doing. He had your mind that night but I had your body. Every soft word he spoke to you was me. I'm unleashed now and there is nothing we can do about it," he said.

"So, where is Akea?"

"The Temple of Afterlife where I used to be. He's the cursed one now but don't worry, I'm going to go back after we find Destiny. As much as I love you, I cannot make you accept me. I have no place here if it isn't with you or Destiny," he said. I walked over to Akea and grabbed his face, forcing him to look me in the eyes. His eyes were in my dreams and I saw them countless times when we made love. I always thought it was magic. I could only come up with one conclusion—Akea had a split personality. Maybe that was the reason he felt incomplete because he couldn't get in touch with his beast side. The dream of Akea and the white wolf was trying to tell me that they were one and the same. Akea's mood swings were also complicated to deal with. One minute he was happy then the next he'd stay to himself. I didn't want to tell him I knew what he was going through so I went along with it.

"What is your name so I can stop calling you Akea?"

"Djet. The gods named me," he said.

"Does anyone else know about you?"

"Just Kanye and Monifa. Fiti and Zaan think I'm using magic," he said.

"I believe you, Djet. Akea's personality is different. Where do we go from here?"

"We start a new journey together after we leave this place with Destiny and my father."

"I'm afraid to find Destiny. I think she's dead. I can't believe I was thinking about forgetting her," I replied.

"Tomorrow night is when Osiris plans to make his sacrifice. We'll have her back. I promise," he said.

"I can't imagine how you must feel because I put her in harm's way. None of us saw Osiris for what he was. He must be stronger than we think to hide it so well. Someone in the pack would've picked up on it."

"Osiris has a lot of strength now. Get some rest. I'll watch you while you sleep," he said. I was exhausted. I haven't had any good sleep since I left home. Djet sat on the bed he made for me and I laid inside his arms. He smothered me against his body. His body temperature was warm—very warm. I rested against his chest and fell asleep...

I woke up inside the pack's mansion. I was in my old bedroom. The house was quiet and it was dark outside. The door to my room opened and Djet stood in the doorway with glowing eyes. He was in mid-shift. He grabbed my hand and pulled me against his body.

"Why do I keep dreaming about you?"

"It's the only way I can connect with you because you don't believe in us in the real world," he replied. Djet turned me around and Akea was standing there, watching us. He smiled at me and I reached out to him.

"You deserve real love, Chancy. I need to figure out who I am. I can't find the love I'm supposed to give you but he can," Akea said.

"I had real love with you."

"You had a fantasy with me. My love isn't strong enough to give you eternity. We're so opposite that I can't give in to the mating for life tradition. Only a beast can you give you that. We both needed each other then but now we know what we want," he said then disappeared...

When I woke up Djet was gone. I was ready to search for him but he came down the stairs with a dead camel. The camel was huge and could last us for a few days. He dropped the animal in front of me and I noticed the legs were missing.

"What happened?"

"The legs were dragging across the ground while I carried it on my back. I didn't want to leave any tracks that would lead them here. I chewed them off," he replied. Djet's face and chest were covered in blood. I never thought the sight of blood would sicken me after seeing so much of it. Djet used his sharp nails to tear at the animal's stomach. He pulled out a chunk of meat and placed it against my mouth. Akea ate human food and couldn't stomach the sight of dead animal carcass. I watched closely to see if he was going to eat with me. Djet shifted into his beast and tore the animal apart.

I haven't eaten in a few days. Don't mind my manners. I'll make it up to you later, he thought.

"I wish I could shift and eat. I can consume more that way. It's going to take me hours to eat this heavy meat with my teeth."

Djet's beast's teeth butchered the meat into smaller pieces. I was able to stuff my mouth with uneven cube-sized meat. His beast winked at me and I blew him a kiss. Something was changing between us and I was frightened. I wanted Akea to be himself but what would happen if I fell for Djet? That would go against everything I told Akea about me accepting him the way he was born. I was more confused than ever.

Arya

B aneet spit the grapes I was feeding her onto the floor. She was becoming a pest. She should be thankful I didn't let her die with the rest of the pack. We were in the Poconos, PA. The pack had a vacation home there for bear hunting season.

"My wrists hurt. Untie me now," she said.

"Would you just put a cork in your mouth already? I've been good to you and this is the thanks I get?"

"I'm uncomfortable! I need to stretch and this position is putting stress on my pup. Then again, what do you know? You're not mother material. You are incapable of loving anyone. I hope someone cuts your head off!" Baneet screamed. I left the room and closed the door behind me. I went into the living room and picked up the spell book Osiris gave me. The book gave me a lot of energy. I was able to practice real spells. Soon, Seth and I would be together again in our world.

Boom! Boom!

There was a loud noise coming from outside. I opened the door and Osiris stood in front of me with five Anubian warriors. He stepped into the cabin with red glowing eyes. His warriors had red eyes, too. His men guarded the front door while Osiris walked around the living room. He picked up a family photo of the pack and hurled it at the wall.

"You had one fucking job! ONE!" he yelled.

"What are you talking about?"

Osiris grabbed me by the throat and slammed me into the wall. He pointed a hunting knife at my neck.

"I gave you power and in return you gave me nothing. The pack isn't dead. I sent my warriors to their domain and guess what? It was empty.

Where are their bodies and, bitch, don't you dare lie to me!" he gritted.

"They probably turned to ashes but I saw them with my own eyes collapsing on the floor through the window." Osiris back-handed me in the face twice.

"Who is the white wolf?" he asked.

"The pack doesn't have a white wolf!"

"You're lying to me. The son-of-a-bitch has the same markings as Kanye and their father. Goon has another son? I know it isn't the magic boy. Not even a witch spell can duplicate those markings. They are a gift from the gods and Akea isn't a werewolf. So, again, who is the white wolf and you better not lie to me! He took my mate away from me and anyone who stands in my way will pay."

"You were at the pack mansion after I was exiled from the pack. You should know about the pack member! Now get your hands off of me!" I yelled. One of Osiris's warriors was ready to attack me but he told them to stand back.

"That spell book you have belonged to my aunt, Meda. She was a very powerful witch. I gave you something so precious to me but I feel like you're lying to me. I will kill Seth if you fucked this up," he said.

"I thought you were going to resurrect him. Why would you harm him?"

"All bets are off if you didn't do your job," he said then pulled away from me.

Baneet began screaming for help and I cursed myself for not gagging her.

"Go eat!" Osiris told his warriors. They went to the back of the cabin in search of Baneet.

"You get that spell book to figure out a way to weaken Goon's pack. This is your last damn chance and you better go out with a bang," he said.

Baneet's screams pierced my ears. Osiris caressed my breast and pressed his erection against my leg.

"What are they doing to her?" I asked.

"It's feeding time, but don't worry. They won't kill her. Just drink some of her blood," he said. The warriors left out of the room and I ran to the back to check on Baneet. They took her clothes off to feed on her. She had bite marks on her breasts, stomach and thighs.

"I don't feel so good," Baneet mumbled.

"You should've just shut the hell up! And be thankful they didn't rape you. Do not put up a fight the next time they need blood. Osiris will not spare us."

I left out of the bedroom and locked the door. Osiris and his warriors were in the living room making jokes about Baneet.

"How long do I have to wait for her to give birth? She's delicious and I wouldn't mind having her locked away in my chamber," one of them said.

"Why have her when we can have this one? She's the whore," Osiris said about me and they laughed harder.

"She can take all of us and still beg for more. Isn't that right, sweetheart?" he asked.

SOUL Publications

"I'll do what you asked but you need to leave," I said without staring at his face. Looking into a bloodsucker's eyes would hypnotize you and that was the last thing I wanted.

"Y'all hear this bullshit? She thinks because she got a little power she can tell the king what he needs to do. I'm not going nowhere, Arya," he said. Osiris told his warriors to go back to Anubi and search for the white wolf while he teaches me a lesson. He waited until the warriors left before he dragged me down the hall into one of the bedrooms. I let Osiris have his way with me so he could leave. After he left, I took a long bath. I wanted him dead but I needed him to change Seth first. I drifted off to thoughts of Taj and wondered what he was doing. My love for Seth caused me to take the worst turn of my life.

My life with Taj would've been much easier. I wouldn't have a spell book nor would I have a demonic bloodsucking werewolf controlling me, but I made the deal with Osiris and it's too late to be broken. But what if Taj can heal me and make me choose him? All he has to do is make love to me so he can surrender his heart.

After my bath, I dried off and got dressed. I sprayed Taj's favorite perfume on my neck. Before I left the house, I grabbed my spell book. Baneet was still sobbing and screaming at the top of her lungs. Taj was four hours away and the fastest way I could get to him was teleporting. I grabbed the elements I needed for the spell out of the woods then placed them inside the vessel in the spine of the book. With a drop of my blood on the page, I teleported. I wasn't exactly near Taj's loft but I was a few blocks away.

Damn this old piece of shit. This book has everything but a GPS system.

I wondered if a pup sacrifice helps the spells stick instead of them only lasting for a few hours. My heels clicked across the pavement as my hips swayed side-to-side. My long and silky hair blew in the wind. The human men slammed on their brakes while driving past me to get a good look at my ass. I hoped I had the same effect on Taj once he saw me.

"Excuse me, miss lady! Can I talk to you for a second?" a black boy asked. He didn't look a day over twenty-five. I stopped walking and turned around to get a good look at him. He was coming out of the Chinese carry-out store which sat on the corner. He was very handsome. His skin was the color of sand and his hair was tapered really low. He had a small gap with full lips that looked darker than they were supposed to be.

He's a stoner.

"I'm kind of in a rush. What do you need?" I asked.

"I won't keep you long. My name is Wyatt and I was wondering if you're single. I would love to take you out one day. I'm so sorry, you're breathtaking. What's your name?"

"My name is Arya. Give me your phone and I'll store my number in it. Maybe I'm free tomorrow night," I said. Wyatt went into his pocket and gave me his phone. Our hands brushed against each other. Our eyes locked and Wyatt froze—he was hypnotized.

Go kill yourself worthless human!

Wyatt dropped his Chinese food on the ground and walked away in a daze.

Two minutes later, I was in front of Taj's building. I walked inside and the doorman recognized me.

"Hello, Mrs. Arya. Is Taj expecting you tonight?" he asked. The doorman was an older Asian guy and he wore glasses two sizes too big for his face.

"Is he home?" I asked.

"Yes, he just arrived a few minutes ago. I'll page him and see if he's expecting you because you're on the block list," he said.

"There must be a misunderstanding."

"Noooo, no misunderstanding," he said.

I checked my surroundings and waited until a couple went inside the elevator. Once the coast was clear and I asked the doorman to send me to the private suite. Taj's loft was on a floor by itself and you needed a security code to take you there. He must've changed the code if he banned me.

"What's the new code?"

"I have to check with Taj first but I will call the police if you give me trouble," he warned. I grabbed him by the throat and picked him up, his small feet dangling as his eyes bulged out of his head.

"What is the fucking code?" I gritted.

"RENA," he said.

"He changed the code to another woman's name?" I asked aloud. I dropped the doorman on the floor. I kneeled next to him and forced him to look me in the eyes.

Disable the security cameras, and after you're done, find a train track and stand there until it comes. Do not move; I want you stand there and let it run your worthless ass over! Now get up and do what I said.

"Anything for you, Arya," he said. I backed away from him and he got up. He walked down the hall to the security room. I got on the elevator and typed in Rena's name on the keypad.

"To Taj's suite," the robotic voice said through the elevator speaker.

When I stepped off the elevator, a weird feeling came over me. I fell in love with Taj but he didn't have Seth's ways that I craved so much. The spell book was my only hope to get Taj on the other side. I had a key to unlock his front door and it still worked. The smell of soap filled his loft.

He's in the shower.

I looked around to make sure there wasn't any sign of Rena; he was home alone. After kicking off my heels, I tiptoed to his bedroom. The bathroom door was open and I caught a glimpse of his tall and muscular body covered in soap. I peeled off my dress and opened the door. My heart sank to the pit of my stomach. Taj wasn't alone in the shower. His arms were wrapped around Rena while massaging her mound. The steam was in the way which made me believe Taj was alone. Rena's eyes were closed and her nipples were erect. Me and Taj shared hot moments but we never had a chance to explore one each other's body. All we did was kiss.

"I can't wait for your sweet pussy to coat my dick," he moaned against her neck while he fingered her. Taj's face was contorted in pleasure.

I could tell he loved the smell of Rena's center and the way she creamed on his fingers.

"Ummmm, Taj, I'm ready to come," she whined. He massaged her breast and rubbed his erection against her backside. I was so focused on Rena's expression I didn't realize Taj was staring at me. He smirked at me to get underneath my skin. Taj knew I was watching for a while but he had to please his precious Rena. He turned her around so she wouldn't open her eyes and see me. Taj waited until Rena came before he stepped out of the shower with a towel wrapped around him. He hurriedly grabbed me by the arm.

"Rena is going to kill you but before she does, I want to know everything you have going on. Where is Baneet?" he asked.

"I cannot tell you that until she leaves," I spat while getting dressed.

"The pack is worried about Baneet. Damn it, Arya. She's pregnant! And what's up with you siding with Osiris? He's only using you, so I'm sure you're his sex slave now," he said.

"Why does it concern you? Tell me something, Taj. How was it so easy to move on so soon? You were just in my bed not even a week ago and now you're playing around in that bitch's pussy?"

"It was very easy for me since we weren't on the same page. Plus, I always had a thing for Rena but I respected you when we started dating so I backed off. And another thing, stop lying to Rena about us having sex. Now, tell me about Baneet," he said.

"Osiris is going to kill me if I don't do what he wants. He tricked me, even framed me to make me look like I stole from Seth. He gave me a spell book and promised to give me what I had in Ibuna if I killed the pack. I need your help." I grabbed his face so he could look me in the eyes.

Kill Rena then join me so we can be together.

"That shit doesn't work on me, Arya. Maybe a weak immortal or a human but never on me. I'm protected from black magic," he said.

"Are you protected from Rena's bite? She's going to feed on your blood during intimacy if she's anything like her father."

"Don't concern yourself with that. But I have to tell Rena you're here since you won't tell me what I want to know," he replied.

"Why? Are you part of a wolf pack? What does this have to do with you? Stay out of our business and serve your purpose as my cat boy."

"You'd be a dead muthafucka if I hit females," he gritted.

Rena walked out of the bathroom and we came face-to-face yet again. She wanted me dead and I wanted the same for her.

"I'm gonna whip your ass!" Rena yelled.

"Come on!" I challenged her. I picked up Taj's bed and hurled it towards the other side of the room. The space was well needed because we were about to get messy.

"She's not worth it, Rena. She's going to shift on you," Taj said.

"I killed a werewolf before and I can do it again," Rena replied. We ran into each other. I jumped on Rena and sank my teeth into her face. She sent two hard blows to my nose.

"I won't forgive you if you break this up!" Rena said to Taj when he tried to pull us a part. Taj backed away. It angered me how much he showed Rena he was attracted to her. I was the beautiful one with a sexy body and all the men wanted me. What did he see in her plain, bloodsucking virgin ass?

Me and Rena rolled around on Taj's bedroom floor, cracking his walls and breaking his furniture. She was strong despite not being an animal but she wasn't a match for me. I wrapped her braids around my hand and pounded her face. Taj paced back and forth, worried about Rena.

"This is who you choose? A helpless bitch, Taj?" I asked and bit her shoulder. She pulled my arm out of the socket and it brought tears to my eyes. My left arm fell limp. Fighting with one arm was a death trap. Rena kicked me into a wall then jumped on me.

"Who's helpless now?" she screamed.

Shifting was my only option. My large beast emerged, and Rena backed away when my arm snapped into place. I growled at her, warning her it was time to kill. Rena crawled up the wall then let out a piercing scream that shattered all the windows in Taj's loft. Taj closed his ears and fell to the floor. Rena's screams sounded like a Banshee. My ears throbbed and the building shook.

What in the hell...

Rena turned into some kind of creature. Her hair was styled into two ponytails, shaped into small horns with a gold clasp holding the style together. She had bat-like wings on her forearms and her body was shapelier than before. Her nipples were pierced and a gold plate covered her vaginal area. Her jet-black skin sparkled. Rena's nails were two inches longer than my beast's.

"I guess now is an important time to tell me you're a succubus," Taj said to Rena.

I disappeared out of Taj's house while him and Rena were arguing.

"Where am I now?" I asked aloud.

I was standing in the woods naked and wounded. Feeling defeated, I sat next to a tree and rested my head. Tears fell from my eyes as I sobbed. I was tired and alone once again. I closed my eyes and thought back to my younger years when I was a little girl. I remember when my father, Dayo, used to read me bedtime stories. Goon's mate took me shopping with her and Monifa's mother almost every weekend. I was the only pup then, so the pack spoiled me. Everyone treated me like an angel. But somehow along the way, I got lost and seemed to have forgotten all they'd done for me. But I had to keep hating them because I'd done so much to them that they'd never forgive me. I felt a small hand touch my shoulder. When I looked up, it was me when I was ten years old.

"You ruined the only family that loved me. What about Anik who raised me? She was my mother and you tried to kill her. You turned out to be just like Sosa and my real mother," she said.

"I'm so sorry. I don't know what to do. It's too late for me."

"We have to tell Anik our secret," she said.

"NOOOOO!"

"We have to tell Anik our secret so we can be free," she said.

"I can't tell her. It won't fix anything. It doesn't matter now. It happened a very long time ago."

"I still feel him sneaking into my bedroom and doing things to me! Tell someone so we can feel better. I don't want to hurt anymore. I don't want to keep feeling his nasty hands on my body," the younger me said.

"Nobody will ever love us! We are whores! That's why it happened to me in the first place because we were born whores. Nobody loves us and never will."

"Taj could've helped us and so could the pack. You betrayed both of them and now nobody will ever know about those nasty hands on my body and all the blood I saw that day. You want to know something? Seth can see everything that happened to you when he feeds on your blood. He knows your secret yet he still treats you like a whore. You know he doesn't care but you hold on to him because he made those nasty hands go away when you were in his world. You were empty and soulless and felt nothing. That's why you want us to go back. You want to hide from those nasty hands."

"You are just a damn kid! What do you know, huh? What in the fuck do you know about life? You laid there and let that nasty fuck touch you and have sex with you! Why didn't you scream for help? Why did you start enjoying it? Why did you ruin me? This is all of your fault! You were weak and now I have to pay for it!" I yelled and threw a rock but it went through her.

" I was scared, Arya. What was I supposed to do? He would've killed me and Anik, so I had to lie to protect us. I'm sorry if I ruined us," she said then disappeared. My eyelids swelled from the tears. I couldn't remember the last time I cried so much. I couldn't breathe. The person I became was a monster.

Should I fight for Seth or Taj?

After going back and forth weighing the pros and cons of both men, I decided it was time to be with someone who could give me everything I needed.

I will get another chance soon...

Kanye

Meanwhile in Anubi...

"This is it," Tiko whispered.

We were inside the temple where they kept my father. It smelled like death. Dead men and women hung upside down by their ankles with bowls of blood underneath them.

"He drains their blood to gain strength. The people think they're doing a sacrifice for the gods. Soon, Anubi will be filled with bloodsuckers," Tiko said.

I gritted my teeth to keep from howling. Veins covered my body, spreading underneath my skin like vines. I was fighting the urge to shift and kill everyone who sided with Osiris by sacrificing their family. A young woman hung upside down with blood saturating her white and gold gown—she was pregnant. Tiko handed me a knife so I could cut her down. Seeing her reminded me of my mate. I'd kill every living being if that was Monifa. The woman's body was cold. I could tell by her complexion she was dead for at least two days.

"Her mate sided with Osiris and sacrificed her. He promised her she'd come back stronger. A lot of Anubians believe what he's doing is a gift but I felt it in my heart that something wasn't right. There has been so much death here the blood is seeping through the walls," Tiko said.

The dungeon where they kept my father was at the bottom of a stairwell. Jasiah was gathering the children, women and the older werewolves. He was helping them to escape through the way me, Djet and Zaan came in. There were fifteen other warriors with Jasiah who had sided with us. It was probably more who were against Osiris's ruling but were too scared to do anything. I thought we could just kill the warriors who guarded my father's dungeon but Tiko informed me we'd die before getting to him. So, we came up with a plan that took hours to formulate. Tiko pulled me into a dark corner.

"Listen, whatever they do you have to deal with it. This is the only way. Do not give in. Are you ready?" he asked.

"Go ahead and do it. Hurry up with it," I replied.

Tiko had a sharp flat dagger inside his knapsack. I held my arm out and he cut through my skin. He shoved a glob of camel fat into my mouth to hush me. I've been bitten and scratched but I've never had someone slice my arm open.

"Don't look," he warned but it was too late. My skin hung from my forearm and my flesh was exposed.

Hurry up before I heal!

Tiko hurriedly laid the weapon inside my arm and it healed afterwards. I spit the glob of fat out onto the floor. Although I was healed the pain was still there because the dagger shifted.

"The dagger is sharp enough to pick the lock on the shackles. The middle lock which is usually around the chest area is what keeps all the other chains together. After you get through that you'll be able to unchain him," Tiko said.

I had to sneak the weapon underneath my skin because the guards searched the prisoners and stripped them naked before going into their dungeon. The only way I could get through without conflict was to be a prisoner.

"Are you ready?" Tiko asked.

"I'm straight, now let's hurry up."

He pushed me onto the floor then held his knee into my back. He blew into a wooden whistle and five warriors ran up the stairwell.

"I caught him cutting down the bodies. What do you want me to do with him?" Tiko asked the guards then they attacked me. They were thirsty for violence. Instead of fighting back, I laid there and let them damn near kill me. The doors to the dungeon were heavy and thick. They were made out of cement and stones. It would've made the temple collapse if we knocked down the doors so it was better to get through without damaging the temple. Also, they were so strict they'd kill anyone who came to the dungeon that wasn't appointed by Osiris to guard it. A warrior kicked me in the face hard enough to break my jaw.

You're gonna be the first muthafucka I kill, bitch-ass punk.

"The king wants him in the dungeon," Tiko interrupted.

"For how long?" one of them asked Tiko.

"Two weeks without food and water," he replied.

"That's if he can make it," another one said then they all laughed.

Once you get inside, kill them! Tiko thought.

Three warriors dragged me down the stairwell. My head hit the stairs. My vision was blurry and my face ached badly, but I wasn't backing down. They could cut my limbs off and I still would've been proud of myself for being the beast my father raised me to be. The stairwell seemed never ending. I held my breath when we got to the very bottom. The stench was worse than anything I smelled, including dead animal carcass. The door opened and that's when I saw two guards sitting on top of the wall. The guards were gigantic. They probably stood at seven feet and weighed six-hundred pounds. They were the ones who dropped the heavy anchor so the door to the dungeon would open. Men and women were chained to the walls. Half were alive but most of their bodies were rotting away. Rats and termites were eating on the rotting flesh of dead prisoners.

"Put him in the cage with the bloodsucker. I think he's hungry," a warrior said. The zoo seemed like paradise compared to their human-sized dog kennels. The floors were muddy soil with all kinds of fluids seeping through it. They opened a cage to a cell and a man was sitting in the corner shaking. The cage across from us was dark, but I saw the same set of eyes I inherited staring back at me. I was in disguise, but my eyes glowed to let him know it was me.

Father!

Kanye?

I'm going to get you out of here.

I want you to save your mother first. She's in Anubi! Leave me here and get her.

WHAT!

"Get in there!" a warrior said to me. One of them pushed me and I head butted him, snapping his neck. The other two tried to jump me, but I was quicker. I bit their throats severing one of the warrior's heads. A fire torch was on the wall by my cell that I used to see inside my father's cage. I dropped to my knees and wept when I saw my father's body. He was frail, almost mummified because of the blood they had drained from him.

"Let me go, Kanye. I'll see you in another life. Usually I overcome things like this, but there comes a time when a man doesn't find his way out, but you can. Get your mother and leave!" he said. Half of my father's face was gray from decaying.

"I'm too late. It's all my fault. I tried, Father. I tried! I'm going to get you out of here so you won't die in this shit hole. I'd rather you die at home. I'm not going to leave you."

"I don't want to go back to the pack looking like this. I will not let them see me broken down. Go home! I'm still your father and you gotta respect me. Your mother and the pack needs you. I'll see you in another life," he said.

"You're my father but as the pack leader I have to make sure you get home. You didn't raise a pussy, Father. I didn't come all the way here and almost get killed to let you tell me what I should do," I replied.

"Give him back his blood. Let him drink his blood to restore his strength before he won't be able to drink it," a voice said. I turned around and saw a familiar face. He wiped his mouth from feeding on one of the dead guards' bodies that was lying next to him.

"Seth?"

"Utayo but you can call me what you want," he replied. Seth broke out the chains and stepped out of the cell.

"You have your strength?"

"They didn't drain me but thanks for the kill. All I needed was something to eat," he said. I slammed Seth on the ground and he yelled for me to stop.

"I'm on your side. Me and your father have a deal," he said.

"Let him be, Kanye. That was a nice move, son. I taught you well." My father cracked a smile. He didn't know it but he was stronger than he gave himself credit for. Another beast would've died a few hours after blood drainage, but my father was still alive. I stepped away from Seth and he grilled me. Seth looked younger than he did when he was messing around with that demonic bullshit. Monifa thought she healed Osiris when in fact she healed Seth. Osiris still had a dark spirit latching onto his soul. Seth went inside the pockets of the dead guards and found a key.

"I have a dagger in my arm and you mean to tell me all I needed was a key?"

"The keys are for the cages. The chains and the locks don't have a key. Once you're in, you do not come out," Seth replied. Seth unlocked the cage and I rushed to my father.

"Stay away from his blood. I don't trust you like that," I warned Seth.

"I'm not interested in your father's blood. It'll make my stomach burn. It's too rich for me," he said. Immortals' blood didn't clot like a human's, maybe because it helped us live for eternity. My father had deep gashes on his legs and other areas; his wounds were deep enough to stick my hand in. I used my nails to pierce through my arm and pull out the weapon I needed for the middle lock. The lock wasn't like a normal key lock. I needed the sharp end of the dagger to pop out the chains. Seth grabbed a rusty bowl and scooped my father's blood.

"Don't fuck with me, bruh. I'm telling you to back up because we don't trust you," I spat.

"I don't have beef with your father anymore. I'm righting my wrongs and I need to get out of here to get to my daughter. So, we're going to help each other now then kill each other later," he said.

"It doesn't work!" I spat in frustration.

"It's probably too rusty to pick. Let's feed him this bowl then he might be able to break away from the wall with our help," Seth replied.

I heard footsteps along with a clanking noise. We listened quietly to see how close it was to us. I sniffed the air to pick up a scent.

"Sniff any louder and they might hear you," Seth whispered.

"Nigga, I'll knock you clean out on your ass if you say something else to me. How about you pick up the scent then, bitch boy."

"I'm not an animal, muthafucka," Seth said.

The noise was louder, but I couldn't pick up a scent. A figure came towards the cage and I rushed to it, knocking the person on the ground. Sharp teeth bit my shoulder. We tussled around on the ground. The stranger was wearing a hood, so I couldn't make out their face, but I saw a reflection of gold eyes. Not too many had those eyes.

"Ma?"

She took her hood off, looking at me in confusion.

"What did you do to yourself?" she asked, observing my face.

"A disguise. It'll wear off soon. Why are you here? Do you know what they'll do to you if they catch you? How did you get in so easily?"

"Naobi showed me the way. There is a hole at the end of the dungeon but I had to go through a lot to get here. The hole leads to a swamp and the alligators are monstrous. They are feeding them Anubians. This place is sick and we need to leave soon. I went searching for something sharp to pick the lock but I can't find anything. He's dying and we need to do something," she said. My mother wasn't telling me everything but that was my father's problem.

"The family reunion is very nice but can y'all help me get this blood back into his body before more of them come and we'll be outnumbered," Seth said. My father was filling out already, but he was still weak. His complexion came back and his ribs filled in but we still had a long way to go. He began choking while we rushed the blood down his throat.

"Damn it, this isn't going to work!" my mother panicked.

"Let him choke. At least we know it's going down. Father won't die from choking on blood," I replied.

"This is going to take an hour," Seth said.

"You would know, bloodsucker," my mother said.

"Why the hate, beautiful?" he asked and my father growled at him.

"Watch your mouth," my father warned Seth.

Seth was an asshole but he was adamant about getting my father back to health. He could've attacked me maybe even got away but he stayed back to help us. I had a new respect for him, but we'd never be friends. We were enemies who were bonded together to defeat a bigger enemy. My mother snatched off the garments the dead guards were wearing so my father wouldn't have to roam around naked. It seemed like hours passed when my father took the last drop. His heartbeat was louder and the veins in his body were filling out and pumping blood.

"Can you break out of these?" I asked.

"Yeah, but I think the dungeon will collapse. The chains are embedded into the cement of the walls. We gotta break the lock unless you three are fast runners."

"Wait, we are leaving out through the swamp?" Seth asked.

"Yes. Why would we go through the temple? My wife isn't going to fight," my father said.

"I can handle it," my mother said.

"Don't get on my bad side, Kanya. I'm still pissed off that you came here. This isn't over," he scolded my mother. She looked at me, wanting me to come to her defense but I couldn't because my father was right. My mother shouldn't be fighting with us. I thought about Monifa and cursed myself for letting her talk me into bringing her with us. After I thought about it, my father didn't make decisions based on if my mother would be happy or not. He made them based on what was right.

"Where is Akea?" my father asked.

"He's here. Me, Zaan and Akea split up. We need to hurry up and make sure they're safe," I replied.

"You know I think the dungeon collapsing will be a good idea. They will think we're dead. So, as soon as you pull, we're going to run," Seth said. My father pulled at the chains. His body was still trying to recharge. It would probably take hours for him to feel like himself again even though he was physically healed.

"Ma, where is the hole?" I asked.

"Run to the left when you leave out of this cage, do not take the hall on the right. It's nothing but a graveyard. Don't stop until you see a statue of a man with a wolf head. Behind the statue is a hole," she said.

"Okay, go and we'll meet you there," I replied.

"Noooo. I cannot leave you and your father. We are leaving together," she said.

"We will get a divorce if you don't listen. This shit is unacceptable. Go, Kanya and we will meet you there," he said. My mother kissed his lips then kissed my forehead before she ran out of the cage.

"A divorce? A human split up?" I chuckled.

"Your mother still lives in human tradition. I still don't know much about a divorce but it must be bad because she hauled ass," he said.

We heard the heavy anchor drop as the dungeon rattled when the door opened.

Oh shit.

My father pulled and we pulled with him. The strength I had wasn't doing much.

"It's the dungeon, son. It's built with strong magic that keeps us from what we are. You have to depend on yourself and not your beast down here. You can do it, trust me," he said. At twenty-one years old, my father was still teaching me about being a beast. Me and Seth grabbed the heavy chains and pressed our feet against the wall.

"On the count of three! We're all going to pull. They'll be here soon," my father said.

"1—2—3!"

All three of us pulled. My muscles tensed up on me and Seth almost lost his balance but he caught himself. The chains shook the dungeon and debris began falling. I could hear the guards shouting and screaming. We kept pulling, my body was drenched in sweat and I felt faint. It was like pulling a cruise ship. My father grabbed the iron cage and pulled his body away from the wall. The chain in my hand broke, causing me to fall against my father. I got up and rushed to Seth because the chain he had wasn't breaking.

"This one is too sturdy," Seth said out of breath.

"Father, this is the last one. It's bigger than the first one. We have to pull until we can't anymore or else we're going to be mashed potatoes."

My father braced himself. He pulled onto the cage while me and Seth pulled the chain. The chain snapped and all three of us stumbled into the hallway.

"Get them!" a guard shouted. I couldn't see how many it was because cement was falling. Seth jumped onto a guard and bit a hole into his neck. My father picked up another guard and slammed him down on his knee, breaking him in half.

"We don't have time to fight! Let's go!" my father yelled.

We ran through the dungeon and the hallway split in two. My mother said take the hall on the left. The ceiling was collapsing; we pressed our bodies against the wall to avoid being smashed by the large pieces of concrete.

"What about the others in the prison?" I shouted.

"They'll be free," Seth replied.

The coast was clear and we made a run for it. I pointed towards the statue, but something fell and damaged it. The way to escape was blocked.

"FUCK!" I shouted. My father was safe and all I needed was Djet and Zaan so we could make it home. I needed to be with my mate.

"We can move it," my father said. The three of us pushed the heavy block of cement away from the opening. It was pitch-dark but we heard water running. We went through one-by-one because it wasn't wide enough. Seth was the last to leave but something fell on his leg.

"Go ahead! I'll find a way out," he said. He pulled on his leg but it wouldn't budge. We could've left him, but we helped him instead. Seth's leg was badly broken up, a sharp bone poked through the skin on his thigh. It was night time and there wasn't much light in the swamp, but I could make out the big alligator resting in the mud. The monster was the size of a dinosaur.

"That is an old alligator. Very old. We have to be careful," my father said.

Seth healed his leg, the sound of his bone shifting in place woke the monster up, but he didn't move. We hid behind a tree. A rock hit me in the face. I looked up and my mother was in the tree.

The alligator is old and blind, but it doesn't move much. The younger ones are very active so be careful. You have to climb up the trees and jump from there.

The three of us climbed separate trees when a few alligators emerged from the swamp water. I shifted into my beast and leapt from tree to tree. They would have mangled me if I fell in human form. My father shifted and my mother climbed on his back. The alligators smelled our animal scents because more came out of the water—it was feeding time.

It's too many! It's like fifty of them! I can't do this, Father. I can't die like this. I promised Monifa I was coming home to her and our pups. Our beast is too heavy for these trees. They can't hold us long.

You've came too far, Kanye. I know you're tired, we all are, but we are not going to give up. We're predators with survival instincts. There is another way out of here.

What if we run on top of them? They're a bit slow. We can use them like a bridge. That's the only thing I can come up with, I replied.

The tree I was in was beginning to snap. The alligator below me opened his mouth wide and I panicked again. I wasn't scared of the animals, but I was afraid to break the promise with Monifa.

After seeing that pregnant woman hanging from the ceiling, I wanted nothing more than to hold my mate and protect her. I was too anxious to return back to her and it was ready to cost me my life.

Seth isn't fast enough. He'll have to ride on your back, my father thought.

My mother told Seth to jump on my back because we were going to run across the gators. Seth was on the tree behind me, swinging from a branch. The gators were waiting for us to fall.

Damn it!

I jumped to Seth's tree and he grabbed a hold of my fur. I leapt onto a gator's head and followed my father across the bridge of gators. Their muddy bodies were slippery, and my front paw almost slipped into a gator's mouth. Seth was yelling we were going to die because large mouths snapped at us. The gators were in a frenzy, they were rolling and twisting around each other. We were almost out of the gator's den when a gator slapped me with its tail, knocking me into the swamp. They disappeared and went underneath. Seth was still holding on, gasping for air because he was going under water. I found a log and lifted my body up. My beast howled when one of them latched on to my side. My father's gigantic beast jumped on the gator's back then tore at its snout; the gator released me.

We're almost out! Shake it off, Son!

My adrenaline and heart raced as I ran the rest of the way. I've run many times but my future with my pups and Monifa was on the line. Maybe I was imagining things, but I saw her silhouette. The faster I ran the further she seemed to be, but it made me pick up speed. Seth was holding on tightly as I hurdled over a large log. After I got over the log, we were no longer in the swamp. My mother ran to me and Seth jumped off my back to puke. I collapsed on the ground, shifting back to my human form. My stomach was ripped apart.

"Baby, don't look at it. Listen carefully, everything is going to be fine. We're done," my mother cried.

"I just want to go home to Monifa, Ma."

My father's beast landed in front of us. He shifted into his human form then rushed to me. He kissed my forehead and forced me to look at him.

"This ain't shit, Son. Do you hear me. We don't die, remember that. You're going to heal," he said.

"He's losing a lot of blood!" my mother said.

My body was going cold and my eyelids grew heavy. I saw Monifa's silhouette again.

This is what I saw, Kanye. I saw your death when I begged you not to leave me. You promised me! You promised us, she sobbed.

I'm sorry, beautiful. I'll come back to you in another life. I love you and the pups. Please forgive me. I won't be able to rest in peace if you hate me for saving my father...

Monifa

"**C**alm down, Monifa," Ula said while pacing back and forth in the middle of her floor. Something wasn't sitting right with me. My pups weren't moving and my head was spinning.

"NO! Something happened to Kanye," I said.

"Did you have a vision?" Fiti asked.

"Before he left. I saw a vision of him dying and he was in so much pain. Sometimes our visions are dreams and I forced myself to get that image out of my head. I need to go back to my house. No offense, Ula, but I need to be around his things so I can feel close to him. Maybe the pups will move again."

"I don't understand why we aren't looking for Baneet!" Geo said.

I almost forgot about Geo being with us. I actually forgot about a lot of things. My body was going through a change and it was difficult for me to function without thinking about Kanye.

"I told you I cannot see any visions of Baneet. My mind goes blank when I try because Arya is messing around with a spell book. You saw it for yourself what Osiris gave her so I don't understand where this is coming from," I replied. Geo stood up and banged on the wall.

"Fuck you! I've been with y'all for hours and still nothing. All of y'all are witches for crying out loud but can't find shit. I thought y'all were supposed to be psychic," he said.

"Are you judging us? Do you want to fight or something? The last time I checked we helped you out! I should've let you die because you have been itching my ass since we found you. You don't like what we're doing? Find Baneet yourself! She's Arya's pet anyway and I wouldn't be surprise if she was in on this with her. Soon, the demons will walk this Earth, looking for bodies to turn, so we need to find the answer to that!"

"Ask the bloodsucker princess. Isn't she a demon?" Geo asked.

"She has demon roots but she's a good spirit. And don't talk to Monifa like that! She's already stressed," Fiti said to Geo.

"I don't give two fucks about that witch!" Geo said.

I picked up a heavy spell book and slammed it into Geo's face. He was ready to charge me but Ula and Fiti stepped in.

"You do not want to piss off three witches. It will demolish you and the rest of your bloodline for eternity. SIT DOWN AND SHUT UP!" Ula yelled at Geo. Geo told us he was going to find Baneet on his own before he stormed out of Ula's small cabin.

"I need to go home. Whatever happens, happens. We lost this war or whatever it is that's going on. I'm pregnant with two babies, I'm barely eating and I haven't slept since Kanye sent me back. I cannot fight anymore. I promised Kanye I was going to stay safe but here I am, trying to save the world."

"I'm going to look for my father's spell book then I'll come to your home with the answers. Fiti will go with you to make sure you stay off your feet, but you're right. You cannot do anything but wait for everyone to return. Your pups are the most important thing, even if Kanye doesn't come back. I know you don't want to hear that, but we cannot always have the ending we want, but we have to make the best of what life gives us," Ula said.

"I'm starting to see that."

Fiti and I hugged Ula before we disappeared and ended up back at me and Kanye's house. A sense of relief came over me because his cologne still lingered in the air.

"Rena has to know something about those demons. She saw a lot when her dad was one of them. There is a key to everything, we just have to look close enough," Fiti said. I texted Taj with my address and told him to bring Rena with him because it was important. He replied and said he was on his way.

"They're coming."

"Go get some rest. I'll wait up for them," Fiti replied.

I thanked her then headed upstairs to the master bedroom. When I opened the door, the first thing I saw was Kanye's Timbs sprawled out across the floor. Everyone was telling me not to worry about him but how could I not? He was my soulmate and we were connected. I had his markings which bonded us together. I peeled off my clothes and pulled the covers back to slide into bed. My pups fluttered when I inhaled his scent on the pillows. They were already bonded with their father while in my womb.

Where are you Kanye?

****

I woke up to rap music playing in the gym room we had at the end of the hall. Kanye woke up every morning to work out before he went to A&K Jewelers. Two blue birds were on the windowsill outside and they were chirping. I opened the window to let the smell of nature come into the house. Kanye was doing pushups with four-hundred pound weights on his back. He was only wearing gym shorts and sweat glistened over his markings, making them appear sexier than they were. I picked up the remote and turned the system off. Kanye stood up, towering over me by nine inches, possibly ten. I stood on my tip-toes and kissed his lips with tears of happiness. I could no longer mask my excitement as I squeezed him.

"You trying to get something early, huh? What are my babies doing?" he asked, caressing my stomach.

"They woke me up to eat. When did you get home? Where is your father and everyone else?"

"My father is safe but they are still in Anubi. I couldn't stay away from you," he said.

"Want to join me in the shower?"

"Yeah, get it started and I'll be in there. Let me finish this up," he said. He smacked me on the backside while I was leaving the room. I couldn't stop myself from blushing. My mate was back home and I wanted to make it special for him. I went into our spacious bathroom in the master bedroom to run our bath water. My pack uncle,

Amadi, made great skincare products. Kanye used his muscle relaxers after spending hours in the gym. I added bath salts with a milk, honey and mint bubble bath. The aroma mixed with the breeze flowing through our bedroom window was relaxing. I stepped into the tub and called Kanye before the water got cold. Our tub was built into the floor, almost like a small pool. Goon and Kanya had one in their bedroom and I fell in love with it.

"Kanye!" I yelled.

He came into the bathroom seconds later with a bottle of cognac.

"This water feels good. My nuts were sweating and shit," Kanye said when he sat in the water.

"Really?" I giggled.

"Really. I missed you," he said.

"I missed you more. Is the pack safe?"

"They were before I left," he replied.

Something was different about Kanye. He couldn't look me in the eye and his skin was a little pale.

"Are you okay?"

"Yeah, beautiful," he said.

The bath water turned red when Kanye coughed up blood. I rushed to him, I was confused. He was in great shape minutes ago.

"Baby, I don't feel too good. I can't feel my legs," he said.

I rushed out the tub then pulled him out. Kanye's left side was almost missing. So much of his flesh was gone except for his ribs.

"I fucked up, Monifa," he said with tear-filled eyes.

"Noooooooo! What did you do? What did you do?" I asked while rocking him in my arms.

"I was so close," he coughed.

I couldn't heal him and I tried everything. No matter what I did, Kanye's wound wouldn't close.

"I don't have much time," he said.

"I'm going to stay here with you and heal you. I'm going to fix this, I promise you. We're going to be happy again. You're going to help me birth our pups. We're going to make love every night and spend hours talking about everything until there's nothing else left to discuss. I won't let you go."

Tears fell from my eyes and Kanye wiped them away. His lips were turning purple and his fingers were so cold. He was shivering.

"I haven't told you this before but one time I snuck into your bedroom. We were seventeen years old. You were sleeping while I sat in the window and watched you. I had a feeling we were going to fall in love before we figured out we were soulmates. I told myself you were the girl I was going to spend my life with. I picked out our pups' names that night. For some reason, I knew we were having a boy and a girl. It sounds silly but I want our son's name to be Moon and our daughter's name to be Venus, since the planet is the closest to the moon," he said.

"I like that. It's beautiful."

"Are you going to tell them how much I love him? I don't want them to think I betrayed them, and make sure they are close. Me and Akea spent years hating each other and I regret that," he said.

"You can make sure of that because you're not going to die. I'm not going to let you."

"I'm already dead, Monifa. You just won't let me go," he said.

"You're not dead, but you're not fighting hard enough to stay alive."

"I'm fighting harder than I ever have, but I just keep getting colder," he replied. I laid Kanye on the floor and ran into our bedroom. He wasn't going to die on me. I went inside the closet and grabbed a suitcase with natural herbs and many other things to heal a wound. My mother gave them to me for when I give birth to the pups. I told her I didn't need it but I was glad I took it anyway. On the top shelf of the closet was a spell book. I rushed back to the bathroom and laid everything out on the floor.

"What are you doing?" Kanye whispered.

"Sshhhhh, save your energy," I replied and covered him up with a blanket to keep him warm.

"You tried to heal me already."

"I'm going to try another way but it might take time. Just hang in there, please!" I begged. Kanye grabbed my hand and brought it to his lips.

"I trust you," he smiled weakly.

I didn't understand what was going on. It seemed like a dream mixed with reality, but the clock was ticking and I didn't have time to figure it out. Either way, Kanye needed me.

Rena

"**M**ONIFA!" I yelled.

Taj and I arrived fifteen minutes prior. When we walked into the house, we heard screaming coming from upstairs. We ran into the direction the noise was coming from and it was Monifa. She was sleeping but she was crying and wouldn't wake up. Fifteen minutes passed, and the sounds stopped. She was sleeping peacefully but we were worried about her.

"Something isn't right. I can't see her visions when I touch her. She's in a comatose sleep," Fiti said.

"How? Was she hurt? I don't understand what's going on?"

"No, she came up here to get some rest. She kept saying she needed to be home to be close to Kanye," Fiti replied.

"Maybe she's dreaming about him," Taj said.

"I communicated with my father on our way here when I took a nap. He told me Kanye and Goon saved him but Kanye was badly hurt. That's all I could make out," I replied.

"His spirit must be trapped. He must be hurt very badly," Fiti said.

"You think he came to her in her dreams?" I asked.

"Mated werewolves' love is like magic, so there is no telling what is really going on," Fiti said. She stood over Monifa and began chanting something in a weird language. I looked at Taj and he shrugged his shoulders. Fiti's eyes turned black and she floated to the ceiling.

"What is she doing?" I asked Taj when Fiti's hands moved in a circular motion. A ball of blue energy shot from Fiti's palms and covered Monifa's bed.

"She's protected while she crosses over. She'll wake up when Kanye is better again," Fiti said.

"What if he doesn't get better?" Taj asked.

"It's up to her to come back..." Fiti replied.

"Whooaaaa, you're telling me Monifa can choose to live or die in her sleep?" Taj asked.

"No, but she can stay asleep for years until she's ready. Your mate will come to you in your dreams for a final goodbye. He wants to make peace with her before he dies, but she's holding on. Give it some time, I trust Monifa knows what she's doing," Fiti said.

In the corner of the room was a black shadow with red eyes. I wondered if I was the only one who saw it.

Go away!

Help us!

"You see something?" Taj asked me.

"I need to get some air."

I rushed downstairs and outside of the house so I could breathe. All the demons wanted was a human form so they wouldn't have to live in the shadows anymore. They wanted freedom but Osiris was multiplying them, infesting Ibuna with dark spirits. There were too many for me to help. He was causing them to rebel, promising them the sacrifices would cure them but it kept them trapped. The front door to Monifa's house opened and Taj stepped out onto the porch with his hands in his pockets. We haven't talked much since he figured out I was a bloodsucking succubus.

"Talk to me, Rena. We have a lot to talk about," he said.

"I don't feel like talking."

"I saw that shadow, too, but it didn't seem threatening. What did it want from you?" he asked.

"Help," I replied.

"A demon that needs help? Are you shitting me?"

"No, Taj, I'm not. Yes, they are demons but those souls were once good people! Have you not been paying attention to anything that has been happening? Those shadows were once alive. They were in love, had children and they even had bodies! They need to be free."

"Then what?" he asked.

"They'll be like my father."

"You can't heal demons," he said.

"They can be reborn."

"Isn't that what the sacrifices are for? To rebirth them?"

"No, it's to feed them. They'll go dormant if you starve them, that's what my father did until Osiris began feeding them again. I don't know the secret of killing them yet.
    "Be honest with me, Rena. Are you a demon, too?"

I dropped my head in embarrassment. The truth was something I couldn't face for many years, but there was something good inside me. I wanted love, marriage and children. If I could spread that to Ibuna, it would be a better place. When me and Arya fought, I revealed myself. I didn't want Taj to find out that way because I was hoping he would fall in love with me by the time I revealed my truth.

"I'm a succubus," I replied.

"Just say it, Rena! Stop beating around the bush and tell me what the hell you are. Come out and say it!"

"I'm a demon, Taj, and I'll possess you if we make love; this is why I'm still a virgin. Are you happy now? I cannot be the woman you want me to be! Do you think I like being this thing? I fucking hate it! You will never put your guard down and see me for who I truly am."

"I'm a demon fighter. How can I be that and stick my dick into a succubus? My ancestors will hate me for this. I cannot love you because what I am won't allow me to. I can deal with you being a bloodsucker and a witch but a succubus? Are you really a virgin or are you tricking me into sleeping with you? Succubus are very conniving and play an innocent role when they are far from it," he said.

"How do you know?"

"I WAS IN LOVE WITH ONE!" Taj yelled.

He sat on the steps in front Monifa's house and massaged his temples. I sat next to him, I wanted to know more. Taj didn't talk about love much and I wanted to know if he had something against it.

"I was young and curious when I met her eighty years go. She was so beautiful and had the sweetest smile. My cousin, Yada, talked me into going to this poker game. I wasn't into dealing with humans back then so I kept brushing him off until one night I decided to go. So, I went to watch my cousin win a lot of money from the humans. Anyway, I was drinking a glass of scotch trying to be cool and that's when she approached me. She was literally a devil in a red dress. But anyways, her dress reeled me in along with the scent of her perfume. There's something about lavender that reels us tiger shifters in and I should've known she was tricking me but I couldn't see it. She had sex with me that night and it was the best sex of my life. The way she rode me while looking into my eyes made me explode so many times until I was drained. Afterwards, we started dating then it turned into something serious. I fell in love with her. I was so in love that I was blinded by it. Things I should've noticed I didn't at the time. Shakira was a whore and slept with all the human men in our city. The men she was sleeping with was giving her money and things I couldn't afford at the time. She made the men violent and a few killed their wives and even children. She had this strong hold on all of her prey, including me. I was lost and my cousin, Yada, warned me. I was losing weight, couldn't keep my food down and my hair was falling out. She was killing me. Yada threatened to kill her. He told me she was a demon in disguise and I couldn't accept it because she was beautiful with a pretty smile and she had a great aura about her. I told him I was sick with the flu and he laughed at me. He said, 'We tiger shifters don't get sick! She knows what you are and she's trying to kill you!' I didn't like him speaking that way about her so I killed him. Later that night, I told Shakira what I'd done and she told me that was what I was supposed to do. She used me to kill my cousin and once I did she had no use for me anymore. My cousin was keeping the other demons away and she was sent to take him out. For some reason, a succubus can walk past us and we not know it. Anyway, I attacked her. Rage overpowered the love I had for her and the possession she had over me. Her ruffled dress was ripped from me clawing at her and that's when I saw she was pregnant. She begged me to spare her and my child's life. I didn't believe she was pregnant for me until I felt her stomach. She was really carrying my seed. I couldn't let a succubus bare my child so I killed her and left her there to rot. The violence in the city stopped and I was back to my normal self. I pledged my life to my god for a second chance because I committed a sin when I killed my cousin," he said.

Taj scooted away from me when I tried to console him.

"I'm not like her. I'll never do that to you," I pleaded.

"I don't know, Rena. I still can't live with killing my own seed. Loving someone for who you think they are will kill you if they turn out to be someone else. What if I love you with everything I have and you eat away at my soul, slowly killing me with no remorse?" he asked.

"I can't make you change your mind."

"No, you can't. I hate what you are more than those black red-eyed shadows," he said.

Beasts 3: Unleashed   Natavia

"Fuck you, Taj!" I yelled.

"Goodbye, Rena," he said. He stood up and went into Monifa's house, slamming the door behind him. I flew away and headed towards my father's club. When I burst through the window, the place was empty. The humans Arya hypnotized were gone.

They must've left out through the back door.

I went to the bar and poured myself a drink then turned the music on inside the club. Dancing relieved stress. I was a stripper before my father opened his club. I wasn't interested in the money, we had a lot of it. The peaceful feeling I had on stage gave me hope and showed me my life had its own path.

"Fuck love," I said aloud.

A raunchy old rap song came on and I went to the center stage. My father was safe and nothing else mattered anymore. I was born in the darkness but had a pure heart. How was that possible? I unzipped my jacket and unhooked my bra to get in a better mood. While I was drinking and moving seductively on the stage, I imagined Taj's hands touching my body. There was something about him and since I couldn't have him, I didn't want to be with another man. I grabbed the pole then dropped into a split, humping the stage as if Taj was underneath me groping my breasts with his strong hands. My essence dripped from between my slit and my body ached for him. I smashed the vodka bottle on the stage in frustration because I was sick of thinking about him. Why did I love someone who couldn't accept how I was born? Black shadows surrounded me when I opened my eyes. The club was filled with them.

"I'm not helping any of you! Y'all ruined my life!" I yelled at them.

A shadow stepped forward. He was the same one in Monifa's room. They all looked alike, but somehow, I could tell the difference.

Help us. We are begging you! Osiris is destroying Ibuna. Soon there won't be enough room for us. Where would we go?

"Go to hell, where you belong. I cannot help you. You all sacrificed yourself to him and now you want help? It's too late!"

We were forced! We didn't want to do it. Some of us sided with him but most of us don't belong with him. He tricked us. You are our only hope. There is a lot of good in you. Come to Ibuna and stake your claim as our new ruler, it's the only way to turn the others against him. We will starve if we have to prove to you we want to change. We are not the real demons, but they do exist. I need to go home to my family, he said.

"I can't do it."

The rest of the shadows disappeared but the one who communicated with me stayed behind.

We worship you, Rena. I'm not asking to free us all, just the ones who don't deserve it. Your lover is keeping you from the right choice. Just because he can't accept your world, doesn't mean you shouldn't be a part of it. You showed your father the true meaning for the vampire god, so show us the way. Darkness can be overcome by light. We just need you to light the match," he said.

"I was naïve and thought we could be different but we are who we are."

We are who we answer to.

"What do you want me to do?"

Kill Osiris and burn his soul with the rest of us.

"I thought you wanted to be free?"

Start your world over and change the image it has of us. Some of us still feel hurt, pain and sadness also love. We are sacrificing ourselves for you, Rena. Take us and do the right thing.

"Okay," I replied.

The shadow thanked me before he disappeared. The gateway to Ibuna was inside the club. I was nervous and even frightened to revisit the dark place where evil consumed you. It was Osiris's world, completely different than my father's even though he didn't make it a great place either. The difference between the two was my father was forced into being that way when he was a little boy and an evil witch kidnapped and turned him, rebirthing him into Seth. Osiris just wanted power—he was born with greed and a wicked heart.

I went to the gate as a succubus. I had a red ruby diamond embedded into my forehead which was connected to a gold crown that framed my head. The gate was in the basement of the club; it looked like a regular exit door which it was if anybody else opened it. But the darkness waited ahead. I had to brace myself for the screams and moans that came from within the halls.

"I can't do this. The lust, the moans and the sex is going to distract me. I'm not strong enough."

The shadow appeared in front of me and grabbed my hand.

If you can't trust yourself, how will Taj be able to trust you? Show him you can succumb to him by facing this challenge.

"Who are you?"

I don't know. I've been here for thousands of years. But I do know we're tired. Walk by faith and lead the way.

I stepped into the door and realized I was alone. I turned around to look for the shadow, but he wasn't there. A woman who looked familiar stood in the doorway. I was more confused than ever.

"I can't go with you, but you are our only hope for both worlds. I'm Naobi by the way. I'm your mother, Keora's, creator," she said.

"You were the demon?"

"Sorry about that but I had to persuade you. All the black shadows out there was my doing. I didn't know any other way. We will get well acquainted very soon. You know the way, Rena," she said. She closed the door and I ran back towards her.

"Let me out! You tricked me," I cried.

The door wouldn't budge. Naobi trapped me with her magic.

"You are stronger than all of them. We will fight in Anubi and you can defeat Ibuna. We will have peace if we stop fearing what we're greater than. I'll see you soon," she said. The door disappeared and I cursed myself for attempting to save Ibuna by myself.

Fuck it. Hurry up and get this over with so me and this Naobi sorcerer can have a talk.

While walking down the hallway, a group of black shadows were taunting a human woman.

Osiris doesn't want you here! Get out or we will feed on you.

The shadow ran towards me and I braced myself.

This is it. They are going to have my soul...

Goon

Back in Anubi...

Hours passed while we roamed around in the forest next to the temples. I tied Kanye to my back with pieces of clothing.

"There is a small temple right there," my mate said.

"Somebody might be in there," Seth replied.

"Then we will just have to kill them. Let's hurry."

I made sure my mate stayed behind me in case warriors were inside the temple. When I approached it, there was a familiar scent. I nodded for Seth to push open the door and we walked inside. The place was a witch's sanctuary. I sniffed the air again to pick up the scent. It was coming from beneath the floor.

"Here we go with the sniffing again," Seth complained.

"Pull the thong out of your ass. Our animal instincts saved your blood-drinking mosquito ass. Lift up the floorboard," I replied.

"Only because I need somewhere to sleep," he said.

He lifted up the floorboard and a white wolf grabbed Seth by the throat and snatched him through the floor. My mate shifted and I hid Kanye behind a pile of skeletons. My beast jumped down the hole Seth was pulled through and I saw Chancy balled up in a corner. The white wolf let go of Seth when he saw me. I noticed his markings which were identical to Kanye's. He shifted into his human form then kneeled in front of me.

"Forgive me, Father," he said.

"This is your son?" Seth asked.

"Akea?" my mate asked.

"Yes, Mother. I'm Akea," he said.

"You look amazing. When did you do this?" she asked then ran to him and hugged him.

"Both of my babies are safe," my mate said.

Chancy ran and hugged me and I kissed her forehead.

"I'm so happy to see everyone. I thought you all were dead," Chancy said.

"We need to get inside the king's temple. I'm going to kill that little son-of-a-bitch nephew of mine," I replied.

"Osiris has a lot of Anubians on his side, but we need to get to Destiny before it's too late. We were ready to leave out until we heard you all come into the temple," Chancy said.

I jumped through the ceiling to get Kanye. We couldn't understand what was happening to him. He didn't have a pulse but he was talking in his sleep. He was speaking to Monifa.

"Kanye! Wake up!" I shook him. His body was cold and lifeless. My mate kneeled next to me.

"His wound is healing. Look, it was bigger than this a few hours ago," she said.

My strength wasn't all the way there, but I could feel it surging through my body.

"Don't worry, beautiful. I'll be back to normal soon. Kanye's body went through a lot in a short period of time. He was beaten before he broke me out of the dungeon and pulling the chains in my cell weakened him. The gators put the cherry on top. He's not dead, his body just won't recharge. Stay here with him and Chancy to keep an eye on him. And whatever you do, don't fuck this up."

My mate mushed me and yelled at me. She was emotional, we all were, but she was hard headed. I grabbed her wrist and pushed her away from me.

"Look at our fucking son, Kanya! You want to fight with me at a time like this? You lost your fucking mind! If you would've stayed your nosey ass home this wouldn't have happened. We had to go through a swamp instead of the temple to avoid you being caught in the middle of a battle. We are alphas! We don't need a fucking jackal to tell us what to do," I yelled.

"Throughout the years you never appreciate anything I do. You always leave me out, even when it comes to our sons. So what, I came here to help you! You were hanging from the fucking wall like a piñata. The man I fell in love with would've fought harder," she said.

"Are you questioning my manhood and how I protect this family? I didn't have nothing in my body and you're going to throw that up in my face as being weak? If I was weak, I would've taken the easy way out. If I was weak, I would've said fuck fate and left you twenty-one years ago! You think being with you is easy? It takes a strong fucking beast to deal with your bullshit. I've spared your feelings so many times and let you say what you want to me, but let's just take a break before we hurt our sons. Stay here with Kanye and do not move!"

She took her ring off and threw it across the floor. We were all upset, drained and tired. We were taking our frustrations out on each other, but there was some truth in her words. For years me and Kanya argued and threatened to leave each other. Being soulmates was challenging, but I wasn't blaming everything on her. I had my days where I wanted to leave for a few months, but I couldn't because I wanted to show my sons the trials and tribulations of being mated.

"I've been unhappy for a long time, too. Go and get our granddaughter. We'll be here waiting," she said. She sat next to Kanye and laid him in her lap. Seth and Akea met me by the door. Akea's eyes were different and we stood eye-to-eye, the same as me and Kanye.

"We have a lot to talk about when we get back. I'm not happy about this but I respect your decision. Be what you want to be, but do it for yourself and not anyone else. Chancy isn't worthy of you if she can't accept who are you."

"I'm starting to see she won't accept who I am, but I'll be fine. Let's go," Akea said.

Me, Seth and Akea headed towards the king's temple. Our beasts ran through the forest and Seth ran alongside us. I had a wakeup call when Osiris had me chained inside the temple. Anubi needed a king—a real king. Their rules needed changing and so did the people. I've run from my destiny many times but this time was the last. I had to accept fate because if not, history would repeat itself and my family would be punished for it. I was partly to blame for Kanye's injuries because he wouldn't have come to my rescue had I not neglected my duties. It was costing all of us our lives. The temple was close by and I ran ahead. A group of werewolves were in the forest. A gray and tan wolf walked ahead of the pack. The wolves kneeled, including the gray and tan wolf.

My name is Tiko. We are not against you. We will fight with you. Where is Kanye?

You know my son?

Yes, I showed him the dungeon. The warriors behind me want to fight for Anubi, but we were waiting for your final word. We helped a lot of Anubians escape. We are ready.

Let's go!

The werewolves scattered throughout the forest. We split up in groups to trap Osiris and his warriors.

Son, aim for the neck when you attack Osiris's warriors. Crush their throats, sever their heads if you have to, but whatever you do, do not let them see fear. Fear will get you killed during a battle, I said to Akea.

I'll be fine. I know more than you think.

The werewolves crawled up the temple's walls to get in through the windows. I came to a halt when I saw a familiar gang run down the hallway of the feast room. My pack brothers found a way to Anubi. Izra howled to alert me of their presence. I ran down the hall and into the feast room. Osiris's face was of my father's when we came face-to-face. I killed my father twenty-one years ago. We fought and I ripped his head off his body. The Anubians kept his ashes instead of burning them because, despite his sins, he was once their king. Osiris was trying to resurrect him.

"I thought you were dead, Uncle. Your father's ashes came in handy. I sacrificed many Anubians to gain his power and strength to defeat you and your pack. This is payback for my parents for you being a punk bitch and neglecting your people. They hate you, Uncle. We all hate you! I'm the wolf god!" Osiris yelled.

"You want to be like him, die like him? You slayed your own people to be like your grandfather? He was nothing! You made your people sacrifice themselves for this foolishness! They thought they were doing it for the gods but everything you did was to possess Ammon's strength. He was weak!"

"He never ignored the throne and that is what you've done! Everything I did was to relive the night you killed my grandmother and turned Meda into a revengeful witch. I will kick your ass to honor them and my parents. You are the fucking problem! Your presence made me sacrifice three-thousand Anubians," Osiris said. Osiris called out to his warrior and told him to bring me my gift. I wanted to crush his neck and rip his torso in half when they dragged Kofi through the crowd of warriors. Kofi's face was badly beaten and he was skinny. Kofi had no life in his body. My pack brothers circled around Osiris ready to attack. Kofi raised me, Amadi, Dayo, Izra and Elle. He was like our father.

"Let him go, Osiris. He's done nothing to you!" I yelled. Osiris pulled Kofi up on his knees and forced him to look at me.

"Look at the punk you raised. I ought to beat your ass again for it," he said.

"I'll be fine, Goon. Do what you have to do for Anubi. I lived a great life," Kofi said to me. I shifted and ran towards Osiris but his warriors protected him. They jumped on me clawing and biting at my throat. Tiko's warriors along with my pack brothers joined the brawl. Blood stained the temple floors from injured and dead werewolves. A werewolf jumped on my back and my pack brother, Dayo, tackled the wolf and they tussled down the stairs. I ran after them, grabbing a hold of the wolf's leg, crushing his ankle between my beast's jaws. Dayo finished him off when he ripped out his throat.

I had him, Dayo thought.

Save Kofi and we'll handle the rest.

We ran upstairs, and the brawl was larger than before. Akea's beast killed two werewolves after they jumped on him. Akea's beast locked eyes with mine and I don't know how I missed it or let it slip past me, but the white beast wasn't Akea. He disappeared into the crowd and I left them to find Osiris. My beast ran through the halls of the temple in search of Anubi's king. Walking past the statue of my father's beast brought back memories of the night I killed him. A gold spear fell to the floor, breaking in half. I caught a glimpse of red eyes looking through the mask of a warrior's beast. The hall was a memorial for Anubi's fallen warriors. I paused in my tracks to listen carefully and heard someone breathing. My beast charged into the statue, knocking Osiris into a wall. He shifted into a werewolf and we tumbled down the stairs.

Where is Destiny? He howled when I wounded his leg, taking a chunk out of his paw.

She belongs to me! Chancy should've chosen me and none of this would've happened. Your pack gets everything! What makes y'all scums so special?

Osiris's hind legs scratched at my torso while I shook him down, ripping the fur off his beast's chest. He howled in pain while his paws clawed at my snout.

You can't kill me. You'll never find her if you do.

I'll take that chance!

Three werewolves piled on top of my beast in Osiris's defense and he slipped from underneath me. Growling, teeth snapping and clawing at the flesh echoed throughout the hallway. The walls were splattered with blood. Three werewolves went for my throat. The white wolf bum-rushed us, tackling a werewolf and ripping out his throat. The two werewolves got up and ran down the hall frightened.

Damn it! Osiris got away. Slippery fucking punk.

The white wolf shifted into his human form and I did the same.

"What is your name? And don't tell me you're Akea. Why do you look like my sons? Who sent you here?"

"I am your son. Answer to the gods and they'll show you the truth," he said. I choked him against the wall.

"Is this some kind of sorcery? Who in the fuck are you? I was there when my mate birthed two sons, not three! There were only two heartbeats inside of her while she was pregnant. Are you fucking with me? Is this some kind of joke or sumthin?"

"You can kill me if you have to but the story will not change, Father. You have to answer to the gods," he gritted. I released him and he looked disappointed in me. Why did he want me to accept him? Was it because he was a copycat of Kanye? Whatever it was didn't sit well in my spirit.

"I've spent years waiting to meet you in the flesh, but you think I'm an imposter? Explain to me why I look like this if I'm not a part of you! Kanye is the only one who believes in me. I'm out of here," he said. He jogged down the hall then took off running when he shifted into his beast.

This place is setting me crazy.

****

The battle was over and the ones left from Osiris's clan were surrendering but I ordered they be burned anyway. Zaan came to me and I ruffled his hair.

"Where have you been?"

"I was around fighting them off but not in that way. Fiti disguised me as a girl," he said. My pack brothers ran to me and hugged me.

"I'm alive, chill out," I joked.

"We came just in time, bro. We flew on our private jet to Egypt. Izra's idea of having one came in handy," Amadi said.

"It's better late than never," I replied.

Elle and Dayo were helping Kofi up. He was weak but he managed to crack a smile.

"You're a tough ancient solider," I joked.

"You damn right I am. That weak son-of-a-bitch came into my room while I was sleep and captured me. He wanted me to help him kill you. He figured I could reel you in because I raised you but I was preparing to go out like a solider," he said. There was an altercation coming from the center of the king's room. I left the group to see what was going on and it was my baby pack brother, Izra, arguing with an elder.

"I'll knock your ashy-kneed ass out if you hit me again. I was on your side, muthafucka. I didn't touch your daughter! She was trying to sneak me into her room because I saved her," Izra said to an elder.

"She's not my daughter! She's my mate and I'll cut out your ungodly tongue," he threatened Izra.

"Your mate is a jezebel and needs to be burn for her ungodly sins! She came on to a married man. She looks like a male warrior anyway," Izra said. The old man grabbed his mate by the wrist and dragged her out of the temple.

"Bro, why must you start shit everywhere you go?" I asked him.

A group of women who only wore silk wraps around their waists walked over to us. Their breasts were exposed.

"We heard all about the black wolf who was going to come and save us. We want to thank you. Come to the king's room and we'll bathe and feed you," one said. They walked away giggling and Izra nudged me.

"My wife will kill me if she knew I had dirty thoughts for a split second. Do me a favor, erase my mind so she won't see my visions. I know she's going to check for them while I sleep," Izra said.

"You need help my brother."

"Welcome back. We're going to throw you a coming home party. It's gonna be the party of the year. Big booty human girls and orgies," he replied.

"Quite an imagination but I'm not trying to get my dick cut off in my sleep. Keep dreaming, bro."

"Where is Destiny?" Dayo asked me.

"We don't know. Osiris got away and I'm certain she is wherever he went to. He's using her as collateral. He knows we can't kill him if she's still missing."
"This is all bad, bro. He's probably not feeding her. I hate my mate for sending Destiny with strangers. I haven't said a word to her since it happened and I honestly don't think I want to," Dayo replied.

After the wounded warriors were treated, we dug a hole in the forest to bury all the dead bodies that couldn't be healed. I pulled my pack brothers to the side and away from the ceremony. An elder was singing and praying for the dead bodies so their souls could go to the Temple of Afterlife.

"I'm going to go home to say goodbye to the rest of the pack, but I'm coming back. I think it's time for me to grow up and do what's right. We have to rebuild Anubi so our tradition can live on. This is my home," I announced. My pack brothers were silent for a while but it was to be expected. I lived enough years with humankind, so it was Anubi's turn to have me.

"We will stand behind you with whatever you want to do," Elle spoke up and the rest of my brothers agreed.

"But we will find Destiny before I give my final goodbye. Osiris knows if he kills her, he will not stand a chance. He's holding her as protection, but if he's in Ibuna, we cannot go in. Magic can't even get us inside. Ibuna will reject us and the only way in is to turn into one of them bloodsuckers. We have to bring him out of Ibuna to kill him."

"He knows we can't get inside and is using this as an advantage. Your father created a fucked-up legacy for this generation," Dayo said and I agreed.

"It'll change. I promise you," I replied.

The pack dispersed but Kofi remained. He was healed and able to stand on his own again.

"Who was that white wolf, Goon?" he asked.

"Probably a witch in disguise. He claims I'm his father but my mate only carried two pups. I know my offspring."

"That boy had your symbols and the eyes of both his parents. We both know magic cannot duplicate those symbols. I was there when your mate gave birth to Akea and Kanye, but what if we missed something?" he asked.

"Missed what? A baby coming out a vagina is something we cannot miss, Kofi. That boy is an imposter and should be punished for wearing my trademark. He's not my son."

"I hope you're right because it'll be a shame if he is your son and you won't accept him. Nothing is impossible with us and our tradition. I watched him fight during the battle and he killed every werewolf that came near you; he was protecting you. Someone with a sinister heart wouldn't have interfered. But worry about it later. You have a granddaughter to find," Kofi said. He walked away leaving me alone with my thoughts. I tried to think of what I'd missed.

Who is this white wolf? And why isn't he black or gold if he belongs to me?

Seth was in the crowd along with the Anubians, singing with them. He had done bad things to Kanye, but should I continue to blame him for it even though he was forced to be the way he used to be? I had a lot to deal with, but I was adamant about handling everything thrown my way.

Kanye

"**K**anye, open your eyes!" Monifa said. The pain I was in made me drowsy and her remedies to heal me didn't make it any better.

I couldn't remember how I ended up with Monifa after the fight with the gators, but it wasn't a dream. Maybe it was her magic that kept me safe. It was almost as if she was preserving my soul. I could be wrong about it all, but she was healing me. My wound was smaller than before and my skin was growing back. While she was wrapping my stomach, I moved the hair out of her face and caressed her chin.

"Your skin is getting warm," she said.

My body wouldn't allow me to sit up but I was feeling better like I could run if I tried. I grabbed Monifa and pulled her down next to me. The pups moved against my stomach and Monifa blushed.

"We should stay here," she said.

"Something tells me it wouldn't be a good thing if we do. I don't know what kind of magic this is, but I damn sure ain't trying to go back to Anubi. That place is like a huge graveyard for immortals. This is my peace right here with you."

Monifa helped me stand, but I wanted to walk to the bedroom on my own. She stepped away from me but she was still too close.

"Damn, girl, back up. I got this," I assured her. She shrugged her shoulders and I headed towards the bed. My side pained me a bit but I felt alive again. She gave me a necklace with a marble that resembled my beast's eye.

"I was going to wait until the baby shower to give you this."

"A baby what?" I asked.

"It's something your mother wanted me to have to celebrate the pregnancy. This is your gift." She put the necklace around my neck and I thanked her.

"It feels good to have gifts like this. We have so much expensive jewelry that doesn't have no true value other than money. I'm not going to take this off."

"Please don't. It took me days to make it especially for you. Never take the necklace off, even when you wear your other jewelry," she said.

"I promise I won't take it off."

"Go back, Kanye. You're fine now. I've been selfish for the past week, but I don't want you to regret anything. Don't stay here because of me." I got up from the bed and walked over to the window. Monifa came from behind and wrapped her arms around me. She kissed my back and massaged my shoulders.

"That place scares me, Mo. I thought I was fearless because of my beast but that place did something to me. The death, my father's appearance when I found him and those gators. If all of those things are in a place we look to as heaven, what does hell feel like?"

"I don't know how to answer that," she replied.

"I just want to vent to you. I'm not looking for any answers, just a way out."

"Did you see something else?" she asked.

"A pregnant woman hanging upside down from the ceiling with her throat slit. A bowl was underneath her to collect her blood. Her eyes were wide open, staring at me. She was cold and hard like a brick. She had a painful expression on her face and both of her hands were cradling her stomach. Even in death, all she wanted to do was protect her pup. I cut her down but that was not good enough. She didn't deserve it, none of them did, but her eyes were the only eyes open. Maybe she was still looking for someone to save her."

"The gods will protect her spirit," Monifa said and I pulled away from her.

"What gods? Those muthafuckas are watching their people get slaughtered and treated like pigs! You still believe in those gods after all I told you?

There isn't a god, Monifa! Believe what you want, just don't put that in our pups' heads when they get older. They don't need to know about their bloodline. Anubi doesn't exist anymore."

"I feel the same way sometimes but I know better than to think they really don't exist. We have to follow our own path and make our own decisions. Ula said life doesn't hold value if you expect things to happen the way you want them to," she said.

"Ula doesn't like Anubi herself. The hell she spreading lies for?"

"We can have this discussion later because the last thing we should be doing is arguing with each other. You have to go back, Kanye. Please go back and come to me the right way. You can do it," Monifa said.

"Oh, now you putting me out of our house? Who are you sneaking in here, beautiful?"

"Oh hush," Monifa laughed. Seeing her smile was a breath of fresh air. I pulled her into me and wrapped my arms around her waist so I could feel her soft round breasts against my chest.

"Ummm, Kanye. Go back," she moaned.

"Let me just put the tip in." Monifa's scent was driving my beast insane. My dick pained against her leg from an erection.

"Noooo," she said and pulled away from me.

"I'm going to leave even though I want it as bad as you do. We need to get back," she said. She stepped away from me and I reached out to her, begging her to stay but she disappeared. She was forcing me to get back to Anubi.

****

"OUCH, SHIT!" I woke up with a stinging face.

"You're finally up! Oh, thank god," my mother said.

"What did you smack me for, Ma?"

"You've been talking in your sleep. Your body is warm again and you're healed minus the little bruising. Does it still hurt?" she asked while examining me.

"Naw, I'm good. Where is Father?"

"Him and Akea left a while ago to get Destiny and Zaan," she said.

The necklace Monifa gave me was in the palm of my hand instead of around my neck. I thought I was dreaming, that I had fallen into a deep sleep because of the stress my body endured. There was something about the necklace because Monifa made me promise her I was going to wear it. Chancy was sitting by a fireplace inside the abandoned temple and my mother was wiping her eyes.

"I'm going to Osiris's temple. I'll be back."

"Just stay here in case some of them come here. Please, do not leave. Your father and brother are gone. I can't lose all of you in case something happens. Get some rest because your body's been through a lot. I know you're grown but I wouldn't be able to take it if you walk out the door. You did your part already," she said.

"They might need my help."

"Your mother is a nervous wreck. Just listen to her," Chancy said.

"Oh, now you want to say something? This shit is half your fault. If it wasn't for you, we could've grabbed my father and left. Where is your daughter at? Do you even know? You and your sister are always in something. I bet you was shocked Osiris killed all them people, huh? We saw you fucking him, too."

Chancy got up and pushed me. My mother got between us.

"STOP IT!" my mother said.

"She needed to hear that. I don't want her butting into my business. We would've been left if she didn't tell Osiris she wanted to come with him, now look, he dragged her here. He done something to her and might be using her as his spy. I don't trust her."

"I already explained myself to Akea. I don't need to answer to you," Chancy said.

"You need to answer to all of us because we risked our lives for you, too! What did Osiris do to you, Chancy? He possessed you, didn't he? Can you shift?"

"No, Kanye, I can't shift yet! He poisoned me, are you happy now?" she asked.

"You'll be back to normal once we get home," my mother promised Chancy. She excused herself and sat in front of the fireplace. Chancy pulled me into a corner so we could talk in privacy.

"What is up with Akea? He seems very different," she said.

"He can show you better than I can tell you. The only advice I have for you is to stop being in denial." Chancy walked away from me and sat next to my mother. They consoled each other and talked about our home back at the mansion. It wasn't usual for me to sit back while pack members were in battle, but I couldn't leave my mother and Chancy. They couldn't hold off a pack of Osiris's warriors. I went upstairs and guarded the door. Thankfully, the temple only had one way in and one way out. The marble rock on my necklace glowed. I held it in front of me, curious about what it meant. Monifa appeared inside the marble. She was in our bedroom back at home with Fiti and Taj. I was able to watch her like a movie. They were talking about something and I couldn't make out what it was but Monifa was excited. I got comfortable near a pile of old bones and watched my mate.

Hurry, Father. I need to get back home.

Rena

buna was back to looking like hell and reeked of blood. When Monifa healed my father, the place healed with him. With a snap of a finger, it was back to darkness. The shadows were still coming towards me, as balls of fire shot from my hands and burned them. Their screams almost deafened me. I've been fighting for a long time but they wouldn't stop coming. When I defeated what seemed to be the last shadow, I stepped into the king's chamber. Where my father used to sit were a lot of dark shadows. Osiris sat in my father's old chair with my father's bat resting on his shoulder. His nails tapped against the arms of the chair and his white fangs seemed to glow in the dark room. On the floor next to him was a basket with a pink bloody blanket inside. I breathed a sigh of relief when I heard the baby cooing.

"You've been a busy bitch, haven't you? How does it feel to burn your own kind?" he asked.

"You're destroying your world and ours! We put them away and you released them again!"

"That's not my issue. Your father should've destroyed them so they wouldn't be released. This is my world now, Rena, and you need to leave before I get really ugly with you. You look spicy by the way. I like the demonic vampire look on you. I heard succubus fuck and suck really good," he chuckled.

"And I heard you like to get fucked in the ass. Give me my father's bat. It doesn't belong to you. He harbors a lot of dark souls that you won't be able to handle," I replied.

"Your father doesn't need him. He turned his back on Ibuna, remember?"

"Trying to do the right thing doesn't mean he turned his back!"

I wanted to burn him, but he had a baby next to him. The shadows behind him disappeared and it was just us.

"Come to me, Queen," he said.

"Return the baby."

"You want to take her spot?" he asked.

"Yes, I will."

The shadows came from beneath the floor and grabbed the baby's basket. I hurled a fireball towards Osiris and he blocked it, sending it back to me. The energy knocked me into the hallway. The bat was giving him his strength by feeding on him. If I destroyed it, I could possibly kill my father. The bat was what made my father immortal.

"You don't want this world. You only came here to gain strength then leave to spread your wickedness."

"You know what you have to do to make all of this go away, but your poor father will burn with us! He might be healed but he is still what he was destined to be, so by all means destroy us all. Either that or you will remain here with me. Ibuna needs its queen, Rena," Osiris said.

"What will I gain if I stay?"

Osiris was smarter than we thought. He figured out the connection between my father and his bat that we called Isis though my father named him Red. Red being in Osiris's possession made him the king, but Red's blood flowed through my father's veins making them entwined.

"I'll let you burn all the demons and I'll give Destiny back to her pack. But I need you here with me so we can start our own legacy. It'll just be us and you can use your gift to win the heart of any man you want. Besides, I wouldn't mind bedding a virgin. You'll be just how Goon's mother was to his father. At one point, before he got greedy, they ruled Anubi together. We can do the same and your father will get to live. Once I enter you, you won't have any desires to kill me," Osiris said.

"Send Destiny back home and do it now!"

"You will have to open your legs for me. You want me to send her home then kill me? A deal for a deal, right?"

"I'll be trapped for ever if you enter me," I replied.

"Is Destiny's life worth it? It shouldn't be, you have no ties to that pack."

"She's an innocent baby!"

"Which is why you should take the deal! Hurry up and figure it out because I'll take what I want from you and force you on your knees," he said. Osiris turned his back towards me and that's when I made my move. I jumped on his back and wrapped my legs and arms around him. He bumped me against the wall but I held on tightly.

"I will find Destiny myself but you have to die!" I screamed. I bit a chunk of flesh from his neck and he dropped to his knees. He grabbed his throat and Red flew to him, sinking his fangs into his arms to heal him. I snatched Red away from Osiris and he fell onto the floor gasping for air.

"Sorry, Red. I can't kill you but I can make damn sure you don't use these teeth again!" The bat flapped its overly large wings and made hideous squeaking noises while I choked him. I ripped his fangs out of his mouth and Osiris screamed.

"You think I was going to submit to you? A fucking punk at that? You're not half the demon you're trying to be. This is my world!"

Osiris got up and charged into me. I threw Red against the wall before I slammed my fist into Osiris's face. He ripped off his clothes to reveal the hairs of his werewolf. Osiris was in mid-shift but he was still wounded. He swung and knocked me into the wall. His nails clawed at my legs while I slashed his face.

"BITCH!" he yelled.

He grabbed me by the hair and pressed my face against the wall.

"I have my grandfather's strength and I will not die easily," he whispered in my ear. Osiris knocked me onto the floor and dragged me across the room by my feet. My fireballs didn't work on him. I had to find a way for him to bleed out.

"We could be married by now but you want to fight your king? You're going to wish you didn't get on my bad side!" he said. Osiris was getting stronger without Red's help. He had another soul living inside of him. I could tell he was no longer

Osiris because he was bigger and stronger. His once brown and tan wolf hairs turned all black.

"Who are you?"

He picked me up and wrapped heavy chains around my wrists so I could hang from the wall.

"You already know who I am," his deep voice echoed.

"You want to be everyone but yourself! Why is that, Osiris? Why are you doing this to yourself? My father possessed you because you were weak and you are still weak! Be yourself and live by your truth before you die a lie! You can perform all the rituals you want but you will never prosper! Do what you want to me but I'll never submit to you," I said. He snatched the gold plate from between my legs and my center was exposed.

"A succubus's pussy is the most fruitful thing on this planet. You stroke it right and she'll make all your dreams come true," he said. He wrapped my legs around his neck, burying his nails into my flesh. I screamed loud enough to make his ears bleed but it didn't stop him from sticking his tongue inside of me. He was weakening me, giving me pleasure when he knew my kind thrived off sex. It was what I feared the most. I wanted to give my virginity to a man who was worthy of me. He pressed his tongue against my bud and slipped his finger into my anus.

"NOOOOOOO!" I cried.

"Shut up!" he groaned against my pussy. His thick animal tongue stretched my lips apart and the tip curved into me. He banged my center against his wet mouth and I closed my eyes and thought of Taj.

You failed everyone, Rena. You were their only hope and you let them down.

I saw a crack in the ceiling where the chains were connected.

If I pull hard enough I can use them.

Osiris was distracted by exploding from the taste of me. His thick wolf cum splashed onto the floor. The taste of a succubus was addictive. He pressed me against the wall while scrapping my back on the uneven bricks. I moved the chain to the right where the crack was and pulled on it. It fell from the ceiling and I wrapped the chain around Osiris's neck to strangle him with it. I drove my nails into his neck, piercing through his flesh. He fell onto the floor and the black shadows came up for him. I burned some of them but they kept coming. They were trying to protect him.

"Get away from him!" I yelled.

I wasn't their queen because I wanted to do good deeds for people I considered friends. In their eyes, I was a traitor. I heard a baby screaming and I followed the sounds instead. The cries were coming from across the hall. The shadows chased me after I grabbed the baby out of the basket. Osiris's voice echoed through the halls, telling the demon shadows to grab me. My heels clicked across the floor and I almost slipped. Destiny screamed and cried when I ran faster. The portal seemed so far away, but I couldn't stop. Something pulled at my hair and I slung it off.

"GET HER!" Osiris yelled. The shadows were climbing on the walls on both sides of me and some were on the ceiling. They wanted the baby. I held her close to me and ran. I caught a small glimpse of the word "Exit." The door was so close but the shadows were closing in on me and crawling over the door. I zapped them with balls of fire and the door opened. Naobi slammed the door shut after I fell through. I rolled into a rack of toiletries and shielded the baby. Naobi grabbed Destiny from me.

"Thank you so much," she said and rocked her.

"I couldn't destroy all of them. There were so many of them and Osiris claims to have the soul of your son's father. What is really going on, Naobi? Osiris's issues are with your people but he's using my world as a weapon to defeat them. This is out of my hands."

"We are going to rest. Everyone is safe now. Osiris will die and take Ammon with him," she replied.

"He's very strong. I couldn't stop him. He's weak when he's himself but when Goon's father's soul surfaces, it's a different story."

"Osiris must've used witchcraft and brought him back by using his remains. I refuse to say his name. And don't you say it either. He wants us to acknowledge his presence so it can stroke his ego. We need to burn this club down so those things can burn with it," Naobi said.

"We can't yet. My father's bat is still down there. If he dies, my father dies with him. Monifa healed his wickedness but he is still a demon vampire."

"Let's get out of here," she said.

Naobi placed a symbol on the door to Ibuna and it transformed into a gate to keep the demons inside.

"That is the symbol of Si. It protects us against wickedness and if they go anywhere near the door, it'll turn them to dust. I don't know how long it'll hold since Ibuna's strength has grown. Osiris on the other hand is the only one who can get out since he's in human from, but it shall last past fourteen moons," she said.

"Two weeks?"

"Chile, where I'm from we say, 'past moons,'" she replied.

A bottle appeared in Naobi's hand so she could feed Destiny. We walked out a back door which led to an alley. I inhaled the smell of Earth. A sense of relief came over me to see cars and the sky. I promised Naobi I'd see her around before she disappeared.

"Hey, baby! How much do you charge?" a young Caucasian boy asked me with pink hair and a lot of face piercings. His car crept alongside of me while I strutted down the sidewalk naked and only wearing heels.

"Fuck off!" I spat.

"I have twenty bucks for a blowjob," he said.

I struck the light pole with a jolt of fire and it fell on top of his car. He screamed for help when his car went ablaze. I ran down the street and through the woods. When the coast was clear, I flew to my father's mansion. After I was safely inside my bedroom, I collapsed. Ibuna physically and mentally wore me out. Osiris took it right from underneath my father's feet because my father was moving on from it. The world had a dark past but we still needed to get it back and control it again. A lot of humans and immortals would lose their lives if my body surrendered to Osiris. I wasn't a succubus with a dark heart and couldn't use my body to make him obey the way Taj's ex-lover did to him.

Father, where are you? Please come home before Osiris gets strong enough to release all of his demons on to the world.

Akea

"You can go home now, brother," Djet said to me.

I was inside the temple praying with the overseer of the afterlife. When I first came to the temple, I was distraught, but after a while I accepted my fate. I didn't want to go back home because I was at peace. Being around the pack would make me feel unwanted again. The overseer hugged Djet in excitement. They'd built a father and son relationship over the years. I was able to learn more about Djet while being in the afterlife temple. He was a religious werewolf. His fur used to be black and gold like Kanye's but it changed when he was twelve years old. Djet bowed his head at the overseer and then they said a prayer together. The overseer was teaching me about the prayers but the language was something I couldn't understand because it was ancient. Their language was ten thousand years old.

"Is the pack safe? What about Destiny?"

"She's safe. I saw it through a vision. She was in Ibuna, a world where none of us are welcomed. She was never in Anubi. The pack is safe as well and your father will celebrate as Anubi's new king," Djet said.

"Wait, he's going to be the king of Anubi?" I asked.

The overseer smiled and danced around the prayer statue.

"He's going to rebuild it, instill old traditions into his people. After all these years and different lives, he is able to see himself for what he was born to do. The gods won't punish him anymore. Come, let me show you something," the overseer said. Djet shrugged his shoulders and we followed the overseer down a cellar. Inside the cellar were our names.

"I thought you said it was forbidden to come down here," Djet said.

"I didn't want you to be afraid," he said.

"What's up with our names written on the wall?" Djet asked.

"The gods wanted all three of you until your father found his way to the throne. But Naobi cast a spell to protect Kanya's womb. It wasn't strong enough so we were only able to take one. Your father was selfish and didn't deserve three strong warriors until he made the right choices. Naobi knew what we wanted from him, but she wanted him to be free. We cannot change fate. If you're born a king, you should be king. If you want to live without following traditions, you will suffer the consequences. I'm sorry Djet about not telling you the whole truth but I wasn't supposed to tell you anything at all. You thought all this time you were being punished when the truth is, your brothers were supposed to join you," he said.

"So, we're free?"

"Yes, you two are leaving and will never come back. Goon broke the cycle and accepted his destiny. He saw how much his people were suffering because of his choices. All is fair now," he said.

Beasts 3: Unleashed   Natavia

"He doesn't accept me. I'll stay here," Djet said.

"You cannot stay here. The curse is broken for good. You don't need to live through your brother anymore. You can live your own life," the overseer replied.

"My life doesn't hold any value in their world. My father thinks I'm an imposter and my mother thinks I'm Akea with a magic beast. I'm neither one of those things," Djet said.

"Were you with Chancy?" I asked.

"Yes, but she loves you. I won't interfere," he said.

"Do you love her?" the overseer asked me.

"I do, but we're not compatible which drove my insecurity through the roof. She deserves to be happy. I'll always hurt her although not intentionally because Jetti is carrying my son. She doesn't need this."

"Destiny?" he replied.

"She's still a part of me. At the end of the day, we all are family for life. Chancy is smart, she'll learn we aren't meant to be."

"Your life will be different when you leave here for good. You'll live like a human and have the things they have," the overseer told Djet.

"I don't know how to live amongst them or the pack as myself. Things were better when I lived through Akea's eyes. I can't explain it but my father and Chancy weren't accepting of me even though I told them the truth. You told me the truth shall set us free, but it didn't do anything. I cannot go back and Destiny is better off with Akea," Djet said.

"Whooaaaa, bro. You can't give up on Destiny. She's innocent," I said.

"You think Chancy will let me into her life after finding out I'm the one who impregnated her?"

"Yes, Chancy is forgiving but you gotta make her believe you. Matter of fact, she'll see the both of us and know the truth. We can sit down with her and tell her about Destiny," I replied.

"You've grown already. See, this place isn't as bad as you thought. A lot of great things come from here, Akea," the overseer said.

"A great place but it doesn't have a great welcoming," I replied.

"I'll deal with whatever happens. I'm going to pray on it," Djet said.

He walked away from us and went to the corner where he prayed. The overseer quietly pulled me out of the room so Djet could speak with his gods.

"The gods won't answer him, will they?"

"Yes, they will. The gods answer those who believe in them. Not too many believe like they used to because of all the bad things that are happening, not realizing the bad things are happening because they stopped believing. It goes both ways. Pity on us for causing problems and telling them to take care of it for us. We have to do our part and let them do theirs like a union. You will talk to them soon. Take this with you," he said. The overseer gave me a booklet and I scanned through it to make out what it was.

"A bible?" I asked.

"That's a human's belief. This will show you visions of the past and how tradition is important to us. You will only see these visions if they know you're really willing to learn. We're done here so it's time to go. I can finally get my rest," he said. Djet came out of the room, but this time he was confident about going back.

"The gods have spoken to him," the overseer said.

Djet thanked the overseer for teaching him the way of life. I thanked him for showing me how much I took everything for granted. It was a short lesson, but he made a big impact on my life. Being different caused me to have self-esteem issues which was poisoning my mind. Now that Djet was free, I could see things from my perspective, not his.

****

We were standing in the pack's mansion after we disappeared from the Temple of Afterlife. My room was the same way I left it. Me and Djet stared at each other for what seemed like forever. Being in the real world with him was still unbelievable. Me and Kanye had another brother from a different world.

"Whoa, this is so surreal," I said.

"I'm nervous. She's going to reject me now knowing we're really two people," Djet said.

"Can I ask you a personal question?" I replied.

"Go ahead, brother."

"Was Chancy the only female you've been with?" I replied.

"Yes, and she'll be my last even if she rejects me. My heart won't allow me to desire another female," he said.

"That's a beastly thing to do. I'm just trying to figure out how I didn't know you were inside me."

"You do know you have to tell the pack about your suicide attempts. That's what allowed my soul to enter your life. I know you want to keep that to yourself but we have to be honest. It's the key to recovery," Djet said.

"Don't tell Kanye I said this but you're my favorite brother already."

"I definitely don't want him to bite your head off. His ego is bigger than his beast," Djet chuckled.

The door downstairs opened and I heard the pack's voices. They were home from Anubi. I cursed the overseer for sending us back the same time they arrived home.

"The overseer done this intentionally," Djet admitted.

"Just when I began liking him. I'm not ready to face them, yet. Are you?" I asked Djet.

"AKEA!" I heard Chancy's voice coming down the hall. Djet looked worried and life almost drained from me again when she barged into my room.

"Why did you leave Anubi without telling anyone?" she asked.

Chancy stopped in her tracks when Djet stepped from behind the door. She looked at us in confusion.

This was bad timing!

Chancy

T he pack had just arrived back home from Anubi. Akea was missing and we figured he went home before everyone to find Destiny. I heard his voice when I came into the house and rushed upstairs to his bedroom. There were two Akeas in the room. I knew the other one wasn't Kanye because he was downstairs with the rest of the pack. The taller one with the different colored eyes was in my dreams. I thought Akea was using his magic to be a beast, but I was wrong. Djet was real and I felt betrayed.

"We have to talk," Akea said. He closed the door and sat me down in a chair while I stared at them in a daze. Djet sat next to Akea.

"Ummm. Uhhh, this is hard," Akea stuttered.

"So, there are three of you and nobody knows about it?"

"Yeah, it's a complicated story, but we can't ignore this issue between us," Akea said.

"Did you create him to distract me from your affair with Jetti? Just tell me we're over for good so I can move on because this is pathetic. I cannot believe you're not taking this shit serious with Destiny getting kidnapped. I'm done, Akea. So, finish experimenting and I'll get out of your hair."

"Can you shut the hell up for a second? Listen to yourself and how stupid you sound. Why would I create someone at a time like this? I was desperately trying to get you back until these past events spiraled out of control. But this isn't what you think it is," Akea said. I listened quietly as Akea told me everything about himself and the first time he met Djet.

I was heartbroken to learn the truth about Akea. I'd always known he had things going on with himself that he didn't like to talk about, but him admitting he tried to end his life more than once was mindboggling. Djet was a third brother who was taken away from his mother's wound before she found out she was having triplets. He spent his life in another world but at times his soul intertwined with Akea's. I couldn't believe how Goon's mistakes effected his children's fate.

"I'm sorry, Djet, but I don't think I can be passed around like this. First Akea, Osiris and now you? How is this supposed to work? I'm not a whore."

"Osiris wasn't your fault. This isn't any of our faults. I hate to blame our father for this, but we were all played because of his wrongdoings. His karma passed down to his kids. Kanye was possessed by a demon, Djet was living in a temple for afterlife souls and I have an issue with accepting myself. Why can't you see the truth? Don't make this about you. If you want to be upset, be that for all of us. I'm tired and we're all drained from the past few months. We need to heal and move on with our lives," Akea said.

"I understand everything now but I thought Djet was your other personality."

"I'm not going to force something you don't want. I'm fine with whatever you decide. All I know is that I'm glad to be here," Djet said. I pulled Akea out of his room and into the hallway for privacy.

"I can't let you go. I love you so much and you know that. Please don't fall into the trap. He wants us to be apart. This has to be a mistake. We had so many moments with each other and the love we made was real. Me and you were real. I can't love anyone else and I refuse to." Akea wiped the tears from my eyes then kissed my forehead. I wanted him to console me and tell me Djet was created by him and their story wasn't real.

"I love you enough to want you to be happy. Djet's love for you will always top what I have to offer. Why settle for less when there is someone who wants to give you more? While I was away, the temple showed me bits of my past. I was mean to you and Djet saw it. You never asked yourself, 'why now?' Look me in the eyes and tell me you didn't notice the sudden change. The way I dressed and the way I talked didn't pique your interest? You've known me all your life and I have never worn a pair of Timbs until that day you asked me to go to the movies with you. You don't want to see it, but you know deep in your heart that wasn't all me. I cannot take credit for everything," Akea said.

"How is it so easy for you, huh? You broke my heart with Jetti and now you're telling me someone got inside your head and made you fall in love with me?"

"I have feelings for you, too, but they are not as strong as his and they might not ever be," he replied.

"He's a stranger to me. I'll never love him."

"I'm seeing visions of the two of you when y'all were in Anubi as we speak. You dreamed about him all your life. You wanted him to save you when Osiris poisoned you. You're aroused for him right now. The scent of him drives you insane. Am I lying? I can see right through you. If we stay together, how would I be able to compete with his scent and the way he cares for you?" Akea asked.

Djet's scent drove me crazy when we were in Anubi. I thought the white wolf was a fantasy of mine, but for years he wanted to show me my soulmate existed. I had a crush on Akea and even thought about giving up because he was so cold to everyone, but something kept pulling me towards him. Maybe Akea and Djet were right, but it was too much to swallow. My reputation would forever be ruined even though it wasn't done intentionally.

"I need some space from all of this," I said. I walked down the hallway to my old bedroom. When I opened the door, I almost had a heart attack. Naobi was sitting on my bed with Destiny sleeping peacefully in her arms. Naobi had a way of appearing out of nowhere like a ghost. I ran to her and picked Destiny up.

"Thank you so much. Goon said she was safe but he didn't tell me how. I trusted his word but I was walking on needles."

"I alerted him the moment he came out of the portal. Rena saved her. Osiris was using her to stay alive. She's getting big," Naobi said. I tried to be strong for Destiny and myself but I couldn't. My life was going perfectly a few weeks ago, then suddenly it slapped me in the face. Tears wouldn't stop flowing from my eyes and Naobi hugged me.

"I just want to be happy. Why is that so hard? Osiris made a fool out of me and it caused my daughter danger. I'm going away for a while. Just me and Destiny," I vented. It seemed as if I was talking to myself. Naobi wasn't listening to me. She was looking at the door.

"He returned?" she asked.

"You know about Djet, too?"

Who else knows there's a third brother?

"This isn't good," she said and panicked.

"Exactly! I told Akea I don't trust him."

"No, his spirit is pure. I can feel it all the way in here. It's not good because my son will hate me for what I did, but it was a sacrifice I had to make to save the other two. He's back because my son will be king. The gods set my grandson free in return," she said. I wanted to ask more questions but I heard screaming and yelling.

"Goon and Kanya are fussing again," I said aloud.

"Oh, trust me, dear. This argument is going to get really ugly," Naobi said. Naobi took Destiny away from me and laid her inside a bassinet. The pack was in the hallway wanting answers from Djet. Kanye stood next to Djet and argued with everyone else in Djet's defense.

"He's our brother! End of story. We know this isn't Akea's magic. Be real with yourselves and accept Djet is a part of this pack. He fought like a warrior in Anubi. Come on, Father. You've gotta know deep down he's your son, too," Kanye said. My heart went out to Djet as he silently stood there waiting to be accepted.

"How is this possible? What did you do? Did you do this?" Goon's mate asked him.

"He didn't do anything. I did this," Naobi spoke up. The pack was silent as they watched Naobi for further explanation.

"I take full responsibility for this," she said and the pack gasped.

Goon's mate sat in the hallway chair and fanned herself. The pack sisters went to her aid and told her to breathe. Naobi's secret shocked us all because she was a genuine being.

"You destroyed this family! I thought he was one of Akea's spells but you're telling me you did this? I missed years. How do we rebuild from this?" Goon asked his mother.

"I saw a vision of you and Kanya heartbroken for not having the pups. So, I protected them while they were inside her womb. I thought Djet was protected, too. Your legacy was to be the king, take the throne from your father who lost his way as Anubi's ruler. You ignored your fate with each life you lived and I wanted you to because I want you to be happy without feeling obligated. I thought I was strong enough to keep your life the way you wanted it but fate is fate. You were so happy when you found your soulmate. I've spent many years watching your different lives but this one really brought out the best in you. The gods wanted you in Anubi but I wanted you to be free. It was the least I could do for you since I let Ammon ruin many lives, including yours. I let him destroy our world when I turned a blind eye to it because I loved him. I thought it would've been unruly of me to have you clean up a mess your parents created. You were too good for Anubi but now I see why the gods are upset. Anubi is our home, it's in our blood and we have to accept it. In the past, they didn't have anything to use against you until you mated with Kanya and gave her pups. I couldn't tell you because I wanted you to experience the happiness you've been searching centuries for," she said.

"That wasn't your call!" Goon growled.

"I was trying to protect them! The three of them would've been in another world! Yes, I could've told you the truth but you had to figure it out on your own! I want to have the answers to everything and find ways to escape this, but no amount of magic can destroy what's destined to be. You were supposed to make that choice on your own instead of doing it for your sons. A real king knows when he's ready," Naobi cried. Everyone was emotional and I felt horrible for not believing Djet. I felt his pain as he stood there listening to his family. I've never experienced feeling someone else's pain before. They say soulmates can feel what the other is going through so I cried for him because he wanted to.

"It's better late than never. We have the rest of our lives to know him," Goon's mate said.

"That's it, Kanya? You've been bitching with me for hours about nothing and my mother just told us she knew about our missing pup! You forgive her so fucking easily but I still have to kiss your ass even though you're the one who came to Anubi, putting yourself in danger? So, let me guess. You two are going to have tea tomorrow while eating fancy human food like you normally do and discussing all the shit I do wrong?" Goon yelled and punched a hole in the wall. He paced back and forth, growling and yelling at Naobi and Kanya. Apparently, Goon and Kanya had hidden issues and Kanya not being mad at Naobi was the icing on the cake.

"I prayed about this and I accept all that has happened to me since it saved my brothers. I was the sacrifice that was needed to heal you, Father," Djet said to Goon.

"The sacrifice to heal Naobi, too, because she worshipped a fucking man who killed his people. This isn't just about me," Goon said.

"Bro, come on. That's your mother," Izra said.

"Not anymore. Go home, Naobi. Take Kanya with you if you want because I need some space. You also betrayed me by sending my mate to Anubi alone. I know you have a weak spot for her but you gave birth to me!" Goon said.

We had witnessed Goon's anger on many occasions but he was beyond angry. He felt betrayed by his mate and his mother. The two women he loved and cherished the most. Goon told Djet to follow him so they could talk about a few things. They went downstairs and out of the front door.

"Whew, now I can finally exhale," Monifa's mother said.

The chatter got louder while everyone was trying to digest everything they'd learned about Djet. Naobi was gone and Akea consoled his mother. Kanye announced he was going home to Monifa as he headed for the stairs. I went inside my bedroom and closed the door. Destiny slept through the commotion. Her small stomach was full of milk.

"I betrayed you when I offered to go to Anubi but I'm going to spend the rest of my life making it up to you."

Destiny opened her eyes and they were Djet's. I'd ignored the signs all along. I tolerated Akea's odd behavior in the past and never gave up on him because of the dreams I had of Djet. After watching Destiny sleep, I took a shower to clear my thoughts and have time alone.

****

I jumped out of bed and tripped over a hamper when I heard Destiny's coos. The light came on and Djet was holding her. He traced a symbol on her tiny forehead while saying a prayer. I silently watched him talk to Destiny in a language I had never heard before. After he was finished, he gave her to me.

"Sorry about that. I didn't want to wake you," he said.

"It's okay. I needed that nap. Well, sleep. I think I've slept for nine hours."

Djet sat on the edge of my bed and observed my room. His muscular back was beautiful because of his markings. His curly coils fell into his face, but hid the gold in his hazel eye. He made me nervous, his presence was different than before. He stood up and towered above me, my frame lost in his shadow.

"I won't do anything you don't want me to do. My father showed me my own room so I'll sleep there until we start over. I have to know if you still feel like I cheated you," he said. His voice and his scent put me in a trance.

"CHANCY!" he said.

"I'm sorry, I'm still a little tired."

"I'll see you in a few. I'm going to hunt with my father," he said.

"How did it go with your father if you don't mind me asking?"

"It was different. Better than our encounter in Anubi. He apologized and promised to make up for lost time. My mother just cried and held me. She's very emotional, isn't she?" he asked.

"Yes, but that's a mother for you. She'll come around in a few days. How did it go with the pack brothers?"

"It went pretty good. Izra gave me a stash of herbs and told me to hide them from my father. Your father told me he'd kick my ass if I hurt you. But I was with them for hours in the man cave. Everyone treated me like I didn't know what to do. Father even tried to show me how to flush a toilet. I know everything about this world. The overseer taught me about it before I got inside Akea," he said.

"How did it feel to be inside him? Did you hear his thoughts? Could he hear yours?"

"It's hard to explain, but imagine being inside someone and they can feel your thoughts but can't hear you. I couldn't touch you how I wanted to. It was like wearing gloves while making love. I know you felt something other than Akea when you got pregnant with Destiny. Your beast saw past the magic and looked further into Akea's soul. Your womb opened for me, allowing me to stamp you," he said.

"That night was beautiful."

"It was the first time I felt you," he replied.

I placed Destiny in her bassinet after she yawned. She was exhausted from being away from home. I opened my robe and Djet's eyes glowed when my full breasts slightly bounced with each movement. He reached out to touch me but pulled back. He was afraid of rejection. I pulled him into me and his strong arms swallowed me. My nails scratched through his hair while he kissed the side of my neck. I wanted to resist him for a while so we could learn each other, but my beast couldn't fight it—she needed him. His canines grazed my skin while he traced his tongue from my neck to my breast. He gently bit my nipple and the beast inside him lustfully growled. My center throbbed out of control and it pained me.

What are you doing to me?

He pulled me to the floor and laid on top of me, massaging my breasts while kissing me. I wrapped my legs around him and rubbed my center against his extra-large erection. Soft wails escaped my lips when he choked me. The kiss was aggressive, beastly, strong and pussy wrenching. I covered my mouth when he placed his hand on my mound. My lower body raised off the floor when his finger entered me. He pulled at my wild mane while playing with my pussy. My essence coated his fingers. I couldn't stand it anymore and needed him inside of me. I pushed him back to be in control. Djet was ready to say something but I placed a finger over his lips. I straddled him and he grabbed my buttocks. His dick stood tall and thick. He freed himself and the size was intimidating. Djet pulled me closer to him. We kissed and fondled one another. My wetness smothered his pelvis area. Djet rolled on top of me and stuffed my breast into his mouth. The tip of his dick pressed against my opening. My nipples ached badly from swelling. He pressed at my opening and I winced in pain. Djet's width stretched me apart. My nails sank into his skin when he pushed further into me. He stopped for a moment and looked into my eyes for reassurance. I wasn't holding back because I needed to finally put my mind to rest. Beasts' sex was like art, an expression of our souls connecting. The scratching, biting, movement and sounds were like a portrait, a representation of our love for eternity. Djet went deeper and at a slow pace. It was too much for me to endure but I wasn't one to back down. He buried his face into the crook of my neck and moaned.

"I want to stay inside you for life," he whispered against my ear, but I was a mute. Djet's lovemaking took my breath away. He raised my leg to kiss my thigh. His moans, grunts and growls were getting louder. My stomach bulged with each stroke. The pressure mixed with pleasure caused me to leak. My nectar poured onto the floor and Djet's nose flared. My scent was heavier because of how aroused he made me. White hair appeared on his arms and his nails scratched at my skin. A trace of saliva slipped from the corner of my mouth while I fought to keep it closed. Each stroke caused my neck to stiffen because his size pressed against my rib cage, but nonetheless I couldn't stop my body from cumming. I was drenched in sweat, turning our room into a sauna. Djet spread my legs wider and I was sprawled out like a "W." My tippy-toes touched the floor and my ass was also spread. He placed two fingers inside my rear end while drilling his hard and swollen dick into my pussy. White creamy cum exploded out of my body.

"DJET!" I screamed when another orgasm rippled through me. The tip of his shaft slammed into my spot and my toes cracked. Djet pulled out of me, leaving me panting on the floor. He laid next to me and pulled me on top of him. He held me in place while entering me again. His hands caressed my body while I rode him. My pussy walls gripped him tightly and he moaned. It didn't matter how fast I went, Djet wanted more. He lifted me until only the tip was in then pumped into me with the head of his squash-sized dick. I rubbed my clit and squeezed my breasts. Djet sat up and hugged me while matching my rhythm. I held his face and pulled his lips between mine to capture his tongue. He kneaded his fingers into my ass and I wanted to scream at the top of my lungs when he sank his teeth into my throat. Djet gave me the intimacy bite where he claimed me. He swelled again inside me then erupted. I fell into his body and hugged him. We fell asleep in the middle of my bedroom floor.

A few hours later...

"URGHHHHHHH!"

I woke up and ran into the bathroom because my skin burned badly. I ran cold water in the shower and hurriedly stepped in so it could sooth my skin but it wouldn't work. The thin snake-like thing moved underneath my skin. I scratched and pulled at but it made the pain worse. It poked through my skin to form patterns on my body. Another one was in my neck and I fell into the sink, knocking it out of the wall. I rolled on the floor, kicking, screaming and growling. Djet ran into the bathroom and scooped me up into his arm. He held me down in the tub and told me it was almost over.

"What did you do to me?"

"The gods stamped you. It's almost over," he said, unbothered. I stopped overreacting after the pain went away. Once it was over, I ran into the bedroom and looked in the mirror. My slim curves were broader and my breasts were fuller. I also had more markings on my body but the one on my neck was too hard to miss because it glowed.

"I gained weight!"

"No, you didn't. Your hips have to be wide enough to take my beast so it wouldn't hurt you like last night. You look beautiful," Djet said from behind me.

"Tell me anything," I replied.

"Take a compliment for what it is and be happy with it," he said.

It reminded me of a time when I was shopping for bigger clothes while carrying Destiny and I couldn't find anything cute to wear. I modeled different clothes for Akea and he told me to take a compliment and be happy with it. When I found out the truth, I was leery about starting the process over, but a lot of things remained the same between us. The only difference was his beast. I playfully punched him in the arm and chuckled.

"I can kick your ass now."

Djet fell into a fit of laughter and I chuckled myself. He grabbed Destiny so I could breastfeed her and she latched on. For weeks, it was hard getting Destiny to latch on because Jetti breastfed her when I wasn't able to. Depending on Destiny's mood, she would latch on but she naturally reached for my breast. At that moment, I noticed something else about Destiny. She was a normal-sized pup instead of the small premature pup I gave birth to.

"I thought spells were too much for a baby. What happened?"

"Prayers. I'm not magical, I'm spiritual. I've been practicing this for many years," he said.

"That's what you were doing when you were chanting something over her?"

"Yes, I wish I could've done it sooner but I wasn't able to heal her being inside of Akea," he replied. My door flew opened and it was my mother panicking about Baneet. Djet covered himself with a pillow and walked backwards into the bathroom.

"Dang, Mother. Why didn't you knock?"

"Baneet is in trouble," she panicked.

"Why is there always something going on? It's pissing me off!"

"We cannot get in touch with her at all like she's dead. Usually the pack can telepathically communicate," she said.

"This has Arya written all over it, I'm sure."

"Fiti is downstairs and she says Arya took Baneet before she tried to kill us. What if she's dead?" she asked. My mother was very passionate about family and sometimes it clouded her judgement. The pack warned her plenty of times about Arya.

"You can stay here while the rest of us go looking for her. We'll be back," she said and stormed out the room. Djet opened the door to make sure the coast was clear.

"Your sister is missing?" he asked.

"That's what my mother said so the pack is out searching for her. I'm going to stay here with Destiny."

"I'll stay with you," he said.

"Let's get some fresh air. I need to get out of this house."

"Cool," he replied.

****

The lake outside was a breath of fresh air. We sat on a log while Destiny laid in her carrier. I was worried about Baneet, too, but I was also concerned about her loyalty with Arya and if they were setting up the pack to finish them off. Djet was lying against a tree with his arms crossed. He was wearing sweatpants, a T-shirt and a pair of tennis shoes.

"Your sister will be safe," he said.

"She's pregnant."

"She will be safe. I promise you," he replied.

"I believe you."

The ducks swam across the lake and I saw a few deer galloping in the grass. We talked about everything, including his life in the temple. It had been a while since I was able to sit and talk with someone other than Monifa. Me and Akea used to talk but the recent chain of events put a strain on us.

"I didn't think I was going to come back after I saw Osiris's true colors. It bothers me how easily I gave up to him. I don't think I can get over that part of my life. I still see those black shadows when I close my eyes begging me to come back. Being emotionless is not living and that's what it was like for me in Anubi. I don't think I'm mentally okay."

Djet pulled me between his legs and cradled me. Osiris ruined my spirt, but the shadows that followed him were too strong to ignore.

"I promise you won't ever have to worry about them again," Djet said. Silence came between us and we found ourselves staring at the lake, waiting for Baneet to get back.

Arya

"**Y**ou have to eat, Baneet."

"I will when you free me. I won't run very far, I'm too weak," she replied.

"It's best you stay here until I figure out what I should do next."

I heard a loud crashing noise come from the living room. It could only be Osiris because nobody else knew where I was hiding since everyone was in Anubi. I sat the plate of raw bear meat on the dresser before I quietly walked down the hallway. Osiris was trashing the living room when I peeked my head around the corner. I wasn't expecting him back anytime soon because he had a long agenda. He threw a couch through the window and I ran back inside of Baneet's room and locked the door.

"We have to go. He's pissed off," I whispered.

The chains were heavy around her ankles and wrists. I searched the dresser drawers for the key but couldn't find it. My hands shook and my heart was racing.

"Hurry up!" Baneet said.

I found the key underneath a pair of sheets and rushed to Baneet. The door flew off the hinges and wood shattered, cutting me across the cheek. Osiris's large frame stood in the doorway. He wore a black suit and a bat medallion hung from his neck with red eyes. It was Seth's necklace. He must've taken it when he captured Seth.

"Did you kill him?" I asked.

"He's alive but I got what I wanted from him," he said.

He looked at Baneet's breasts and smirked at me.

"I like my women chained and in distress. The fear in their eyes always gives me an erection. But I didn't come here for you. I came for her," he said, pointing at Baneet.

"What do you want to do with her?"

"The blood of the pup will open the demon's gate. I need her baby," he said.

"I did what you wanted me to do! Please leave her alone."

He slapped and kicked me around the bedroom, my body sailed through the air and crashed into the mirror on the wall. Shards of glass pierced through my back but I managed to get up to defend Baneet.

"Your whore ass had one fucking job! You haven't done nothing! The spell book was to strengthen you but it made you dumber! Is it that tiger boy you're worried about? I should've known you were weak when you fell for the trap. You really thought I was going to make Seth demonic again for you? Why in the fuck would I do that if I want to rule Ibuna myself!" Osiris yelled then punched me in the face with a closed fist.

I stopped caring about Osiris's plan to take over Anubi and Ibuna the moment I realized Taj was the one I wanted to be with. At one point, I wanted Seth to be the man he used to be, but that person wasn't coming back. Taj made me feel important whenever he was around and I took it all for granted because of lust. I hurriedly got up when he snatched the chains and locks off Baneet's limbs and pulled her off the bed.

"Please, just let her go!"

"Let her go? Let her go for what? That bitch Rena stole my prisoner and now I'll use this one. I doubt your life would mean anything to your pack if I take you with me," he said. I charged into him and he grabbed me around the neck and slammed me to the floor. Osiris was too strong and he sorta didn't look like himself. He was starting to resemble his uncle Goon. Baneet broke away from Osiris and headed for the door but he caught her by the neck.

"LET HER GO!" I screamed.

"I want Goon's pack dead! They ruined my plans! My clan cannot come out of Ibuna until I break Naobi's curse on the gate. This is all your fault. They were supposed to be dead!" Osiris yelled with spit flying out of his mouth.

"She's carrying a pup," I pleaded.

"Were you not thinking about that when you had her chained for days? Now you have a heart because you want that tiger boy to accept you? It's too late to do the right thing."

"I chained her here for my personal reasons. She's all I have left and I didn't want her to leave me after finding out all that I've done. I fed her and bathed her, but you want to kill her. I can't allow you to do this," I replied.

"You took a demonic witch's spell book. Your fate is sealed! I own you and everything else in your possession. You should've been wiser. Seth was going to die either way because I want his world. This was never about you, whore!" he said.

"I'll do anything, please don't take her. Take me instead."

"You're of no value to me, Arya," he said.

Osiris ran out the door dragging Baneet by her feet; I chased after them. My beast emerged and I ran faster. Osiris shifted into a huge black wolf; his size made a few trees tumble over, knocking me down a hill. Osiris and Baneet were gone when I ran up the hill. He took her to Ibuna.

Without knowing where to go, I ran back to the cabin and grabbed the spell book Osiris gave me. I lit the fireplace and tossed the book inside but it wouldn't burn. There was no way I could escape him. Taking the book was a sacrifice of my soul. I sat in front of the fireplace and wept. Baneet cared about me and I betrayed her. I hurt her so much that she would never forgive me. The ten-year old Arya sat next to me and watched the fire.

"We will never be free now. You sold us to a man who can do whatever he wants with us," she said. My conscience was allowing me to see and hear things I tried to keep in the dark over the years.

"I know that. Why do you keep showing yourself?"

"Because you forgot the promise you made to me. You weren't supposed to let a man use you for your body ever again. After Sosa did those things to you, we were supposed to stay away from them until we found someone who loved us. We weren't supposed to be like this," she said.

"I got lost."

"You wanted to be lost," she said then disappeared.

I grabbed the book out of the fire after it died down because I needed it for a spell. Driving to Taj wasn't an option because it would take hours. He was the only one who I trusted to help me despite his ill feelings towards me.

****

There was a new doorman in the lobby when I walked into Taj's building. He asked me what floor I was going to, but the elevator door opened. Taj stepped off the elevator with a scowl on his face. He pulled me into the corner and the doorman asked Taj if there was a problem.

"No, she's fine," he said.

"The pack is looking for you because they want Baneet. Monifa had a vision of Baneet inside of a bedroom. What did you do?" he asked.

"Did you know I was coming?"

"Yes, the demon inside of you is growing. You know I can feel when they're near. I need to know what is going on with Baneet. So, I hope there is a spec of good in you left," he said.

"Monifa saw a vision? A spell shielded Baneet's thoughts. What else did she see?"

"It doesn't matter. They are going to the family's vacation home if they haven't gotten there already. Listen to me, Arya. Whatever you're connected to is feeding on you and once it finishes, you're either going to be dead or dead inside. You won't know who you are and the need for sex will deepen. Be honest with me, is Baneet dead?"

"Osiris took her to Ibuna as a hostage. He wants to proceed with his plan without the pack butting into his business. If they do, he's going to kill Baneet but her pup is what he really wants. He said something about a witch casting a spell on the gate to Ibuna and locking his clan in."

SOUL Publications

"Well, go to Ibuna and save her. You know where the gate is. You can get through, can't you?" he asked.

"Not if there is a spell on the gate, Taj. Someone who is born a part of that world will have to go. Maybe Rena?"

"Or Seth. I heard he came back with the pack from Anubi," he said.

"Well, let's go to his house."

"I'm not using that sorcery to teleport. I'll drive there," he said and I shrugged my shoulders. I followed Taj downstairs to the garage. He had his own section of cars. His favorite was a truck because of his long legs.

"Ride in the back. I don't want Rena getting any ideas," he said.

"This isn't about you and Rena. The brat will get over it."

"And this isn't about how you feel about Rena. Ride in the back," he spat.

"I can find my way there."

Taj grabbed me by the arm and pushed me against his truck.

"You're coming with me. It can be a trap for all I know. Now, get your ass in the back of the truck," he said. His body was close to mine and his cologne tickled my nose. All I ever wanted was for Taj to make love to me, but something was holding him back.

"You haven't been thinking about me?"

"Not anymore," he said and backed away from me.

"You slept with Rena?"

"How is that your business again?" he asked.

"We were together at one point and I still have feelings for you. I'm sorry, Taj. I'm truly sorry for not being the person you deserve but neither is Rena. She harbors a dark soul. Me and her are just alike, you can do better." I saw an emotion in his eyes when he looked into mine—he was sad.

"Let's run away after we save Baneet."

"I'm too damn old to run away and I cannot be with you. I'd rather mate with Rena before I go back down that road with you. The way you betrayed me was enough."

He opened the back door and told me to get in.

"This doesn't make any damn sense how insecure you've gotten. Are you afraid of little ol' me?"

"Have you seen what Rena turns into? Get your ass in," he said and pushed me into the back seat. He got in the driver's seat and grabbed his keys from the visor. I crossed my arms and pouted as Taj drove out of the garage like a bat out of hell.

"I'm not giving up on us."

Taj stopped at a red light and looked into his rearview mirror. I caught a glimpse of my reflection and my eyes were red. Taj chuckled to himself.

"Shut up and ride, demon," he said.

I was going to be better for Taj because I loved him. Seth's sex caused me to be submissive but Taj could lay next to me for hours, making love to my mind. It's sad to say how much I had to go through to realize sex and love weren't the same. I want love to capture me, save me from myself.

Rena

"Come to me, Rena. Be my queen so we can run this world together. This is your home."

"I don't want to be a part of it anymore."

Osiris's voice filled my head while I was sleeping, but I was too exhausted to wake up. I tossed and turned until my body hit the floor with a loud thud. When I opened my eyes, the sun was setting.

I've must've slept for over a day.

I grabbed my robe and headed down the spiral staircase of my father's mansion. There was a noise coming from the family room. I crept inside and there was a figure sitting in my father's chair. I couldn't make out the body but his arms hung over the arms of the chair. Once I caught a glimpse of the tattoo, I knew who it was. I ran to my father and hugged him.

"When did you come home? Why didn't you wake me?"

"I wanted you to sleep. I've been here for a day, just sitting here and thinking about the ending. I had to prepare myself for what I had to tell you," he said. He picked up a bottle of aged whiskey and guzzled the rest of it. I sat on the rug in front of him, the same way I used to when I was around eight years old. My father used to tell me stories about my mother. I looked forward to those nights but then it stopped. His soul had gotten so dark that at times, he forgot he had a daughter. The older a demon gets, the more their appetite for blood grows.

"I want you to understand something very important, Rena. I love you very much and I'm thankful to have a daughter like you. Me and your mother both had dark spirits, but somehow, we created an angel. I'll give anything to stop you from having nightmares and get rid of that sexual desire you have to fight every day. I can heal you so you can have a normal life. But in order for that to happen, I have to sacrifice myself by burning my soul," he said. I wished I didn't wake up and stayed to asleep forever. The thought of not having my father was enough to stop my heart.

"No, Father. NO! We can lock them away or something. Please, don't do this. I'll be alone in this house by myself. What other family do I have? You're trying to hurt me!" Tears fell from his eyes and he sobbed.

"Anubi is ruined because of what I created. You didn't see what I saw there. It was a slaughter house. Osiris is trying to follow in my footsteps because he thinks it heals the feeling of being lost. I showed him that world so I have to do what I have to do to make sure Ibuna doesn't ruin Anubi again. I felt their tradition when I was there and I prayed with them. I've never prayed in my life. Me and Goon found our legacy. He is to be king of his world and I need to destroy mine. That's what we learned when we were in the dungeon together. It was fate, Rena. I'm not sad about this. These are tears of joy because I can finally rest in peace and take all those shadows with me. You don't need me, I always needed you. You're going to find love, have babies and they will have babies. They don't need to be attached to those shadows that follow us around even when we don't want them to. I'm going to Ibuna and I'm not coming back. I have to kill Red because he's the key to it all," he said.

I buried my face in my hands and my father rushed to me and held me. He rocked me in his arms and kissed my forehead.

"It'll be okay. This is why I didn't wake you up. I wanted you to rest first," he said.

There was nothing I could do but respect his wishes. My father wanted to cure Anubi because Ibuna damaged it.

"I want to go with you so I can see you one last time. That's all I ask."

"Fair enough," he said.

The doorbell rang and my father looked at me in confusion.

"Expecting company?" he asked.

"Nope, but it better not be Arya. I'm sure she was stalking this place. I have a feelings it's her."

I got up and ran to the door. Arya was trying to keep my father from doing things right and she needed to be punished for it. When I snatched the door open, she hid behind Taj. Jealousy and raged consumed me. I struck Taj in the face and he picked me up and carried me into the house.

"Get that bitch away from here! She's trying to stop my father!" I screamed.

"Chill out, Rena, damn!" Taj shouted while I swung and kicked.

"We were fucking in the car before we came here. Thank me later!" she said.

"STOP LYING!" Taj shouted.

Taj dropped me on the floor when I bit his forearm. I ran to Arya and she threw a hallway table at me, but missed. She made a run for the door but I grabbed her by the hair and slammed her into the wall. She clawed at my arms and bit my shoulder. She was slightly taller than me and stronger because of her beast but my anger wouldn't allow me to stop. Arya bit my shoulder and I scratched her with my razor-sharp nails, putting deep gashes into cheek. She held her face and blood dripped on to the floor. My father and Taj broke us up, but Arya shifted and attacked me. She laid on top of me using her beast's weight. I spit a ball of fire into her face and she swiped at it with her paw and shook it off. Arya ran out of the house and I flew after her. She howled when I swooped down and grabbed her by the tail, slinging her into Taj's truck, setting off the alarm. She laid on the ground with a bloody snout and broken arm. I pressed my pencil-shaped stiletto nail into her throat and through her flesh.

"I told you I was going to kill you, bitch!"

My father pulled me away from Arya and she shrank into her human form. Her leg was twisted and her face was almost unrecognizable.

"That's enough, Rena. You did what you wanted to do, now it's over," my father said. My father helped Arya and Taj pinned me against what was left of his truck so I wouldn't attack her again.

"I'm fine now, Taj! Let me go!"

My father carried Arya into the house and it pissed me off even more. He helped her and she didn't have his best interest at heart.

"Are you okay now?" Taj asked.

"Go home and take that bitch with you. You and her don't belong here. You stated how much you hated those with demon blood, so why come here?"

"Because Baneet is in Ibuna and only two people can get in: you and your father. The pack wants her back that's all and I brought Arya with me to keep an eye on her. I wasn't sure if she was telling the truth or if it was a trap. I didn't come here to beef with you and your father," he replied.

"My father will go soon, so tell your friends Baneet will be home if she's still alive. In the meantime, leave and never come back."

"I also wanted to talk to you about going to Ibuna. Did you, ummmm. Did you..."

"Did I what?" I spat.

"Give into temptation. In other words, did Osiris get inside you? Are you still a virgin? Were you able to resist him because I'm sure he was trying to weaken you so you could be on his side."

"Why do you want to know? You made yourself clear about me, so please leave!" Taj stood there for a second not knowing what to say because I'd never yelled at him before. I was so angry with Taj, and my father sacrificing himself didn't make my mood any better. Tears stung the brims of my eyes and Taj reached out to me.

"What happened? Did he do something to you?"

"You wouldn't understand since you don't care for us," I replied and snatched away from him. Taj called my name but I kept walking. I closed the door and leaned against it for a few seconds, thinking about what just happened. Noise came from the kitchen, so I headed there. My father was lying on the floor next to Arya. I reached out to him but a force pulled me back. A hand covered my mouth as a voice whispered in my ear.

You belong to me.

A tiger burst through the kitchen's window and attacked Osiris. Osiris turned into a black beast with red eyes. Taj and Osiris rolled around on the floor, clawing and biting each other. Arya mumbled something but I couldn't make out what she was saying. I helped my father up and he was confused. There was a bloody sledge hammer on the floor. Osiris didn't come for my father nor Arya, he wanted to kidnap me, too.

Taj's oversized tiger pounced on Osiris. His paw struck Osiris's snout and he rolled across the living room. The house was a mess almost like a tornado came through. I cringed when Osiris's teeth punctured Taj's ear. Both animals stood on their hind legs and wrestled while biting and clawing at each other's flesh. I ran to my father's weapon case and grabbed a gold sword with spiked ridges. Osiris was on top of Taj, aiming to snap his neck. I flew into them and stabbed Osiris in the back. He fell into the wall and I dropped the sword. Osiris shifted into his human form and grabbed the sword.

"I'm not trying to kill my wife but I will if I have to," he said.

"You're a sick bitch!" I screamed.

Taj punched Osiris and he fell over a shredded couch. I screamed when Osiris plunged the sword in Taj's throat. Osiris kicked me when I crawled to Taj.

"Do you submit to me now? Tell me or I won't let you save him. Look at him gasping for air like a human's pet gold fish," Osiris said. Taj grabbed the sword but it wouldn't budge.

"Please let me help him! Why are you doing this to us?"

"Because my grandfather wants payback!" he said.

"Your grandfather is dead! You might have his beast and strength but he's not inside you. This is all your doing!"

The house rattled and pictures fell from the walls. I rushed to Taj and dragged him somewhere safe. His eyes were bloodshot red and he was losing color. He tried to talk but I placed my hand over his mouth. I pulled the sword out of his throat and pressed down on the wound to stop it from bleeding. Werewolves came in the house through the ceiling and windows. I counted seven of them. The biggest beast was Goon. He shifted into his human form and the pack stood behind him growling.

"Where is Baneet? We know you have her! End this now, nephew. Your issue is with me," Goon said. Another wolf shifted into human form and it was a woman.

"Where is my daughter? Give her back to me!" Baneet's mother yelled at Osiris.

"Says the bitch who gave her grandchild to me. Now you don't trust me?" Osiris asked. Arya crawled out into the living room and I hated she was still alive, but something told me she contacted them. Five witches appeared in the living room. The witches were Akea, Fiti, Monifa's mother, Naobi and Ula. Osiris didn't back down even though he was cornered. Taj wounded him badly and he lost a lot of blood. He could barely stand on his own.

"You all are pathetic! I came here for Rena and I will leave with her! You want Baneet, you can have her but the succubus is mine! We'll figure out another way to rule both worlds in due time. So, do we have a trade?" he asked. I pulled away from Taj and he grabbed my arm.

"No, Rena. We will figure out another way. I won't live with myself if you don't return. The fear of you kept me guessing about us but I'm over it.

Just stay here with me," he choked. My father stumbled into the living room and looked around.

"What in the fuck did y'all do to my house?" he yelled.

"Go ahead and sacrifice yourself, Seth. Baneet will disappear with Ibuna. You're a fucking traitor! The demons hate you for bowing to Anubi's feet and kissing the wolf god's ass," Osiris said.

"I'll go with you but let the girl go!" my father shouted at Osiris. Baneet appeared in front of Osiris and he held a dagger to her throat.

"Stay the hell away!" Osiris shouted when the pack closed in around him. Akea disappeared and Osiris missed it. He appeared behind Osiris and knocked him onto the floor. The pack rushed to Baneet. Everything was happening so fast I couldn't wrap my mind around it. My father standing with Goon's pack showed his growth since he used to hate Anubi. I accepted his reasoning for wanting to get rid of Ibuna; it could never be a good place. Osiris was losing more blood, which made it hard for him to disappear to Ibuna—he was too weak. A cage appeared around Osiris. His body convulsed from electrocution when he grabbed ahold of the bars.

"He will be punished in Anubi so the people can see his death. He owes it to them since he caused so much pain. My father, Kofi, is waiting for you," Goon told Osiris. Osiris yelled and screamed curse words at the pack.

"Killing me doesn't take away the lives I took! I made my stamp in Ibuna and Anubi for life! They will tell stories about me and how I used magic, power and strength to kill thousands of my people. I will be a part of their history," Osiris said.

"I'm going to make sure they forget about you. Erase your existence," Goon replied. Osiris went insane inside the cage. Fiti came over to us and kneeled next to Taj. His wound was healing since the sword was out.

"We still have a problem. The demons are going to seek revenge since Osiris portrayed as their ruler," she said.

"My father will take care of them. Thank you all for coming."

"Can you believe Arya contacted her mother and told her what happened? She's trying to save her ass. She told her mother Osiris made her do it so he could stop raping her. She's up to something so keep an eye on her. Arya is vindictive when it comes to the men she wants," Fiti said and disappeared. Goon yelled out words I couldn't understand, but whatever it was made the cage disappear with Osiris inside.

"He sent him to Anubi as a prisoner. They are going to slaughter him in front of the people," Taj said. I helped him up and he wrapped his arm around me.

"You saved my life."

"I sensed him when you went inside the house. There was no way in hell I was letting him take you away from me. I want to be with you," Taj replied. The pack left the house but Goon stayed behind to speak with my father.

"We promised each other a fight," my father said to Goon.

"We fought already, just not each other. No promise is broken," Goon replied.

"Cut that muthafucka's head off," my father said with venom dripping from his voice.

"I planned on it," Goon replied.

They thanked each other before Goon left out of our house. My father picked up a broken chair and looked around. I walked over to him and hugged him.

"I have a lot of money in the wine cellar I've been collecting for years. Gold, too. It'll all belong to you," he said to me. Taj was standing behind me and my father gestured him over.

"I'll haunt you if you treat my daughter like a piece of ass," he warned Taj.

"That's not my character, but I understand," Taj replied.

"We have to get to Ibuna so I can destroy it," my father said.

My stomach formed a knot as I thought about what was about to happen. My father walked outside, leaving me and Taj alone.

"You'll have me, I promise. But your world is corrupt and there is always going to be an enemy who will use it against you because they don't have real loyalty. The demons worship anyone who is able to feed them. You know in your heart it was either this or he'd die by Goon. A man should die to save lives instead of being killed for ruining them. His soul will be spiritually cleansed and protected," Taj said.

"I'll be fine. He's lived a very long life— thousands of years. He's tired."

I walked out of the house with Taj tagging along. My father didn't look stressed like I thought he would be. His handsome youthful face looked peaceful, but I was still a nervous wreck.

****

The gate of Ibuna opened when the bars Naobi placed on the door disappeared. The sounds of screaming and the smell of dead bodies spilled into the room. I'd dealt with this scent all of my life but it was beginning to make me sick.

"I'm going to wait for you here," Taj said. He kissed my lips but he wouldn't let my hand go.

"I'm coming back."

"Right, my bad about that," he said.

Me and my father stepped through the door and it slammed shut. The shadows disappeared into the walls when they saw us.

"What is happening?"

"I don't know," he replied.

We walked further down the hall and into the king's room where my father used to sit. Behind the chair was a pit where he used to burn souls. The bat flew to him and landed on his shoulder. The dark shadows came through the floor and surrounded us.

They think I came back to feed them. They are hungry, my father thought.

"You sure about this?"

"Positive, I have to do this. You're a strong girl. You will be relieved when this is over," he said. My heart raced, almost pounding outside my chest. He pulled a dagger from behind his pants and drove it into the bat's chest. There wasn't a drop of blood in sight. The fire from the pit behind him sprouted up and wrapped around the walls. The demons scattered but the fire captured them. The fire was the color of blood.

"When it takes me, run as fast as you can so it won't get you. There is no coming back from this. This world is ending," he said. The floor split and I pressed my body against the wall so I wouldn't fall in. My father's body was changing. He was turning to black dust.

"See, it's painless. It's almost over," he said with tear-filled eyes. He shouted that he loved me before he disappeared. The fire spread through the tunnel, collecting all its demons. I did what my father told me and ran. My legs burned from the heat. The walls inside the tunnel were sweating and soon the whole place would blow. Two shadows ran on the side of me, looking for a way out.

BOOM!

"SHIT!" I panicked and sped up.

"OPEN THE DOOR! THE FIRE IS SPREADING!" I yelled, hoping Taj heard me. The noise was drowning out my voice. I banged on the door when I reached it, the fire was only twenty feet away from me.

"TAJ!" I screamed.

The door wouldn't open on my side so no one could escape. The sacrifice my father made trapped everyone inside with him. The fire was two feet away from me when Taj snatched me out of Ibuna.

"How do you feel?" he asked.

"The same."

Taj opened the exit door and we were in the alley in the back of the club. My father's demon nest Ibuna was gone.

"I hope this is the end," Taj yawned.

"I have to crash at your place. My father's house is ruined."

"Bet," he replied.

We left out of the exit door and Taj wrapped his arm around me. He still had dried up blood on his neck. We were both dirty and in need of a bath.

Forty-five minutes later...

Taj helped me out of what was left of my garments and dropped them to the bathroom floor. We both smelled sweaty and Taj smelled like a musty animal.

"You stink," I giggled. Taj threw me inside his diamond-shaped whirlpool tub.

"I could've hit my head!"

"You'll be alright," he replied, stepping in.

I slid between his legs and he wrapped his arms around my hips. We were quiet for a minute. Talking about my father was a sensitive subject but it was hard not to talk about since it was still fresh.

"I just want to chill here for a week. Lose communication with everyone so we can meditate. What do you think?"

"I have a club to run. I think I should remodel it. Livin' it up a little bit," I replied.

"I think you should leave it the way it is. It has a dark sexiness to it. It's like dragon demon slayer meets urban life. Gothic with a hood feel," he said.

"Hood?" I asked and burst into a fit of laugher.

"What?"

"What do you know about the hood?" I replied.

"Yo, I know shit," he said and I believed him.

"You're right though. A lot of people love the scenery. I'm thinking about changing the walls and turning them to stone. It'll look like a cave inside."

"Now that'll be dope," he said.

A slight moan slipped from his lips when I straddled him. His dick rested between the folds of my slit.

"I think you should stop if you want to keep your hymen intact," Taj joked and I playfully bit his neck. "You're still a bloodsucker?"

"Yes, but the demon spirit that was connected to it is gone. I'm all vampire now, oh and a witch but I haven't practiced any spells, yet. I wasn't interested in learning in the beginning but now I want to try it out. Monifa is going to show me," I replied. Taj grabbed the back of my neck and brought my face to his. He kissed me so passionately, my pussy throbbed against his shaft and made him moan. He cupped my breasts and brought them closer to his face.

"Your skin tastes so good. Damn, I want to eat the hell out of you," Taj groaned with a nipple in his mouth. The desire for Taj didn't go away. I wanted him even more. Maybe it was just him all along. I'd been with men before but none of them drew me in like Taj. He slid his girth back and forth between my slit while biting my neck. Whimpers and lustful groans escaped my lips. I was on the brink of exploding. Taj applied pressure to my breast while purring my name. He was coming too.

"Ohhhh, Tajjjjjj, babbbyyyyyyy!"

"I'm so hard for you. Shitttttt, Rena," he groaned.

I closed my eyes and enjoyed the pain from him biting my shoulder. My legs fell lazily to the bottom of the tub while my pussy throbbed and squirted on Taj's shaft. He pulled me into him and wrapped his arms around me. His dick was still planted firmly between my slit.

"You should've entered me," I said in a whisper.

"I want it to be special because it will be more than sex. It'll be mother and fatherhood for us. I'm ready to be a father and I have to know if you're on board with that. But there is no rush. We can please each other without intercourse," he said.

"Okay."

Taj grabbed a sponge and some body wash to wash my back. I was still holding on to him when he tried to move away to wash himself. I couldn't let go. My breasts were pressed against his chest and I could feel the beat of his heart.

"Rena, I gotta wash, too," Taj's husky voice whispered against my ear. I was getting emotional again because of my father. Taj realized what was happening and dropped the soap and sponge in the water. He rocked me in his arms while I cried like a baby and promised he wasn't going to leave me. I didn't have anyone but Taj.

Akea

Four days later...

Jetti was sitting on the front porch of Geo's new house. Her stomach was starting show. She wore a sweater dress with a pair of boots. Her hair had also grown a few inches and was styled in a curly fro. After spending time with my family and father before he left for Anubi, I was able to face my other fear. What I did with Jetti was a mistake regardless of Djet being inside my conscience. All she wanted from me was to inherit my family's business through my offspring. She was a disloyal gold-digging leech. I opened the fence and she shifted in her seat.

Beasts 3: Unleashed   Natavia

"You weren't nervous when you trapped me," I called out to her. Before I walked up the stairs to the porch, I observed the house. Geo's pack was poor so I couldn't understand where the mini mansion came from. I sat next to her and she scooted away from me.

"How did you find me?" she asked.

"My seed is in your womb. I didn't come here to break peace with you though. I came here to tell you that my son will come with me once he's born, and before you object, hear me out. He will not be a part of this pack. I don't trust any of you. You came into our house and led us to believe you were a good person but you used me to gain access to something my father worked hard for! While I was away, I had time to think about everything that went wrong in my life. At one point, I used to let people take advantage of me, but no more. You don't have a choice in this matter. You will not live off my fucking son. Not you or none of those scraggly dirty werewolves in your pack. I'm going to show him things you can't."

"You can't take him away from me!" Jetti screamed.

"Like you give a fuck. You don't care about him. I can see right through you and this pregnancy. He will not be the answer to your prayers."

"Are you doing this because of Chancy? I'm going to kill her!" Jetti said.

"Me and Chancy are not together anymore though I doubt you can do anything but open your legs and use my sperm for a better life."

"I told you I was sorry for what happened but I was tired of living in a fucking swamp while your family lived in a castle that looked down at us. Somebody had to bring your stuck-up ass down a notch. I nursed your daughter Destiny back to health like a house slave and this is the thanks I get? I'm entitled to everything you have!" she yelled.

"I paid you for it and let you work at our store. We're not responsible for your pack. If you're looking for a handout then maybe Geo isn't a real alpha."

Jetti slapped me in the face. She swung a second time but her fist froze in mid-air. I instructed her to have a seat and she cried about not being able to move her arms.

"How dare you use your witchcraft on me!" she screamed.

The front door opened and Geo's other mate stepped out onto the porch. She was nowhere near as pretty as Baneet. As I observed her, something caught my eye . The bracelet she was wearing was one of ours. It was a gold Cuban link with red and yellow diamonds. Each diamond was worth close to a million dollars. It was our top of the line jewelry. She caught me staring at her bracelet and pulled her sleeve down.

"Take it off!" I gritted.

"Take what off?" she asked.

Brother! I know who took our shit!

Who? Damn it, bro. Me and Monifa been locked up in the house since I came back. She don't want me to leave. I can't do shit! You might have to do this one alone.

Seriously?

Akea, my brother. That jewelry doesn't mean nothing to me right now. Monifa is crazy! She is lying on me right now fake sleeping with one eye open.

You're supposed to be big bad Kanye.

I'm a bitch right now.

I know you, Kanye. It's probably the other way around!

What's wrong with that?

Forget it.

"Is this how y'all were able to afford this house?"

"Some of us are fortunate," she said.

"Not this fortunate. Bring me what is left, including the Pharaoh's necklace. You'd be a dummy to sell that."

"We didn't take anything!"

She turned to walk into the house but I grabbed her arm and paralyzed her. Jetti screamed for me to stop and I paralyzed her, too. I saw a vision through Geo's mate's eyes. He didn't know about the missing jewelry. Baneet gave Geo the code to our safe but he declined and said he'd rather starve than steal. Geo's mate overheard them. She had a few male wolves from the pack help her. She hid the jewels in the swamp and inside a tree next to what was left of their old house. I took the bracelet off her arm before I let her go. This was all Baneet's fault. She was a traitor.

"Did you steal from them?" Jetti asked Rachel after I released her.

"What different does it make? You trapped him! I was sick of that bitch sitting in our house with her nose frowned up. Geo didn't need two mates! I was good enough for him. I'm the one who put us in a better house and you want to question me? What has Geo done for us besides chase after that prissy bitch, Baneet? Besides, Baneet gave the code to Geo so he could take it but I did it instead. Either way, Baneet helped us so they should be angry with her," Rachel said.

"You have one day to get out of this house and then I'm coming through and turning everyone to dust with a single snap of my finger."

"Where will me and my pup go?" Jetti asked.

"We'll temporarily work something out until my son is born. As for the rest of you, y'all can go back to the swamp," I replied. Jetti and Rachel yelled and cursed at me while I walked down the porch stairs. Geo's mate threw something at me when I walked through the fence.

"Save that rock, y'all gonna need it to start some campfires!" I called out.

"Go to hell, Akea! You ain't shit, moron!" Jetti yelled back.

"Be safe, Baby Mama!"

Damn, it feels good to be free.

****

The mansion was filled with laughter when I walked in. In my hand was a muddy box with our missing jewelry. Everyone but Monifa and Kanye was in the den drinking and dancing around. My father came over to me and pulled me out into the hallway.

"Everything okay? We were trying to get in touch with you," he said.

"Baneet didn't steal the jewelry but she gave up the code. She's a traitor, Father. Her and Arya side with the enemy."

"I'll talk to her father but in the meantime, let's just be thankful for what we have now," he said. I noticed my mother wasn't around and Djet was missing.

"Where is Mother and Djet?"

"They went to talk. We can't talk to Djet around a crowd because there is so much to discuss. I don't think we're ever going to make up for the time we've missed. This is something I will have to deal with but Djet is forgiving. He calls it a sacrifice. If I never taught you anything valuable, remember this. Everyone has to make a sacrifice in their lifetime whether it's for yourself or someone else, but change won't come if you don't. Our tradition is built on that and I want my sons to understand that when I leave for Anubi in a few days and take the throne, I don't want to stay gone long again. This family has been through a lot," he said.

"We haven't talked much but I don't know how to tell the pack Jetti is carrying my child."

"I dreamt about it. He's going to be your twin," my father said and patted my back. I almost slipped into the wall because of his strength but he caught me.

"You and Kanye gotta lay off the red meat, geesh."

"Come on downstairs. We're about to smoke," he said.

"Smoke?"

"Yeah, you grown now aren't you? Just hide the smell from your mother. She still doesn't see her sons as men, yet," he replied.

I told my father I was going to meet them in the basement when Chancy stepped into the hallway with Destiny in her arms. She gave me Destiny and I held her.

"We're still friends, right?" I asked.

"Of course. I'm happy the truth came out so you can be yourself. Nobody should ever have to force marriage and a lifetime commitment on you, and me being what I am did that to you."

"I've seen how mean I was to you, to all of you. I was mentally sick and I didn't notice how bad my issues were until I ended up in the place Djet lived in. It was like therapy. The afterlife temple also helped me understand that I'm not one of those guys who wants a soulmate yet. I have many, many years to pick someone to spend my life with and for the first time I'm good with that," I replied. Chancy's pretty face lit up and she smiled. She was still beautiful and had an aura about her that gave off good energy.

"Awww, Akea, you sound so happy," she sang.

"Whelp, I think Destiny needs her diaper changed." Chancy took Destiny out of my arms and went upstairs. I walked into the kitchen and stopped in my tracks. Zaan and his girlfriend were kissing while he fondled her. He pulled his hand away from her pants and she fixed her shirt.

"When did you get back?" Zaan asked as if it was his first time seeing me.

"Bro, I been back. You forgot already?"

"I thought I heard something about you being in a temple of before life, something like that," he said.

"It's the Temple of Afterlife and Akea came back last night," his girlfriend said.

"The both of y'all are dumb as hell. I know the pack doesn't want to come out and say it but y'all know I was there when we saved Baneet from Osiris like four days ago. We made jokes about it when we came home that day."

"I thought that was Kanye," Zaan said.

"Kanye's been in the house with his mate. Nobody has seen them since he came back from Anubi. So how did you think I was Kanye?"

"I think they're twins," Fiti whispered to Zaan.

My father's pack brother, Izra, walked into the kitchen and grabbed a pitcher of water out the fridge.

"Does anyone know what Baneet is having?" Fiti asked.

"A crack baby with rabies. Don't tell anyone I said that though," Izra said, leaving the kitchen.

"A crack baby? Ohhhh, I know what that is," Fiti said in excitement.

Please don't say it!

"What is it? My girl is smart," Zaan bragged.

"It's when a baby comes out of their mother's ass first. Get it? Crack baby," she said.

"I think I heard something about that before," Zaan replied.

Zaan's mind always ventured off because of how much he smoked. Fiti picked up his habit, too, so the two of them together was bad for the brain. I told Zaan the fellas were going to hang out in the basement.

"This looks so boring, bro," Zaan said when we entered the basement. My father's pack brothers were just sitting around drinking and smoking.

"We need some music," Zaan said.

"I hope it's orchestra," Zaan's father, Uncle Elle said.

"Isn't that a bird or sumthin, Father?" Zaan replied.

"That's an ostrich, son," Elle laughed.

"I ate one before and couldn't stop shitting everywhere. Kofi had to put newspaper in my bedroom like I was a puppy. It happened when I was sixteen. Kofi really did raise us to be great wolves. I lost it when I saw how they did him in Anubi. Osiris gotta die bad," Izra said. I sat next to Uncle Dayo and he passed me the blunt.

"Am I a bad father?" Dayo asked everyone out the blue.

"Of course. Your sneaky daughter was out screwing that swamp wolf and letting them pimp her out. Arya is a serial killer and Chancy was in Anubi with Osiris and Goon's other son that we still don't know like that. Me and my mate raised our daughter right. She's a good wholesome woman. Y'all need to take notes," Izra said.

"Take notes? Your daughter is a reincarnation of Keora. What about Keora's daughter, Rena? Isn't she your grandchild? I could've sworn she was a succubus which in short terms means demon whore. Your daughter isn't shit, Izra, and I'm not going to keep reminding you," Dayo said to Izra.

"You know Rena isn't no real kin to Monifa in this life. You asked a question and I'm telling you the truth. It's pack love," Izra said. Dayo and Izra really hated each other's guts. Their beef would never end.

"Back to Djet. What you say about us not knowing him like that? Muthafucka, you got something you want to get off your chest?" my father asked Izra. Zaan slid off the couch and headed upstairs. Everyone wanted to avoid fights with my father because they always got ugly.

"Chill out, bruh. I didn't mean it like that. I'm just saying we don't know him like that. He only talks to you, his mother and Chancy. The fuck you getting mad for?" Izra asked.

"Cause it's a sensitive topic, Izra. He's still trying to deal with his mother's betrayal. I agree with you about Dayo and his daughters but we should leave Djet out of it. It doesn't matter if we don't know him like that yet, we do know he's Goon's son. Stop being a dick all the time," Uncle Amadi said. Everyone was drunk and not realizing the tension in the room. Amadi never got into the mix of things, him nor Elle.

"Fuck y'all! I'm not a bad father!" Dayo yelled and knocked over a table.

"Nobody said you were, but your daughters are a problem. Not Chancy, her actions were because she was hurt but Baneet and Arya are problems. Everyone knows she betrayed us so why aren't we talking about that? Osiris was able to kidnap Baneet because Arya took her. Do you believe she wasn't a willing participant? She didn't leave with us from Seth's house. She went her separate way instead of coming here and telling us the truth. Baneet belongs to another pack so her loyalty is to them. It doesn't make you a bad father but maybe you and your mate need to figure out where y'all went wrong," Uncle Elle said.

"Shut the fuck up, Elle! You always have to be the wise one but your son must've missed that gene. Him and his girlfriend both need reincarnation for a new brain because this life ain't for them," Uncle Dayo said.

"Is that supposed to make me mad? Zaan has his moments but he's loyal! Something Baneet and Arya don't understand," Uncle Elle replied back.

"Arya isn't my daughter," Uncle Dayo replied.

"Can we just take a chill pill for a second? Weren't we just fighting together days ago and now we're enemies. My father will be gone to Anubi in a few days and y'all want to spend his little bit of time left arguing about bullshit? We all have issues, get over it," I said and Amadi agreed. Izra apologized to my father but said nothing to Uncle Dayo.

"I'm going to sleep," Dayo said and left out of the basement.

"Akea is right. We shouldn't be arguing with each other. I think we're still pissed about everything that happened. Me and my mate hate to be around each other. I think we're over for good," my father said.

"Wait, what! Y'all always argue and make up," I replied.

"We had a big argument in Anubi. We said some things to each other we shouldn't have said but we meant it. My main focus is building a bond with Djet. I don't have the energy to work on our marriage," my father said.

"Marriage? That's human talk. Y'all are bonded for life," Uncle Amadi said.

"It feels more like a marriage if you ask me. I think a break will be good for me and her. We did agree on that," my father said. My parents argued a lot lately. When my mother pissed off our father, it pissed off Kanye, too. I knew there was another reason why Kanye wasn't coming around. He thought our mother treated our father like shit but I saw it differently. I saw them having problems because they cared for each other. They always made up afterwards as if it never happened. Zaan ran downstairs and told us to come quick because Baneet was in trouble. We rushed out the basement and followed Zaan up the stairs. Baneet was lying on the floor bleeding from between her legs when we got to the bedroom. Her father was trying to calm her and her mother had a lot of towels underneath her. The pack watched her while we tried to figure out what was happening.

"She's losing her pup!" Baneet's mother yelled out. Amadi ran to his room to get some natural herbs for the pain.

"She's done something the gods don't approve of," Djet said when he came into the room.

"Not now!" Baneet's mother said.

"She doesn't deserve happiness until she learns how to be loyal to those who are loyal to her," Djet replied.

"Get your demonic son out of here! I'm sure he's the problem. Everything is ruined because of him. He just comes out of nowhere and you accept him because he looks like Kanye and Akea? Well, I'm not buying it and I don't want him with my daughter!" Baneet's mother said.

"He's a messenger from the gods, dumbass! I've had it with you!" Ula said and was ready to charge into Baneet's mother but Zaan took her out of the room. Baneet was yelling and screaming about cramping and her mother cursed at Djet because she thought he was responsible.

"Babies are a gift and she doesn't deserve it. Be mad at me all you want but she has to answer to her gods," Djet said.

Chancy pulled Djet out of the room because Baneet was yelling and throwing things at him. A few of the pack members thought Djet was crazy but I knew he spoke the truth. Babies are a gift and we don't deserve them if our souls aren't pure. The gods believed that what goes on with us passes on to our seeds, making history repeat itself; and so on. It was a cycle and it had to be broken for cleansing.

"Djet is right. I was in his world and they believe in spiritual cleansing. Her baby is too precious for her. She's not dead, Baneet. Her soul will go to the afterlife. She'll be born to someone who deserves her," I said. Baneet's parents told us to get out of her room. We left and waited in the hallway for an update.

SOUL Publications

"Have you ever seen the gods?" Ula asked Djet.

"No, but I hear them. I didn't mean to upset anyone. Baneet needed to know what was happening to her so she could learn from her wrongdoings. It's a harsh lesson but we cannot escape destiny," Djet said and we all agreed.

"That was so beautiful. I need to pray more often," Fiti admitted.

"We all do," my mother said.

An hour or so later, Uncle Dayo came out of the bedroom covered in blood. He announced Baneet lost her baby. It was a sad night in the pack's mansion but a strong lesson was taught. Never underestimate the power of the gods. I went inside my bedroom and laid across the bed. Baneet's miscarriage made me think of Jetti. She wasn't of Anubi tradition but I was and so was our seed. Time could only tell our seed's fate. I prayed on it but I had to accept their decision; I was a firm believer in fate.

Tomorrow morning, me, you, Kanye and Djet will go to the mountains so I can spend time with my sons and we bond more with Djet, my father's voice came into my head.

I will get some rest now, then.

Okay, love you.

Love you, too, Father.

Arya

My nights have been lonely. Seth was dead and Taj was with Rena. All I had left was a spell book but it was useless. The wind blew and the sticks from the trees smacked against my window. The pack was still done with me even though they believed my story about Osiris. I couldn't admit what I'd done to them. The clock read midnight and I was still wide awake after not sleeping for days. All I could do was lay in bed and cry my heart out. I called Taj's phone ten times a day until he changed his number. Feeling restless, I went into the kitchen in my small country cottage to warm up a glass of milk.

Hopefully this will work.

While I was preparing my milk, someone knocked on my door. I peeked around the corner and saw my mother looking through the glass on the door with her hands pressed against the window. Her hair was matted to her face because of the heavy rain.

"Open the door, Arya! It's about Baneet," she said.

I opened the door for her and she left a puddle on the mat when she stepped inside. She took off her coat and hung it on the coat rack. I wanted to tell her to leave it outside because it was making a mess but I couldn't form the words.

"Do you want some milk?"

"Sure," she replied.

Anik followed me into the kitchen and sat at the small table I had in the corner.

"Baneet lost her pup a few hours ago," she said.

"Sorry to hear that. She's been through a lot and I take full blame because I couldn't protect her. Osiris tortured the both of us."

Anik thanked me after I set the cup of warm milk in front of her. I sat in the other chair at the table but Anik didn't pick up her cup. She held a blank stare.

"Is everything okay?"

"Have you ever lied to me?" she asked.

I chuckled, "What?"

"You heard the question very clear. Have you ever lied to me before? You know me and you always shared things. I want to know if you left something out. I'm just trying to understand how I failed you," she said.

"Tell her the truth. Anik has always been good to us. This is your chance to come clean so you can move on," the ten-year old me said. She was standing next to me but Anik couldn't see her. I was going crazy.

"Yes," I admitted.

"When?"

"When I was ten years old. Sosa locked you up for ten days and I was alone. He did things to me I don't want to speak of but I lied to you when you asked me. I didn't want you to think you failed me. I'm not mad at you for him molesting me. I'm angry with myself because I should've said something instead of letting it haunt me for years. You always wondered why I was so advanced when I was young. Remember the time Dayo punished me because I used to sneak and drink liquor? Well, I drank because Sosa forced me to get drunk so he could enter me. He said I was too tight and he'll hurt me. I had to drink to ease the pain."

"Why did you lie to me, Arya? We could've ran away from him sooner. I was young myself but I would've done something. The pack used to tell me about your advanced thoughts but I thought it was because of what we were exposed to. He did things to me, too, that affects me every day because he mentally tortured me. Sosa was sick but it was never your fault," she said.

"He made me think about sex. I know it sounds insane but he brought pleasure to my body. I knew then something wasn't right in my spirit. Sosa knew I was becoming aroused at an early age, Anik. That's why I hate witches! A witch cursed my bloodline, making us all whores. He knew exactly what I was going to be and he was right. I was only meant to breed like my real mother. The only difference is our names." I wiped the tears from my eyes and Anik reached out to me but I pulled back.

"I don't want sympathy."

"You are what you answer to. Nobody is stopping you from creating your own path. You have to want it to see it. Sosa has been dead for over twenty years now. You're giving a dead spirit power to control you. You've hurt so many people who loved you, including me. The pack tried to warn me but I couldn't face it. I didn't want to face it. In my eyes, you were my little Arya. The first child I raised as my own even when I wasn't old enough to be a mother myself. I've been so worried about you over the years that I forgot about my own daughters, but it was you I always felt the need to protect. I loved you too much. I had to watch my daughter go through a lot of pain earlier while she lost her pup. Someone told me what we give to our pups they give to the world. I gave Baneet disloyalty and she gave it back to us. I was disloyal to her when I put you first. Now, she's in love with a wolf whose pack constantly hurts her but she's still trying to give to them, even if it means stealing from her own family. We love the wrong people more than we love ourselves. The picture has never been so clear until now. But I forgive you," Anik said and I sobbed.

"I'm so sorry. I promise I'll do right. I know I don't deserve you but I swear I can't help what I do. I'm sick."

Anik got up and hugged me while I cried on her shoulder. She rubbed my back and whispered how much she loved me.

"I love you so much that I'm going to free you from it all. You're rotten on the inside and nothing will ever change you," she said. I pulled away from her and she stabbed me in the neck, twisting the knife into my throat. I knocked over the table when I hit the floor. I pulled out the knife and it burned my throat. My body was burning but I wasn't on fire.

"You can't hurt us anymore. You tortured Baneet and you tried to poison us. I'm free now, Arya. You have to pay for your sins. I dipped the tip of the knife in snake poison. You will not heal from that," she said. When I looked next to me, I saw my ten-year-old body lying beside me. She grabbed my hand as blood seeped from the wound on her neck.

"We won't hurt anymore," she whispered.

I closed my eyes as my heartbeat slowed down.

I always wanted to know what the other side was like...

Goon

"Finally," Kanye said when he got out of the truck.

"That was a long trip. We couldn't use magic to get here?" Akea asked.

"I wanted to drive and talk. Y'all complaining or sumthin?"

"Naw, Pops. Monifa wants me back home already," Kanye lied.

"She was excited when we pulled up to the house. You are getting on her nerves, bro. Your bags appeared in the trunk the night before. She used magic to get you out of the house," Akea said.

"Nigga, shut that shit up. Monifa cried like a baby when I told her I was leaving.

She was like, 'Kanyeeeee, I'm going to miss you so much. The pups aren't going to kick while you're gone and I have to sleep with your pillow between my legs because you do me so good down there.'"

"She said all of that, Son?" I asked.

"Plus, more, Father. Y'all know she's d—I mean penis-whipped," Kanye replied.

"Let me see your thoughts," Akea said.

"Y'all smell that? It's a lot of meat out here," Kanye replied.

We were in the mountains, five hours away from our mansion. Kanye grabbed a football out of the trunk and tossed it to Djet who caught it with his mouth.

"He got you beat, Kanye!" Akea bragged.

"Oh, don't worry, Brother. My lock jaw game is intact. The gods must've helped him," Kanye joked.

"Just accept my beast is as good as yours and we're even," Djet said to Kanye.

"Can I call your beast Cocaine? You whiter than coke," Kanye said.

"I think Kanye is really Izra's son, Father. You should get a DNA test," Akea said.

"That'll mean I'm banging my sister. You just hating because I'm slick. I see you back to the khaki pants and button-ups again. Djet didn't have a mall in his temple and still made you look more appealing in this world. How is that, Akea?" Kanye said.

"These shoes protect my arch. Tell him, Father. These shoes cost two grand," Akea replied.

"Father should've kicked your ass for wearing those old senior citizen human shoes. Two grand, my ass, you traded those with Bengay, peppermints and church hats," Kanye said.

"This is going to last all day," Djet said.

"I'll crack on you, too, god whisperer. Nobody is safe around me. Tell him, Father. I can bury Uncle Izra under the table and he got mad jokes," Kanye bragged.

"But you're still dumber than Zaan," Akea said and I chuckled. Kanye growled at Akea and they were ready to go at it.

"ENOUGH! Damn, have some respect for Djet. This is our first trip together. Just me and my sons but y'all are about to ruin it."

"Akea always gotta run off at the mouth. With his hoe-ass baby mama," Kanye said.

"I can't agree with you more," Akea replied.

The boys grabbed the rest of their things out of the trunk and I punched in the code to me and my mate's vacation home. We had other homes but this house was just for us. Her heels were still by the door and I remembered our last night here together. We were in our own world and it was just us.

"This crib is phat! Father held this one out. It's a glass house surrounded by woods and a big lake. We are definitely going to have fun," Kanye said.

Djet pulled out a rug from his backpack and sat on it to pray. I gestured for Kanye and Akea to pray with him, too. Kanye was ready to protest but I grilled him. They sat on the rug and I joined them. The prayer lasted for fifteen minutes although sometimes Djet prayed for hours. He called it meditating and cleansing his soul for the animals he had to kill for food.

"That actually felt good. My body feels lighter like I can jump fifty feet in the air," Kanye said.

"Meditating my brother. It's good for the soul," Djet said.

Akea and Kanye went upstairs to claim a bedroom. Me and Djet stayed downstairs. I poured him a glass of whiskey and sat across from him. The way I treated him in Anubi kept me up at night. I was mad at everyone when I know it wasn't anyone else's fault. I created the problem so therefore I had to fix it. Being hard headed and selfish towards my kind put me in a dangerous place. Djet needed all of my time and my mate felt some type of way about it because I was stealing time from her which wasn't true. The guilt I had caused me to smother Djet. He had been around us plenty of times through Akea and vice versa but it wasn't the same.

"I was thinking about going to Anubi with you to live," Djet said.

"Chancy wants to go, too."

"I will talk to her about it soon. I don't want to put a lot on her. Sometimes I think she's trying to deal with me and Akea being two different people," he added. Akea and Kanye came downstairs with red eyes and silly facial expressions. It was sure going to be a long two days in the mountains.

****

Stay low, Djet. The one to the right is closest to you. Me and Kanye will grab the other two.

Djet wasn't a great hunter, yet. He didn't plan out his attack and the prey sometimes got away. Twenty feet away were three deer. Djet was hidden behind a tall oak tree in the woods. I gave him the que to make the attack and he rippled through the bushes. The deer almost got away but Djet caught the meal with his teeth, crushing its neck. The other deer ran away and we chased after them. Kanye's beast almost collided into mine while running between the trees.

I'm faster, Father.

Stop talking shit, Kanye. You're nowhere near as fast as me!

I took a shortcut, speeding up and running around the deer. My beast crouched behind a tree waiting for them to fall into the trap. Out of nowhere, Kanye's beast wrapped his arms around both deer and tackled them to the ground. He went in for the kill, snapping their necks in mere seconds. Djet dragged his kill to the pile and we had our lunch. Akea stayed back at the cabin. He couldn't stomach seeing us eat raw meat. Beasts didn't have table manners. We tore into a kill, ripping body parts away, the sound of large teeth crushing bones echoing throughout the woods. We didn't return to the cabin until we made six deer kills. Our beasts ate two apiece. On our way back to the cabin, three miles away, I picked up a familiar scent.

This can't be.

I ran the rest of the way back with Kanye and Djet behind me. Once I got back to the cabin, I shifted and grabbed my sweatpants by the side of the house. When I walked in, I heard her sultry voice. She was sitting in the living room with a glass of wine. My mate was still able to take my breath away and her scent still weakened me. She stood up to greet Kanye and Djet and I couldn't keep my eyes off her. Her jeans hugged her voluptuous curves and her off-the-shoulder sweater accentuated her waist line. Kanya's hair was in a wild mane that reached the middle of her back.

"I didn't know you all were here until I got closer. I came up here to get some fresh air. There is a hotel an hour away. I don't mean to intrude," she said.

"I'm glad you came," Djet said.

"Yeah, Mother. I think this will work out better," Kanye replied.

"Your father might want some alone time with you all," she said.

"It's not a problem, Kanya. Are you hungry?" I asked.

"Akea is in the kitchen fixing me something," she said.

Unlike me, my mate could stomach a lot of human food and Akea was the same way. Djet and Kanye went upstairs to shower, leaving me and Kanya standing alone in the living room. I was surprised to see her wearing her ring. She threw it inside a temple in Anubi and I thought she was going to leave it.

"We have a lot to talk about tonight when the boys go to sleep," she said.

"They're men."

"And yet you still call them boys. They're our boys, Goon. I said it right."

"I can't argue with that," I replied.

We had been avoiding each other since we came home from Anubi almost a week ago. We even slept in separate bedrooms. I'd said things out of anger that hurt Kanya and she hurt me, too.

I kissed her ring finger and Kanya got emotional. We missed each other but were too stubborn to admit our wrongs.

"I knew you all were here. I just wanted to be with my family," she admitted.

"We need to stop fighting. Kanye absorbs more of our energy than Akea and Djet doesn't need to see it especially since he's not accustomed to our arguments. We gotta draw the line, beautiful, before we hate each other."

"I know but sometimes I wish you'd take my feelings into consideration. This might sound selfish but every once in a while I want you to put the pack aside and think about me. I'm not asking that you do it all the time because as their leader you can't but I feel neglected when you make decisions based off their well-being only," she said.

"I can work on that if you can work on your smart mouth. The tongue is a lethal weapon and can do a lot of damage. Respect me as an alpha and I'll give it back to you."

"I apologize," she said. Kanya wrapped her arms around me and I kissed her soft pouty lips.

She giggled when I grabbed a hand full of her juicy round ass.

"Stop before they see us," she whispered and I released her.

"Naobi feels bad about everything."

I walked away from Kanya because she wanted to talk about Naobi. I didn't want to discuss her while spending quality time with my family.

"Seriously, Goon?" she called out.

"We just put our differences aside and you want to bring her up!"

"I'm not trying to make you angry but you're thinking about time being missed with Djet when we could've not had any pups at all! Djet was in a safe place and look at him. He's the most spiritual one of us all. He's perfect," she said.

"It just doesn't sit well with me, Kanya. You're the mother and I thought you'd be heartbroken about this since he was created in your womb."

"I'm heartbroken, too, but there is nothing we can do but move forward. Djet is at peace with it and this is about him before anyone else. He said it himself he would do it again if it meant showing you your destiny. Djet is what we needed to believe in our tradition again. He would've been lost like us if he had come out of my womb with Akea and Kanye. You're the only one who doesn't see this as a blessing but I'm very thankful of him. He's like a guardian angel," she said.

"I see your point but she should've told me the truth."

"She couldn't. You had to see it on your own. All I'm saying is Djet is here now and he loves us. There isn't a spec of resentment in his body. I'm done talking about it now so I won't bring it up again," she said. She went to the kitchen with Akea and I headed to the master bedroom for a shower.

An hour later...

The dinner table was loaded with food especially meat and fruit. Kanya broke the news about Arya.

"Her mother did it? I'm surprised," Akea said.

"Yeah, me, too, but she had to go, bruh. She was rotten and it was starting to spread," Kanye said.

"Her soul won't be reincarnated," Djet said.

"Great riddance. But Kanye was in love with her at one point so I know he's going to cry about it later and pretend hair got in his eye," Akea said.

"Y'all see that? I don't always start it first. Beat his ass, Mother. Knock him clean the hell out. He's the only immortal I know with a STD," Kanye said.

"I don't know if I want to deal with this for a few days," my mate said.

"Me, neither," Djet chuckled.

"Me and Monifa's pups' names are Moon and Venus. I can't wait until she goes into labor. We have a month and some weeks left," Kanye bragged.

"Moon and Venus? What's the cartoon Arya used to watch again? Was it 'Sailor Moon?' Those names, bro. Come on, you can do better. Moon and Venus? Is it because they're close together?" Akea asked Kanye.

"Those names mean a lot to me. Last time I checked, you pissed standing up. No man is supposed to be messy like a bitch," Kanye replied.

"Stop it, Akea!" Kanya said.

"Kanye would've made every joke there is if I picked one of those names for my son," Akea said.

"It might not be your son just like Destiny isn't your daughter. Talk about that if you want to know something," Kanye said to Akea.

"Do you feel better now? Destiny is still connected to me whether it's daughter or niece. I'm not bothered by that the way you're bothered by those hideous names," Akea said.

"I wish Djet was still inside you or whatever he was doing to you because you're still the same punk-ass nerd I hate looking at it! Nigga, fuck you!" Kanye growled and made his mother nervous. Kanye went upstairs and Djet followed him.

"I got a belt in my bag. I'm going to whip your ass when I come back into the kitchen," Akea's mother threatened him.

"Talk to us, Son. What was that about? Something bothering you? Cause that shit you said about Kanye's pups' names wasn't cool. Those names mean a lot to him."

"I was wrong and I'll apologize to him. Me and him always argued but that's how we bonded. I want us to be close considering we were when Djet was latching on to me. Being rude and throwing insults is how Kanye communicates with me. It's been happening since we were little. I'll go up to talk to him but we both know Kanye would've clowned me for naming my son, Moon," Akea said.

"I have a serious headache. Kanya, go get the belt," I told her. She got up from the kitchen table and Akea disappeared. When she came back into the dining room, I roared in laughter.

"Where did he go?" she asked.

"He's hiding from you."

Kanya sniffed the air, "You smell that?" she asked.

"Naw," I lied.

"No, seriously. I smell weed burning. They upstairs smoking weed in the house? Go do something about it," she said.

"Let them be. Weed is a natural plant. You smoked all the time. Remember when I first saw you? You were peeing in the woods when you saw me hunting. Those were good times, beautiful. You gave me the ass on the first night." Kanya playfully smacked my arm and I pulled her onto my lap.

"Don't lie like that. It happened on the first date," she giggled.

I placed her hand on my erection and asked what she could do about it. She purposely showed up to flaunt her curves and full breasts around me. She knew the beast in me wanted to be inside her. She pointed to the closet next to the kitchen. It was a walk-in pantry. She climbed off my lap and strutted to the pantry, her ass jiggling with each stride. Kanya pulled me into the pantry and unbuckled my pants. She knew exactly how to tame the beast. Kanya took off her pants and slid her thong down her legs. She was naked from the waist down, only wearing red stiletto heels. I grabbed a fist full of her hair when she took me in her mouth. She held my piece in her hand and made love to it with her tongue. She wrapped her mouth over the head of my dick, glossing her lips with pre-cum. Kanya was very promiscuous in the bedroom and did things I would be too ashamed to admit. She slid me to the back of her throat and wrapped her lips around me, swallowing every inch of me.

"FUCCCKKKKK!" I groaned when she jerked me off while slurping me down her throat. She loved when I was aggressive with her. I grabbed her hair and pushed myself down her throat, slowly fucking her wet mouth. She rubbed her pussy while I went insane and slammed my dick down her throat. She rubbed her clit faster, making her pussy drip on the floor. The scent of her sex and warmth of her mouth made me crave her. I pulled my dick away and picked her up. She wrapped her legs around my neck when I held her firmly against the wall. Her pussy was spread open, dripping with sticky essence. I called it "Fruit Honey." Her center reminded me of a peach with honey dripping down the center. My tongue explored her, entering her sugary walls and slurping her female juice.

"Goonnnnnnn, I'm about to cum!" she squealed. My beast growled while eating her. She pressed my face into her and rode my tongue. Her thick thighs draped lazily over my shoulders while I feasted without showing her any mercy. She squirted down my throat, teasing me because she knew I wasn't satisfied just yet. My mate was ready for pups but I wanted to wait until we returned back to Anubi. She screamed and I covered her mouth while she experienced another orgasm. I pulled my tongue out of her and lowered her against the wall. She grabbed ahold of my dick and stuffed her walls. I pressed into her and her pussy squeezed me. Kanya didn't want me to make love to her, she wanted to be fucked but I think I wanted it more than her. Canned goods fell onto the floor while I hammered her. Handcuffs appeared around her wrist and stuck to the wall to keep her hands above her head.

"Nooo, Goon, wait! You cannot paralyze me in here! I'll scream too loud," she said but I muted her.

Asshole! I told you not to use sorcery while we have sex with our kids in the house.

"They can't hear you."

I ripped off her sweater and bit off her bra. Her beautiful brown breasts bounced when I stroked her body. I captured her erect nipple between my lips. Her face was contorted in pleasure but she couldn't move nor make a sound. She had to deal with me being disrespectful.

"I'm gonna bust you open so we can deal with this behavior of yours. You're going to cum so hard that it's going to make your heart stop. But I'm going to bring it back to life when I slam into your spot."

Her eyes fluttered after I pulled her away from the wall and slammed her onto my dick. The sight of her pussy swallowing my veiny girth hardened me, causing me to swell between her walls. The only muscle she could use was the one inside her. Her pussy squeezed my dick, locking me inside of her while her warm wetness flushed over my shaft. I grabbed her around the neck and sank my teeth into her as I pushed my way deep inside of her until I saw the tip of my dick in her abdomen. She was being pinned, a strategy male beasts used to warn their mates they were superior. She was getting wetter and tighter when I bit then licked around the bite mark.

I love you so muchhhhhhhh!

Kanya's sweet pussy caused me to mid-shift inside of her, making me grow a few inches. I hooked into her and tears ran down her cheeks. Blood rushed to the tip of my dick when I gave off two deep pumps. The veins in my shaft swelled and throbbed inside of her. The throbbing grew stronger causing her body to tremble. My beast howled when I exploded inside of her and dripped onto the floor. Kanya's pussy made me cum so much that even while still inside of her it seeped out. I fell into her and waited until the swelling went down before I pulled out. She landed in my arms after the handcuffs disappeared.

"I better wake up pregnant with your pups," she mumbled while closing her eyes.

I snuck into our bedroom's bathroom and turned the water on in the tub. After the tub was full, I laid her down in the water and propped her head up. She opened her eyes and gave me a lazy smile. Her nipples were still erect and I forced myself to turn away. Kanya opened her legs and a cute growl slipped from her lips.

"I'm still aroused," she said.

I climbed into the tub with her and she straddled me.

"You're my king, husband and alpha. You lead and I'll follow. I promise I won't hurt you again. You're far from weak and I'll cut my own tongue out if I ever tell you that again." I cupped a handful of water and washed her lips off before I kissed her.

"What did you do that for?" she asked with a raised eyebrow.

"I can taste you all day but I'm never tasting my own nut. The animal in me still won't allow it." Kanya pinched my shoulder and I rolled her over in the tub. I entered her from behind but that time I made love to her, promising that I would do what I had to do to make her happy. She gave me some bad times but she also gave me a lot of good ones. I couldn't live without her or my offspring. They were me and I was them, we were all connected for life.

Kanye

"I think our parents are fucking. It might be the weed but I know a nut howl when I hear one," I told Akea as I passed him the blunt. He came to my room to apologize but it wasn't that deep. Akea was right, we bonded through arguments and a lot of the males did that in the pack. I needed an excuse to get away so I could check up on Monifa without everyone telling me how much I'm obsessed over my mate. It was true to an extent. Monifa was the best thing any beast could ask for and I loved her. I probably was going a little too overboard but being in Anubi made me realize death can easily take love, family and happiness away from us. So, I wanted her to feel loved every day for the rest of our lives. The way my parents argued made me take a better look at my love life.

"They were definitely fucking," Djet replied. His eyes were bloodshot red. We trapped ourselves in the bedroom and Akea created a five-foot-long blunt.

"I'm higher than a giraffe's pussy," I exhaled.

"That sounds good right about now," Djet said with his eyes closed.

"We should go to Africa and get one. Akea can kill it for us," I joked.

"I told Father I was going to Anubi with them. I want to help spread tradition," Djet said.

"Nigga, you just got here from a twenty-one-year flight. Don't pass it to him, Akea. He doesn't need anymore." Djet sat up and rubbed his eyes to wake himself up.

"Seriously. My plan was to get my mate and Destiny then go to Anubi. You two are more open to this world," Djet said.

"We can still visit them whenever we want to but I'm staying here," Akea said.

"Yeah, me, too, since I'm officially going to be a pack leader when Father goes for his throne," I replied.

"I'm going to miss you two. It was short but nonetheless worth everything that I endured," Djet said.

"So, let's talk about this. Which one of you strangled Chancy's mother?" I asked.

"That was me," Djet admitted.

"Get the hell outta here. You serious?" I replied.

"Dead ass. She sent Destiny with strangers and didn't see anything wrong it. She had to repent for that bullshit," Djet said and I slapped hands with him.

"I love that, Brother. I love you, too, Akea, but he's actually my twin, twin. You're just a lookalike."

"I'll be that. I'm relieved I'm not a beast. Just think about it, I can do what I want to do. There isn't a mating ritual for me nor marking tradition to tie me down for life. Picture me on a beach with twenty beautiful women of all races catering to me," Akea bragged.

"We don't care, bro. Humans don't know how to accept immortal dick. You'll kill one with all that electric energy shit you got going on. Me and Djet are good," I replied and Djet agreed.

"I'll have to date a witch. Someone who can see life as I see it but all the witches I know been here for ages. I need someone around my age who resembles Ula," Akea said and I choked on my weed smoke.

"You are lusting after your uncle's mate?" Djet asked.

"No, but we can't deny how sexy Ula is and we done all looked at someone in the pack reaching puberty," Akea said.

"That's how I felt about A—..."

Go ahead, I'm listening, Monifa's voice yelled inside my head. My brothers were waiting for me to answer.

Oh, hey, beautiful. When did you wake up?

Don't make you bite your dick off! Which one were you peeping at?

That's not what was said so stop lying on me!

Listen to me, Kanye. I'm not in the mood for the mind games. I'm literally inside your head, so tell me.

Promise you won't get mad.

I'm waiting...

Your mother had a phat ass but I swear I only looked once! I was young. Why are you trippin'?

I'm not, your father is hungggggggg. Don't worry though, I saw it by mistake when we were playing in the woods while he was hunting.

"Bro! You aight?" Akea asked and I cleared my throat.

"Yeah, I'm cool. That weed got me trippin'. What were we talking about again?"

"I forgot myself," Akea said.

SOUL Publications

I sat up with my brothers all night until the sun came up. We smoked, drank and talked shit to each other. We built a strong bond and it was a blessing to know I had real blood brothers who had my back. I loved them.

Two days later...

The trip seemed like it lasted for only five minutes when we arrived at the pack's mansion. It was time for my father to go to Anubi. Monifa greeted me when I walked through the door and I hugged her. The pups moved around a lot whenever I was close by. They were another reason why I smothered Monifa.

"I complained about you getting on my nerves but I missed you. Those two days were long," she pouted.

"I'll break your fucking jaw bone if you disrespect me again. I'm not playing, aight?" I said between kissing her.

"You are so fine when you're angry," she said to get on my good side.

Beasts 3: Unleashed   Natavia

The pack crowded the hallway when my parents walked into the house. My father pulled Naobi into his arms and apologized for disrespecting her.

"The power of alpha female pussy," Monifa said.

"Come again?"

"Don't act special, Handsome. Obviously, your mother gave your father some good sex. You're the same way. All I have to do when you're mad is be a submissive little freak and you become putty in my hands. Y'all might be alphas but the real power lies within us female beasts. You don't have to admit it but we are tamers," Monifa said.

"Fiti must've told you that stupid shit," I replied and Monifa held her side when she laughed. We stood to the side and watched my father and Naobi make up. He didn't want her to apologize to him because she had his best interest at heart. Monifa got emotional when my father gave his mother gold roses and two jewelry boxes filled with diamonds.

"That is so sweet. Naobi raised him right," Monifa said.

Someone rang the doorbell and I answered the door. Geo and his pack of wolves were on our territory.

"Baneet! 101 Dalmatians is outside waiting for you!" I called out.

"You got jokes?" Geo asked.

I stepped outside and closed the door behind me.

"Why are you on my territory? I spared you and your pack too many times, bruh. Get your wolves and go home."

"I've been searching for my mate for days! I haven't been able to sleep. I'm not leaving until I take her home," Geo seethed.

"What home? Bruh, check this out. You wouldn't be doing all of this if you really cared for her. You fucked up! She gave y'all codes to our safe because your pack made her feel some type of way for having a wealthy family. You did nothing about it! Y'all pushed her and nobody protected her but she still was trying to help. Naw, she ain't going with you. You want to do

Beasts 3: Unleashed   Natavia

something then fight me. You're not a bad wolf, bro. You just don't have nothing to offer my pack sister and I'm not talking about money. You already have a mate. Stop being greedy."

"I love her but I can't choose her over my pack. I know they don't like her but it shouldn't matter because she's there for me," he said. The door opened and Baneet came outside. Geo noticed she wasn't pregnant anymore and yelled at her.

"What did you do? Why would you kill my pup, Baneet?" he asked.

"I lost her but that's not why I came out here. I came here to tell you that I'm done. Our marking ritual wasn't even real because you already have a mate. I have no real ties to you so please just leave. I'm choosing my pack this time and forever. This is my real family. Besides, I'm tired of fighting with your mate who doesn't want me there. Your pack hates me and you stood by and did nothing. I'm done for good. Our pack won't be so nice the next time you come through," Baneet said. Geo let out a howl and his pack brothers howled with him before he left. Baneet hugged me and kissed my cheek.

"I was listening on the other side of the door. Thank you, Kanye. I haven't always been a fan of yours but that's because I thought you were going to be with Arya but it took me a lot to see the truth. Arya didn't deserve you one bit," Baneet said.

"Appreciate it but you still owe me and Akea some money. Don't worry, I'll set up a payment plan agreement later."

"Fair enough," she said.

We went back into the house and everyone was in a circle holding hands. Me and Baneet joined the circle. I grabbed her and Monifa's hands. I was ready to ask Monifa what was going on but a gold light appeared in the middle of us.

What is happening?

We're going to Anubi, Monifa thought.

Already? We just walked in the house.

They have been waiting for him for a few hours now. He's late, Monifa said. The gold light spread into a ball. The bright light pained our eyes and Naobi told us to close them. My body was falling, and by the time I opened my eyes, we were inside the king's temple in Anubi. There were hundreds of people waiting for us. My father was already dressed for the occasion, all of us were.

When you go through the portal during an occasion, you come out already dressed for it. They are very impatient, Monifa thought. Everyone from our pack was in Anubi. We took a seat on a rug in the front row of a crowd. Our father dressed in gold along with his wolf crown which made me proud. I wasn't sad he was leaving, none of us were, because it had to happen. My mother stood next to him and Monifa grabbed my hand.

"They look so beautiful," Monifa beamed.

"I raised him right," I joked.

The ceremony only lasted for two minutes. My father had to give his blood to a bowl in the floor. They said his blood would travel though the temple and rebirth Anubi. My mother had to do the same because they swore her in as their queen. After they gave their blood, the ceremony was over. My parents ruled Anubi. Akea was crying and Monifa's mother rubbed his back. My father announced that his pack brothers and their mates were staying with him. Pack brothers were forever, the same as your mate. Wherever you go, they go.

"Prince of Anubi," someone said from behind me. I turned around and it was Jasiah and Tiko. They gave me a brotherly hug and I returned the gesture.

"Everyone is happy," Tiko said.

"Who is that?" Jasiah asked me. He was referring to Baneet.

"She doesn't have a mate. Go ahead and do us a favor. Just playing but I don't think you can handle that attitude."

"I'll take a chance," Jasiah said and walked away.

"Baby brother's feelings will get hurt," Tiko chuckled.

I pulled Monifa to the side and introduced her to Tiko. She knew about him and his brother because I always talked about the two warriors from Anubi who helped me. Jasiah came back over to us with a blank expression on his face.

"She's evil," Jasiah said.

"Baneet?" Monifa asked.

"That's cause you ain't broke. Anubi is sitting on diamonds," I replied and Monifa elbowed me.

"She might be playing hard to get. Give her a pretty pink diamond and tell her you don't want nothing from her, just her presence. She'll have a different respect for you," Tiko said to his brother. Jasiah thanked us and rushed off.

"He'll be back," Tiko laughed.

I introduced Tiko to the rest of the pack and he blended right in. Him and his brother were both strong warriors. Fiti and Zaan snuck off to smoke and fondle each other. Ten warriors brought out a cage covered with a red silk sheet. Kofi pulled the sheet off and it was Osiris. My father promised he'd be punished as soon as he stepped foot in Anubi and he kept that promise. The Anubians threw things at his cage and Osiris told them all to suck his dick and burn in hell.

"Fuck all of you! You let my parents die and did nothing about it! Goon is the enemy, not me! I was trying to heal all of you but you'd rather side with a punk!" Osiris yelled. My father screamed out a word in the ancient language and the cage disappeared. Osiris stood between an army of guards. Kofi forced him down on his knees and chained his arms behind his back.

"Ibuna is a better world! Resurrect it to defeat the enemy! Goon is going to send y'all straight to hell like he did his own father, King Ammon! He's the real wolf demon!" Osiris screamed. My father shifted into his beast and walked over to Osiris. I covered Monifa's eyes so she wouldn't see the gruesome scene that was about to take place. Kofi raised his hand to silence the crowd. A warrior forced Osiris's head into the mouth of my father's beast. My father's teeth sliced through Osiris's neck, severing his head clean off his shoulders. Kofi held up Osiris's bloody hair and the crowd cheered. My father's beast towered over the crowd, and they resembled ants compared to his tall stature. He was still like the tall statues in Anubi's temples—he was a legend.

"This is our wolf god, Anubi! He will protect, rule and rebirth our home! Everyone who was banned from Ammon's laws is allowed to come back home!" Kofi yelled and tossed Osiris's head into a fire pit along with his body.

"Anubi is reborn!" Monifa pumped her fist in the air.

My father shifted back and walked through the crowd of people. We all circled around him.

"The portal will open every full moon to my temple but only for our offspring. We have to get you all back before you are stuck here for a while. But listen to me, Kanye. You are an alpha now, the leader of your generation. Monifa, Akea, Baneet, Fiti and Zaan are your responsibility," my father said.

"What about Chancy?" Monifa asked.

"I'm staying here with Djet but you'll still see me. Just think of us as living long distance," Chancy replied.

"You all can stay," my father said, getting teary-eyed.

"No, Father. I'm going to take your spot and take over the family businesses. I'm a man now and you said it yourself. I can do this, trust me," I replied and we hugged. My mother and the rest of us joined in on the hug. My pack walked away to head back home and my father's pack stood next to him watching their kids lead their own destiny. My chest got heavy with emotion but I was a leader and had to show strength. My father wouldn't want it any other way.

"Hey, wait up!" a voice called from behind us.

"What's up?" I asked Tiko and Jasiah.

"Your father sent us with you. He said we need to look after you," Tiko said.

I trust them. There's not too many of you and, remember, my pack brothers grew to be my family, my father thought.

I'll see you soon, Father. Love you!

Love you more. Goodbye, son.

The portal took us back home in the same spot we left.

"This is it. We're on our own," I told everyone.

Beasts 3: Unleashed   Natavia

"The ending to a new start," Monifa replied.

Epilogue
Monifa

Two months later...

"Push, Monifa. Are they stuck?" Kanye asked.

I was sitting inside the sauna pool in the basement with the pack surrounding me. I'd been in labor for two days and it was taking a toll on me. The cramping and vaginal pain was worse than anything I imagined. Kanye was in the sauna with me. He yelled he could see a head. Baneet wiped my forehead with a rag and Fiti got into the pool with us to help Kanye pull out the baby.

"Don't touch my baby's head, Fiti. Just be the towel girl. You don't have enough common sense for this. GET BACK!" Kanye growled at Fiti. Fiti hopped out of the sauna and almost tripped. Kanye was yelling and fussing with everyone because he was anxious. We waited for two days for our pups. The cramping was getting worse and I was too weak to push.

"Come on, Monifa. Just give me one more strong push. They aren't comfortable like this," Kanye pleaded. Fiti grabbed my leg and Baneet grabbed the other so I could push out our pup. My ears popped as I strained. I heard soft wails and Kanye was holding our daughter. Akea cut the cord and wrapped her up in a towel.

"Hold her head, Akea!" Kanye shouted.

"I know how to old a baby!"

I wanted to hold Venus so she could latch on for breast milk but Moon was being stubborn.

"One more, Monifa," Kanye said, crouching into the water. Baneet and Fiti pulled on my legs and I screamed for them to let me go but they couldn't because Moon's head was coming out.

Kanye pulled him out and ripped the umbilical cord with his teeth. Akea gave Kanye our daughter and he was holding both babies, planting kisses all over their small faces.

"Give me the babies, Kanye!" He was being stingy with our pups and they were only a few seconds old. He placed them inside my arms and they were beautiful. Moon had a light spot underneath his left eye the shape of a moon. Venus had one, too, but hers were round. Their birthmarks were symbolic of their names.

"You gave them those names for a reason, Brother. You must've seen a vision," Akea said to Kanye.

"I thought it was just a daydream," Kanye replied.

Venus looked more like her father and Moon resembled me.

"What are they? Witch or pup?" Zaan asked.

"They are both beasts. Pure-bred beasts," Kanye said in excitement. He ran out of the book door to the sauna room and howled. He was outside for a few minutes before he came back inside. The pups were nursing and I couldn't stop staring into their small faces. Kanye got back inside the pool with me and thanked me.

"So, when are we going to do this?" Jasiah asked Baneet and she playfully rolled her eyes. They weren't dating yet but they flirted a lot. Jasiah said he'd be patient because they were in a pack together and didn't need to rush. Jasiah and Tiko were easy on the eyes. They both had long locs with greenish-grey eyes. Their skin was the color of chestnuts and both of them had strong cheek bones. Human women couldn't get enough of the new brothers in town and the unmated female beasts were extremely jealous behind it. But, Tiko had several sex partners and Jasiah was waiting for Baneet.

"You're a pup yourself," Tiko said to Jasiah.

"I'm nineteen. That's old enough," Jasiah replied.

Everyone congratulated us before leaving out of the pool room. Kanye's necklace glowed and he held it so we could both see. His parents and the rest of the pack were watching us through the marble eye. Kanye's mother was carrying another set of triplets. According to Kanye, Goon impregnated his mate the same day he returned to Anubi. Kanye had two necklaces, one for me and the other for his father.

"It's like they were here with us," Kanye said.

"We'll see them soon. I miss them, too."

We moved into a new house a few weeks prior. The mansion was bigger than our last. It had thirty-five bedrooms, three basketball courts and five big pool rooms. Each couple's bedroom was set up like a condo. We inherited Goon's father's businesses and Amadi's. Both companies combined made us the richest family in the world but we were still a normal pack. We all dropped out of college to focus on what our family worked hard for.

"I can't wait to fill this house up like your father's pack. We're going to be a big happy traditional family."

Kanye grabbed Venus from me after she finished nursing and I told him to rub her back. He was gentle with her. There was something addictive about a beast being gentle and loving. Maybe it was because they can also show a terrifying side. I rocked Moon in my arms and kissed his cute puffy cheek.

"How many more sets do you want to have?" Kanye asked.

"Five."

"I hope they're spaced out but I'm down for it. We're going to create an army," he joked but I was serious. I wanted a very big family with a lot of pups.

"Do I make you happy?" I asked.

"You didn't hear my beast howling? Of course, you make me happy. I love you to death, Mo," he said and kissed my lips.

Our fate was sealed and our destiny was complete. There was nothing else to fulfill but following tradition and loving one another. We were Anubians until our souls were sent to the Temple of Afterlife.

Chancy

Djet held my hand while walking down the hall to the garden for a picnic. Being in Anubi rebirthed me. I couldn't explain the feeling but love never felt so good. Destiny was with my parents so me and Djet could spend some time alone. I missed Monifa and the rest of the gang but we were both happy in our lives and knew everything was worth it. Djet told me to close my eyes after we left the temple.

"Okay, open," he said.

I opened my eyes and there was a canopy-style bed lying in the garden with wine, grapes and cubes of meat. The beautiful roses were sprawled out on the bed and the waterfall behind us set off the mood.

"This is so beautiful."

Djet untied the long and flowing dress from around my neck and I was naked like the day I was born. His large hands cupped my breasts from behind and he kissed the back of my neck.

"I'm addicted to you," he said, and smiled against my ear. The butterflies were trying to blow me away. He sat on the bed and pulled me towards him. His soft coils fell into his face and his hair smelled like pine and fruit. He was shirtless and was only wearing silk pants. I grabbed his face and kissed him, but we didn't come there to make love. Djet felt if his body wasn't cleansed he could pass it to me through sex because he missed a prayer. I respected him and his way of life. It didn't matter to me because we always made up for it and spent days making love until my legs were numb. He pulled a sheet back and we slid underneath the material. It was night time and the moon was bright in Anubi, whiter than snow. We drank wine and fed each other grapes. I loved romantic dates, the kind of dates that put you in another place with nobody else but you and your partner. Djet kissed my neck and I snorted from giggling because it tickled.

"Why are you so perfect?" I asked.

"I don't think I'm perfect. There are things I need to work on. For example, I need to balance my tradition and love life better. Sometimes I spend hours away from you and Destiny praying, but I have to keep reminding myself the gods understand my life outside the temple isn't the same because I'm with family. It's just hard breaking habits but I promise I'll fix it," he said.

"A man admitting his faults before being scolded about it. It's like a dream."

"But to answer your question I'm perfect to you because I'm for you," he said and I blushed. I playfully pushed Djet and we spilled the wine on the sheets. He turned me over and gave my ass a hard and loud smack.

"OUCH!" I growled and he threw his head back in laughter.

"Extra dramatic. I smacked you harder the other night when we were, you know," he said.

"You know I still dream about you even though you lay next to me every night? I get to have you both ways."

"Maybe it's another brother," Djet said.

"What?" I asked, ready to attack.

"I'm just kidding. I'm going to always be in your dreams to protect you from nightmares. The first time I came to you, you were young; I was young, too. You were picking flowers in a white dress that matched the fur of my beast. I thought you were an angel. I asked the overseer why was I seeing an angel and he told me one day you were going to need me but I had to wait," Djet said. I laid on his chest and toyed with the medallion around his neck that he had to wear because he was a prince. He rubbed his fingers through my hair while we stared at the moon.

"This is forever."

"Eternity. I couldn't wait to be unleashed. It feels so good being able to love you with my body and not just my soul," he said.

I pulled him close to me and held on to him tightly. I wondered how many people had to wait for the man they saw in their dreams hoping and praying that he was real. Either way, I was a lucky woman. Djet was literally the man of my dreams. We had our family, love, peace and serenity. We were whole again.

SOUL Publications

Akea

"**Y**ou're late," Jetti said when I appeared in the room.

She went into labor three hours after Monifa had her pups. Geo's pack moved eight hours away but Jetti stayed back with a female cousin to give birth to my son. I made her stay at a hotel room with her pack cousin. It wasn't hard to convince her because she didn't have a place to go. Her hotel room was paid up for a year which was enough time for her to find a job. The hotel-style resort served three meals a day, snacks and it was an open bar free of charge. That was the least I could do for her. My son was wrapped in a blue blanket sound asleep on his mother's chest. I picked him up and pulled the blanket back to reveal his face. He had my nose and eyes and his mother's lips. I named him Nile Akea Uffe.

"I can't believe you're taking my baby away from me," Jetti sobbed.

"You can visit but he's not living with you. What part don't you understand? Do I have to travel to the past to show you how many times I repeated that to you? Your pack is going to take food from his mouth to feed everyone else. They'll kill you if you leave them for a better house and not take them with you. Or I can get rid of them all. Which one is it?"

"I'll visit him," Jetti sobbed.

"Your family has billions of dollars. It's in the newspaper and you can't supply anything for her and your son?" her cousin asked.

"My son is not a fucking meal ticket! You can visit him in a few days," I told Jetti.

"Who will nurse him?" she asked.

"Human formula. I'll see you in a few days."

Nile was awakened when I stepped onto an elevator down the hall from Jetti's room. The doors opened to a lobby and I stepped off with

Nile tucked firmly into my arm. A taxi driver was sitting in front of the hotel and I asked was he available. He unlocked the door and told me to get in. I gave the address to the pack's mansion as he pulled out into the busy downtown traffic.

"Just born, huh?" the cab driver asked with a sultry voice. I looked into the rearview mirror and pretty slanted eyes were staring at me. She adjusted the mirror to get a better look at me. She was the color of nutmeg and had jumbo braids in her hair with shells at the end. Her nails had a French tip and her hands were small and probably soft like her voice.

"Yeah."

"Nile is a nice name, Akea," she said.

"How do you know me?"

"Let's just say we're one in the same if you know what I mean," she said with a southern twang.

"You're from the bayous in Louisiana? Your name is Keisha but they call you Black Rose? I guess we can both read minds." Keisha laughed.

"I beat you to it. You were so distraught that you didn't know who was driving you. Your son's mother is a shifter and you took him from her because of her family. You made the right choice. No need to beat yourself up about it," she said.

"Do you have any kids?"

"No. I'm a workaholic. I'm too busy for kids. I do fortune telling in the morning, clean schools during the evening and drive a cab at night," she said.

The drive was only ten minutes away from the hotel but me and Keisha talked about a lot in a short period of time. It was the first time I ran into a witch who didn't have any ties to Anubi. Keisha pulled up to the gate of our property and I punched in the code through the window. The gate opened and she drove up the long driveway.

"Beautiful home," she said.

"Thank you. We just moved in not too long ago."

She pulled up around the circular driveway and the front door opened. The pack was waiting to meet Nile. I got out of the cab and walked to the driver's seat to get a look at her. It was true, I had a lot on my mind when I entered her cab and didn't pay her any attention. I don't know how I missed her beauty. She smiled and her teeth were pure white and even. She had a mole on the top of her lip and the pink lip gloss brought out her pouty lips.

"See you around, Akea," she said.

"Can I have your number?"

"You know my number. You know a lot about me," she said.

"Can I call you?"

"You know the answer to that, too. I'll see you later," she replied and pulled off.

"We're waiting!" Baneet yelled out.

"Shut up, I'm coming!"

She took Nile away from me as soon as I stepped into the foyer. Monifa was asleep but Kanye brought his twins into the family room and placed them inside their bassinets. Nile's bassinet was aligned with theirs. Baneet laid him down and she was fascinated by him.

"I would love to spoil Kanye's twins but he has too many rules," Baneet said.

"So, who was the pretty witch you were talking to?" Fiti asked.

"What witch?" Kanye asked.

"Out of everything you can't remember and that's the only thing you can bring up?" I replied to Fiti.

"She's pretty and I saw the way she was looking at you. You should've invited her in. I hope you call her," Fiti said.

"She's just a friend. Y'all are buggin," I replied.

Kanye picked up Nile and sat on the couch with him while his twins were sleeping.

"What's up, nephew?" Kanye talked to him.

"Meanwhile, I can't hold your twins. Put my son back, bro. Give him here," I told him. Kanye handed me Nile and Baneet came back with a bottle and a baby onesie he could wear.

"Welcome to parenthood, bro," Kanye said.

"Same to you, too."

It's just me and you, son. I'm going to make sure you are a better man than me because I failed myself plenty of times. But you're going to be stronger than that. We will be stronger than that.

SOUL Publications

Rena

"**Y**ou gotta come and see the twins, Rena. They are so cute," Monifa said over the phone.

"I promise I will come first thing in the morning. Taj can't wait to meet them, either. We wanted to come a few days ago but I know you're busy and want to bond with your babies."

"I'm definitely busy but you're always welcomed. You know you can move in and bring Taj with you. I wonder how a cat shifter and werewolf will get along in a pack," Monifa said.

"Tiger shifters are loners. Taj will go crazy living around a bunch of wolves, especially your mate. Kanye is very, very self-centered and doesn't like outsiders."

"I know but we're working on it," she said. The front door unlocked and I told Monifa I was going to call her back. Taj walked into his loft with a sexy grin on his face. I moved in with him until my father's house was finished being remodeled. Living with Taj flowed so naturally. I had a surprise for him and I hoped he enjoyed it. Taj wore a pair of fitted jeans, leather Timbs, a black shirt and a leather jacket. His dreads were braided back and the Cuban link around his neck gave him a rugged sex appeal. I jumped in his arms and wrapped my legs around his waist.

"You happy to see me? I need this more often when I come home," he said, kissing my lips.

"Sooooo, I've been thinking for the past few weeks about this. I know you said we should wait but I want to...you know."

"You want to what?" he asked.

"Have a cub, vampire, witch? I mean I don't know what it'll be."

Monifa was teaching me witchcraft but I wasn't completely there yet. It was harder than it looked. You had to unlock certain parts of your body to produce energy and many other things that was too hard to remember.

"You want to get pregnant? Are you sure about this?" he asked and sat me on top of the kitchen island.

"Yes, I want us to be a family. I love you and I don't need to wait to give you my gift. Our lifespan is very long and I'll be waiting forever. I want to do this, Taj. I'm not going into the club tonight so we can you know."

"Make love?" he asked.

"Yes, that."

He took his shirt and jacket off and tossed it over the couch. I was a neat freak and clothes lying around bothered me.

"I'll pick it up later. Take a shower with me," he said.

I was only wearing a lace bra and matching thong. Taj loved when I walked around the house in stripper attire. He smacked my bottom while heading to the bathroom. He unclasped my bra and pulled off my thong. He stood behind me in the mirror and his eyes glowed at the reflection of us. It had been a while since I was able to smile again after my father's death. I couldn't get out of bed for a month but Taj went through it with me. Every morning he pulled me out of bed so I could see what I was doing to myself. But this time, my skin was glowing and I wore a smile ear-to-ear while Taj whispered dirty things in my ear. His hands went from my breasts to my center. He rubbed my slit before placing his fingers inside his mouth.

"Get away!" I said and he picked me up.

"Taj, put me down!" I screamed. I was hanging upside down while he kissed and bit at my ass cheeks.

"I can't. You made me like this, Rena. I'm happy as hell around you like a little playful cub," he said. Taj flipped me up and caught me before I hit the floor. I bit his ear and he let me down.

"What did you do that for?" he asked.

"I'm already nervous and you're flipping me around like you got ahold of cat nip."

"Okay, you got jokes I see," he smirked and pulled me into him.

We played around and Taj went as far as tickling me until I couldn't breathe. The bathroom was a mess by the time we were done. He turned on the shower and I stepped inside. My mind was wandering about the decision I made. I didn't want to chicken out because it was something I wanted but what if Taj didn't enjoy me? How could I please him by lying there not doing anything?

"Second thoughts?" he asked.

"What if you don't enjoy it? Are we going to be over?"

"Why wouldn't I enjoy it? Your scent is heavenly and you get extremely wet. That's enough for me. I'm not worried about you being inexperienced. I actually dig that I'm going to be the first and last man to enter you," he said.

"Can we skip the foreplay? We've been doing a lot of things to each other. I just want to get straight to it."

"No foreplay? Now, I feel bad. Your first time needs to be special," he replied.

"And it will be but we've already explored each other's body. All I want is that thing down there."

We washed each other in silence before we stepped out of the shower. Taj grabbed a towel and dried me off. Once he was finished, he massaged my body with sesame and coconut oil. Taj was a caterer but he was slightly aggressive with it. He went into the hall closet and grabbed two handfuls of candles. I followed him into the bedroom. Taj's bed hung from the ceiling. I remodeled his room after me and Arya messed it up. He lit candles around the room, making the setting romantic. Stairs were built alongside of the wall that led to the bed. Once we were on the bed, I caught chills and butterflies again. Taj laid on top of me and I pulled his face into mine to kiss him. Our lips locked while our tongues danced around. Taj rubbed my pussy and a wet spot formed underneath my bottom. He slipped a finger inside me to prepare me for his entrance. I held my breath when he rubbed his head against my virgin entrance. He licked my breast to distract me from the pain. I hissed when he pressed his head against my opening.

"Relax. It's going to hurt for a little while then the pain will go away," he said. It was hard relaxing knowing Taj's dick was going to squeeze into me. He pushed further, I covered my mouth to mute my cries. He removed my hand and kissed me while going further and it hurt worse than the last time.

"I'm in," he said.

It was uncomfortable for a few minutes until he worked up a rhythm that wouldn't hurt me. He kissed, sucked and licked my neck, breasts and lips. My nails scratched at his back when he picked up the pace. He pulled my hair and suckled on my earlobe. My breathing deepened when the pain finally subsided and was replaced with pleasure. He held back a lot. I know he wanted to do more but I was fragile to him. Taj's strokes were smooth, deep and slow. If I was still a succubus, I would've been tortured from arousal but I was able to enjoy Taj without biting him unless he gave me permission. Vampire bites were like cocaine, almost similar to a beast's bite. Taj pressed against a sensitive spot and I moaned loudly.

"That's your G-spot," he said and repeated the movement. He kept hitting my spot until I bit his neck. His body turned orange with black strips and his teeth sharpened. He clawed at the sheets and shredded the mattress. He swelled inside me and I pulled away from him. His blood gave me a rush and laid still in a trance. We both were in a daze. Taj wasn't angry about the bite, in fact he wanted more. I pulled him into me and punctured holes through his neck. He sped up his rhythm as he scratched my body. I pulled away from him, licking my lips and he kissed me. My bite made Taj more aroused—too aroused. He turned me over and entered me from behind. I grabbed the chain to the bed and he grabbed my neck while he gently slammed into me. He plunged into my wetness and the sounds echoed throughout the room. I buried my face into the mattress and screamed when something hooked inside of me and expanded.

"ARRGHHHHHHHHHHHHHHH!" I pulled away from the mattress and screamed. My throat swelled from the pressure and my stomach cramped. Taj pushed further into me and warm liquid spilled inside me. He laid on top of me and I wanted to rip his face off.

"Get it out of me. Please, pull it out. It hurts so bad."

"We're mating, Rena. I can't just pull out of you until my sperm finds an egg," he said.

"I'm never doing this again," I panted.

"You'll get used to it," he breathed.

Taj's dick swelled again, shooting sperm into my womb. I closed my eyes and prayed it was over....

****

I sat up in bed and realized I wasn't in Taj's room but the guest room instead. My stomach ached and my mouth was dry. I covered my eyes with my forearm when the sun shined through the window. Taj came into the guest bedroom with a glass of blood he kept in the fridge from the blood bank. He sat the glass down on the small table beside me and pulled the cover back. I was wearing a negligee.

"The bed is messed up. I know I should've warned you about mating but I didn't think it was going to hurt you. I couldn't go to sleep last night knowing you might wake up hating me," he said. Taj was very upset but I couldn't hate him because of something I asked for.

"I still love you. I actually feel fine, just a little sore and my mouth is dry."

He pulled up my negligee and my eyes almost popped out of my head. I had three tiger stripes across my stomach which had a small bulge but nothing too noticeable. Taj kissed my midsection while I told myself to wake up because I was dreaming. I covered my face to hide my emotions.

"Don't cry, baby. What can I do to make you feel better?"

"I'm happy, Taj. Look at the cute little pudge like I drank a case of beers. I always wanted this, especially with you."

"We won't know the sex until after the baby is born. We're not as lucky as the beasts with early sex of the baby signs. Drink up," he said and gave me the glass.

"Are the stripes permanent?"

"Yeah, we're permanent but it doesn't make you a tiger shifter," he said.

Taj climbed into bed with me and watched me drink the glass of blood.

"That bite you gave me last night was crucial. I had to jerk off twice. You can sell it to old humans as Viagra and make a killing. Don't do that anymore, warn me next time," he said.

"I'll think about it."

Taj fell into a deep sleep after staying up and watching me. I snuck out of the bed and opened the balcony doors in the living room. Taj's loft overlooked the city and the scenery was relaxing.

Thank you, Father, for everything you have given me. I'm going to speak to you every day and tell your grandchild everything you did to give us a better life. I couldn't have done this without you.

SOUL Publications

You gave me wings so I can soar high and I promise I won't stop flying. I hope I'm having a boy so I can name him, Utayo. He's going to carry your name to honor and represent you the right way. Love you, Father. I have to go but I'll be back soon.

I went back inside and closed the doors. Taj was sleeping on his back when I entered the bedroom. I climbed on top of him and rested on his chest. He wrapped his arms around me and pulled the cover over my body. We were officially together forever like he promised.

The End

Made in the USA
Columbia, SC
29 August 2024

41286003R00286